The Last
SUMMER
SISTER

a novel

RACHEL CULLEN

For my daughter, Emily

The oldest Cullen Sister and my first-born,
I love you more than you will ever know.

This is a work of fiction. Names, characters, places, and incidents are of the author's imagination or, if real, are used fictitiously.

Chapter One
Jennifer

Although the black wool suit has been hanging on the back of my closet door for the past two days, and it seemed perfect when I put it on this morning, now it just feels tight and itchy. I can't remember the last time I felt so uncomfortable. I have a sudden urge to rip off my stockings, Escada skirt, and Armani silk blouse and run around in only my bra and underwear like I did that one Thanksgiving when I was four, and my tights and corduroy dress were giving me hives. But I doubt anyone would find it cute this time, the way they did then, especially during my father's funeral service.

"Are you okay?" Mark whispers in my ear.

"Of course, I'm not okay," I whisper back, shooting him a look that has unfortunately become all too familiar these past few days. "Sorry," I mumble, attempting a feeble grin as an apology for my behavior.

"That's not what I meant," Mark offers. Hopefully, he is trying to remember that I'm going through one of the most challenging weeks of my life and I'm not usually this much of a bitch. "It's just that you're squirming in your seat..." Mark says, not finishing his sentence.

"I'm fine!" I whisper back, regretting the harsh tone and my words as soon as they leave my lips. Unfortunately, my voice comes out much louder than I expect it to, as evidenced by the curious looks I receive from my aunt and uncle across the pew. I give them a sad smile that hopefully conveys grief, sympathy, and love for my husband if it's possible for one smile to wear three different hats.

"When is this going to start?" Ryan complains, trying to speak softly, but as that's almost impossible for a six-year-old boy, I'm quite certain that everyone in the back of the sanctuary hears him, and that's the reason for the quiet chuckles as the rabbi makes his way to the front of the massive synagogue in Glencoe.

Rabbi Saunders welcomes everyone and then speaks for several minutes about the sanctity of life and the tragedy that occurs when a life is lost before its time. He adds that this is especially sad because we also lost our mother before it was her time to go. I keep trying to pay attention, but I can't focus on what he's saying. As ridiculous as it seems, I keep picturing Dad sitting at the end of the row, shaking his head and clucking his tongue every time Rabbi Saunders says the word "God" or "Adonai." The last time David Summer was in a synagogue was for his own wedding, and before that, for his bar mitzvah, he would find it absurd that this is the selected location for his funeral.

"I think you're up next," Mark says quietly, attempting not to upset me. I know he's still impressed that I chose to give the eulogy. He told me how brave he thought I was, but then Mark took that encouragement several steps too far when he said I would "crush it" - who says that about a eulogy?

"Thanks," I say quickly, as I stand up and straighten the offending skirt and make my way to the pulpit at the front of the sanctuary.

I take a deep breath and offer the same sad smile to everyone in the pews in front of me. I'm never nervous, and certainly never at a loss for words, but just in case, I wrote some bullet points on a piece of stationery last night, which is currently folded into sixteen tiny squares in my left hand. Looking out at the mourners, the words I planned to say about my dad no longer seem quite right.

The paper has all the expected talking points. I planned to highlight David Summer's impressive track record as the CEO of a massive insurance company, which he built from the ground up after graduating from Ohio State. Then I was going to add a few anecdotes about his prowess on the golf course and tennis court, where he loved to win, but not as much as he loved the camaraderie and fresh air. I had a few notes to remind myself to talk about the boards that he sat on after he retired four years ago, giving back to the hospital and the Boys & Girls Club and the community in Winnetka. And of course, I would end with a tribute to his magnificent role as a father and grandfather. It's true that he wasn't always around when I was growing up, but he tried hard, and he certainly made up for it with his grandkids.

But now that I'm standing here, I can't get any of the words out. There's a sudden burning in my stomach, and I feel like I might throw up right here in front of everyone. Mark is staring at me with a quizzical expression and mouthing the words, "are you okay?" which is infuriating, comforting, and hysterical at the same time. Isn't it obvious that I'm not okay?

Lynn appears at my side without warning and envelops me in a bear hug, which isn't difficult since she is seven inches taller and at least fifteen pounds heavier. However, considering she is built like an actual model, I know I'm the only one petty enough to think of her weighing more than I do. Lynn gently scoots me to the side and apologizes for my inability to perform the eulogy. Considering we were still arguing about who should do the eulogy last night, and I only *won* because I played the older sister trump card, Lynn must be overjoyed with the current turn of events. She doesn't even have the decency to bring her husband and son to the funeral, but she has no problem jumping in the limelight to give the eulogy? I guess always being *camera-ready* is one of the perks of doing years of cut-rate modeling work, movies, and sitcoms, I think angrily.

"Thank you all so much for coming today to mourn with us and to remember our father on this sad day," Lynn begins. I have no idea what she is going to say next, but I am confident she is not going to give the speech the way that I wanted to give it, seeing as she as spent the past twelve years living out in California, coming home only once in the last five years to visit. Meanwhile, we lived a few streets away from Dad, and I've seen him almost every day for the past fifteen years! I want to push my baby sister out of the way because I know she's going to get it wrong, but my feet are glued to the floor.

"I didn't spend as much time with my dad as I would have liked to over the past several years," Lynn begins. "But although I couldn't be here, we always made sure to talk on the phone once a week. No matter what was going in our lives, we never missed carving out at least an hour for our Wednesday night phone calls," Lynn says, and the crowd audibly sighs in approval while I try to wrap my head around this shocking news. I didn't know that Lynn ever spoke with Dad, let alone once a week! I'm suddenly desperate to ask Dad what they talked about for an hour every Wednesday when I realize that I'll never be able to ask him that, and it's almost too much to hold it together in front of everyone.

"Dad would have done a much better job of writing this speech, and certainly of delivering this speech – it felt like his whole life was spent giving speeches, but you can't give your own eulogy, can you?" Lynn says, her voice cracking, with the first trace of emotion. Rabbi Saunders takes a step over and squeezes her arm to provide comfort and lets her know that she can wrap it up at any time, and he can take over. At least Lynn was able to get out a few sentences. When this is all said and done, everyone will remember that I stood there like a statue, unable to say a single word about my father. At the same time, Lynn shocked everyone with her revelation about being the dutiful daughter all these years.

I hear Lynn's voice as she begins to speak again, and the mourners' collective laughs and tears, but it all blends into a dull hum as if I'm wearing noise-canceling headphones. And then before I know it, Rabbi Saunders kisses me on the cheek, and Lynn takes my arm to walk me back to my seat – I haven't said a single word.

"It's okay, you did great," Mark says, as I slide into the pew next to him and he reaches for my hand.

"That was hardly great," I whisper back at him, and I almost snatch my hand away, but I know it's misplaced anger; instead, I leave my fingers in his warm grasp and will the funeral to end quickly.

I try to focus on Rabbi Saunders as he finishes the service with the closing prayers, but it's been so long since I've been to a service at a synagogue that I can barely follow along in the prayer book. When I was little, I used to ask my parents why we didn't go to temple if we were Jewish, and my dad said, "we weren't those kind of Jews." My dad was the kind of guy who was first in line to speak out if he thought he heard the slightest hint of an anti-Semitic slur, who insisted we host a Seder every year for half the Jews in Winnetka, and who paid colossal sums to have the best bagels, lox, and hamentaschen shipped from Zabar's in Manhattan. However, whenever I asked if we should go to services on Rosh Hashanah, or light candles on Shabbat like my friend Rebecca, or have a bat mitzvah like my friend Shana, Dad scoffed and told me that we were cultural Jews and if he never stepped foot in a temple again it would be too soon.

8

All of this makes my current surroundings even more ironic. I can't imagine that Dad would be too happy right now, but what choice did I have? Even if we're the least observant Jewish family around (and I'm sure that's not the case), we're still Jewish, and he still needed a funeral, so I had to do something. The decision also fell squarely on my shoulders, with Mom gone and Lynn out in California until yesterday. However, it didn't stop her from swooping in and taking over today after I've spent the past thirty-six hours pulling this together.

"Jen," Mark says, tapping me on the shoulder.

"What?" I reply sharply, upset that he interrupted my walk down memory lane.

"The service is over, honey," he says cautiously, probably worried I will bite his head off again, and who can blame him? I make a quick mental reminder to be more patient with him and generally less of a bitch.

"Oh," I mutter, glancing around at the guests rising from the pews.

"Do you want to ride in the car with Lynn, and I can take the kids?" Mark asks as we file into the aisle, and I subtly readjust the waistband of my infuriating stockings while fighting the urge to rip them off once and for all.

"Lynn can go with Aunt Judy. I'll go with you and the kids," I say to Mark, taking Ryan and Harper's hands to show him I don't want any part of a car ride with my sister and to guard against unwelcome condolence hugs on my way outside.

Unfortunately, my trick doesn't work, and I am inundated by hugs and kisses and handshakes and backslaps as I make my way from the synagogue to the parking lot. The large turnout is not a surprise given Dad's role at the company for over forty years and his place in the community. Although he was an only

9

child, there are also distant relatives and second cousins and, of course, Mom's sister, Aunt Judy, and her children. By the time I get to the car, I'm exhausted. "I can't believe we still have to go to the cemetery and then back to the house and pretend to be social – this is brutal," I comment to Mark.

"It's surreal to think that he's gone," Mark says, "I don't think it has hit me yet," he adds, making my comment feel shallow.

"Who was the woman in the back?" I ask him, attempting to change the subject.

"Whom do you mean?" he asks, as he reverses his new Tesla out of the parking spot.

I exhale loudly before I reply, so I don't snap at him again. "The lady in the back row, who was still sitting there when we left and crying. She was probably in her fifties. She was likely a natural blonde at one point, but now it's certainly out of a bottle. I think she was pretty, but hard to tell with all the crying. I assumed she was someone from the office," I say.

"I feel like I've seen her somewhere before," Mark says. "Maybe she's one of those distant relatives who show up at funerals?" Mark adds. "Whoever she was, she seems to be pretty upset about your Dad," he says, but we've both forgotten about her by the time we pull out of the temple's parking lot.

Chapter Two
Lynn

I know I should be thrilled with my luck that I found an apartment for short-term rental on two-days' notice, but now that I'm here, I'm rethinking the wisdom of my impulsive decision. It's crazy to think that I've only been back to the North Shore suburbs of Chicago a handful of times in the eighteen years since I graduated from New Trier High School, but once you move to LA, why would you come back? However, this might explain why I didn't remember that an apartment in Evanston off Sheridan Road wouldn't be ideal for a thirty-six-year-old single woman when everyone else in the building is a Northwestern student! I'm not sure how I didn't realize that this apartment was three blocks from campus, but I'm stuck with it now. Mostly because I've paid three months' rent in advance and I can't afford to find somewhere else.

I collapse on the brown leather couch and try not to think about what might have transpired here previously. It's always a gamble when you rent a furnished apartment, but even more so when there were twenty-one-year-olds living here a couple of weeks ago. I've decided to believe that the previous tenants were the ultimate nerds who never drank, partied, or had sex, so the worst thing that could have happened here was too much highlighting.

It's hard to believe that I was in my apartment in LA seventy-two hours ago trying to decide if I should order sushi or meet Ali for Thursday night happy hour. But then Jen called and said an aneurysm burst in Dad's brain and he was dead, just like that. I talked to him the night before, and everything was fine, and now he's gone.

I wanted more time to get everything wrapped up in LA, but Jen insisted we have the funeral right away. She claimed that we should have had the funeral within twenty-four hours, but because it was almost Shabbat, we could wait until Sunday. It's hysterical that she is suddenly some sort of "Super-Jew" when she's the WASP queen of Winnetka. At least that's how it seems – her house was written up last year for Best Christmas Decorations for God's Sake! But suddenly, we all need to adhere to Jewish customs, which Dad would have hated, so I had to pack as much as I could, ask Ali to water my plants and check on my apartment, and here I am.

I know I didn't need to rent an apartment here for three months; I could have just stayed in a hotel for a few days and then gone home. But after everything that's happened in the last two years, it feels like it might be time to get out of LA. So, I decided to take this opportunity to give it a try. I can't imagine what Jen will say when she finds out that I'm not going right back to LA. She always pretends that she's upset that I don't come home more often, but I know Jen feels like she owns Winnetka and Dad and the whole fucking company. But even *I* knew that today wasn't the day to throw this on her.

Just as a small stain on the rug catches my eye and seriously makes me rethink my hypothesis on the no-party theory, my phone chimes to distract me.

Ali: How are you doing? How did everything go today? I'm so sorry I couldn't be there!

Lynn: It was okay. It doesn't feel real. And you couldn't have come out here and left your family, but I love you for saying that ♥

12

Ali: I feel terrible that you are all alone out there! If Wade didn't have to work, I would be there!

Lynn: I know you would

Ali: How was it with Jen?

Lynn: Fine, I guess. I didn't see very much of her, there were so many people at the service and then after at her house

Ali: I can't believe you're not coming back right away ☹ I'm going to miss you so much

Lynn: I know, me too ☹

Ali: What did Trevor say?

Lynn: I haven't talked to him

Ali: You didn't even tell him about your dad??? What about Declan?? Did you tell him?

Lynn: I texted Declan on Friday, but he never responded

An instant later, the phone rings and I know that it's Ali. She's decided that texting is no longer sufficient for this conversation. "Did you tell him that his grandfather passed away in a text?" Ali asks the second I answer the phone.

"Hello to you too," I respond.

"Sorry. Hi. But seriously, did you really tell him that in a text? And then he didn't respond?" Ali asks, sounding incredulous.

"No," I reply sheepishly. "I texted him to give me a call. And he didn't write back or call me," I murmur.

"Lynn! Declan doesn't even know that his grandfather died?! And he missed the funeral? Are you kidding me with this?" Ali says.

"Trevor would never have let him come anyway," I protest. "And Declan hasn't talked to me in months; there's nothing I can do anymore," I say, the tears welling up in my eyes as I rip the Band-Aid off yet again, and it's no less painful than it's been any of the previous times.

"Did you tell *Trevor* about your dad?" Ali asks, trying a different tactic.

"No," I admit, sounding defeated. "But it wouldn't have mattered. You know that he has full custody, and he would never have let me take Declan out of California! He wouldn't even let me take him for ice cream this summer!"

"I know, I'm so sorry," Ali says, softening a little bit. "But still. It's your dad. And it's *his* grandfather. He never even got to meet his grandmother. And Declan is only twelve. He doesn't know what he's doing right now. He's only acting this way because he listens to what Trevor tells him. Someday he'll figure it all out for himself," Ali assures me.

"And then he'll realize on his own that I was a shitty mom," I say sadly.

"Stop. Don't say that," Ali says. "Listen, I have to go get the kids ready for bed; the nanny is off tonight," she adds. "You must be exhausted. Try to get some sleep," Ali advises.

"I'm almost too tired to sleep. The past few days have been one big blur. It's been the longest three days of my life," I say.

"Get some sleep, and I'll give you a call tomorrow, okay?" Ali says.

"Okay, I'll do my best," I tell her. "Thanks for calling."

"Of course. I love you," Ali says.

14

"You too," I tell her, and I end the call.

I look around the apartment to properly take stock of my surroundings and try again to wrap my head around the situation. Thankfully, this small apartment building appears to have been gutted in the recent past. With the exception of some of the furniture and the aforementioned rug, everything in the cozy two-bedroom apartment seems to be brand new. The more updated apartment means that the rent is likely higher than other places in Evanston, but it's nothing compared to rent out in LA. Perhaps it also means that my new neighbors are graduate or MBA students, rather than undergrads, I think to myself hopefully.

As much as I try to fight it, exhaustion takes over, and the lack of sleep these past three days combined with the emotional trauma from today means I can barely keep my eyes open. Fortunately, I brushed my teeth and washed my face before Ali called, so all I need to do now is stumble into the bedroom and fall into bed. Although the full-size bed feels tiny, compared to the king I'm used to at home, it's surprisingly comfortable; and as I drift off to sleep, I almost manage not to think about what a disaster my life has become.

Chapter Three
Jennifer

I wake up to Harper's warm little body glued to my side and her hot breath on my neck. I don't need to look at the clock to know that it's just past six in the morning. I don't remember exactly when this started; it's probably been six or seven months now, but as soon as she wakes up, she crawls into bed with us, and this is how I wake up. Mark isn't thrilled with the development, but it's far better than her coming into bed with us in the middle of the night, and it's a much nicer alarm clock than anything I could buy in the store or any setting on my phone.

"Momma, what's for breakfast?" Harper whispers in my ear.

"Hmmm," is all I can reply. It's still too early to form words.

"I want waffles," Harper says.

"It's a school day," I manage to say.

"But grandpa died. I don't wanna go to school," Harper says.

"I know, baby," I reply, and I roll over so I can scoop up all thirty-eight pounds of her four-year-old body into a gigantic hug. It's been three days since the funeral, and we've kept the kids home from school since then, so I can understand why Harper feels like she shouldn't have to go to school today – it's pretty reasonable logic even for someone twice her age. But unfortunately, Mark and I both have to go to work today, and I have to meet with Dad's lawyer, so even though it feels like I'm abandoning his memory by resuming everyday life, I don't think we have a choice.

"So, no waffles?" Harper asks, pouting.

"Not today," I tell her. "We can have waffles this weekend," I promise.

"Who's having waffles?" Mark asks, coming into the bedroom in his sweaty workout clothes. I assume he went for a run, but he might have also worked out with his trainer in our home gym – I try not to keep track of his schedule. When we first met nine years ago, I was more than a little starstruck. After playing eight years in the NFL as a second-string wide receiver, Mark had recently retired due to a devastating knee injury. I was in awe of him, his friends, physique, and crazy commitment to his workouts. But eight years into marriage, I no longer find it quite as impressive, and honestly, it's pretty annoying. He's never going to play football again, so why does he have to look like that? He just makes me feel like I have to keep up with him, and every day I skip a workout, I feel fat and guilty.

"Mommy says no waffles today," Harper says, pushing out her lower lip in an attempt to gain sympathy.

I wait anxiously to see whose side Mark is going to take. He casually pulls his sweaty Chicago Bears Dri-Fit shirt over his head, revealing a six-pack that could rival a Calvin Klein underwear model's. Those abs used to make my stomach do somersaults, but now they just make me think about my love handles.

17

"You know we don't have waffles on school days, silly bunny," Mark says. "And you should still be asleep and letting your mommy sleep too," he adds.

"Hmmph," Harper says, defeated by both parents. "Is Liliana coming today?" she asks hopefully.

"Yes, she'll be here soon," I tell Harper. "Why don't you go brush your teeth and get dressed? I put your outfit in your room. That way, you can be ready when Liliana gets here, and you can help her make breakfast," I suggest.

"Okay!" Harper says joyfully, and she bounces off the bed and runs down the hall, all thoughts of waffles forgotten, as she focuses on her absolute favorite person in the world coming over to see her. I like to think that she likes us more than she likes the nanny, but most days, I'm pretty sure Liliana is her first choice.

"How do you feel about going back to work today?" Mark questions as he strips off the remainder of his sweaty clothes and tosses them in a heap on the floor for Rose to pick up later this morning when she cleans our room and does the laundry.

"I don't know. I would rather stay in bed all day," I reply.

"I'm sure they can manage without you for a few more days," Mark offers. "You should at least take the rest of the week off," he says, trying to be kind. "I wish I could stay home with you, but I've already been gone three days, and I don't think your dad would approve," Mark says, trying to make a joke, but it falls completely flat.

He's quite generous in comparing our jobs, and we both know it. I know this isn't the time to pick a fight with him, and I made my choice long ago, but it's times like these that make me want to scream. He's going to go to work today as the CEO of the largest family-run insurance company in the entire

18

Midwest, the one he began working at shortly after we started dating and then took over from my father after he retired. I'm going to stop by the boutique I own in downtown Winnetka that sells overpriced sweaters, jewelry, blankets, and other items that no one needs.

"I'll probably run into the shop for a few minutes just to check-in, but I have to meet with Dad's lawyer later this morning, so I won't stay for very long," I tell Mark.

"Why do you need to meet with the lawyer?" Mark asks, still standing buck-naked in the center of the bedroom.

"He sent me an email and asked if I could stop by today. He said there were a few things he wanted to go over with me before we went through the will," I tell him, hoping that this will end the conversation so he can proceed to the shower.

"Do you think there's a problem?" Mark asks, suddenly concerned.

"I'm sure there's nothing wrong," I reply. "Maybe Dad decided to give all of his money to Ohio State, and he's giving his seat on the board to Chuck, and he wants to break the news gently," I joke.

Mark offers a small laugh, but I can tell he doesn't find it remotely funny.

"I have to get in the shower," Mark says, finally making his way to the unnecessarily large master bathroom. I'm pretty sure it was one of the selling points for Mark when we bought the house three years ago, but I've always felt it's a colossal waste of space. I believe the realtor told us that the overall square footage of the bathroom alone was five hundred square feet, and the Jacuzzi in the center seats six – are we supposed to be inviting friends over to take a bath with us? I know that no one would believe me, but I honestly think the entire house

19

is ridiculous. Mark said I could never understand why the place was so important to him because *I* grew up with money, and *he* grew up clipping coupons for his mom and gambling on three-day-old, expired meat. We fought about it at the time, but then I gave in because it just wasn't worth it, and it seemed to make him so happy.

***

Before the bell can even jingle to alert anyone that the shop door is opening, Stephanie is on top of me. "I'm so sorry about your dad, Jen. And I'm so sorry that I wasn't at the funeral, but I know you wanted me here to manage the store, but I feel terrible that I couldn't be there," Stephanie rambles, still crushing my ribs.

"Thanks, I appreciate it," I say, returning her hug and also trying to disentangle myself from her embrace. "It was great of you to be here on Sunday and take care of the store," I assure her. Stephanie was recently promoted from sales associate to store manager, and I know she takes her responsibilities very seriously. I also understand and appreciate her fierce loyalty after helping her out with an unfortunate personal issue a couple of years ago. Still, sometimes I wish she weren't quite so dedicated.

"How are you doing? How are the kids?" she questions.

"We're doing okay. It's still a shock, but I think it's best for Harper and Ryan if they can get back to normal as soon as possible," I try to explain while absentmindedly re-folding a pile of alpaca throws that were already perfectly folded.

"If you don't want to stay today, I'm sure we'll be fine. Grace is coming in at eleven-thirty, so you can go home if you'd rather," Stephanie says, and then she must see the look on my face and panic that she's said the wrong thing because she quickly stumbles to correct herself. "But of course, everything

20

is always better when you're here, so whatever is best for you. I just want you to be happy," Stephanie says, and then her pale, freckled face winces as she realizes what she's said.

"It's okay," I try to reassure her, although it seems ironic that I should be comforting her. "I only came by to check in quickly. I have a meeting in a little bit, and then I have a few other things I need to get done. I might come back in tomorrow, or I'll come by Saturday with Harper," I promise her.

"She's such a doll," Stephanie says, her face lighting up at the mere mention of Harper's name. Even though I own the shop, I spend the whole time following Harper around and telling her to put things back and keep her hands to herself. However, Stephanie has the patience of a saint and lets her play dress-up with the costume jewelry and the fancy hats while still ensuring nothing gets broken and attending to customers at the same time.

"Thanks for everything Stephanie, I really appreciate it," I tell her again as I make my way toward the door.

"Of course! I'm happy to do it. Let me know if I can do anything else," she calls out.

As I exit the store, I hold the door for three women who are laughing and chatting excitedly on their way inside to do some mid-morning shopping. I envy the carefree atmosphere that surrounds them and wish I could rewind the clock a few days when I felt like that, or at least when I occasionally felt like that. If I'm being honest, it's been a long time since I've felt like those women. Although what do I know? Maybe they are just better actors, and they feel shitty about their lives, too.

The lawyer's office is only a few blocks away down Elm Street and around the corner on Green Bay Road. I know I should probably walk, but then I run the risk of running into familiar faces, and that's the last thing I want to do right now. As I head back to my car, I try to capture the picturesque beauty that our town has to offer, and one of the reasons it is continuously named one of the best places to live in the entire country. On this early September day, a few of the leaves have already fallen from the trees. The grass is starting to dull from the brilliant green color it had all summer long, but the sky is a perfect shade of peacock blue. Mothers are running around with strollers, trying to hold toddler's hands as they cross the street, the sidewalks are full of commuters grabbing a juice or coffee before they catch the late train into the city, and the UPS delivery person is carrying packages into the hardware store; but only after she stops to chat with the owner of the dry cleaner on the corner.

All in all, I've always thought the scene was reminiscent of small-town America from the 1950s, only now we have iPhones and Teslas, and some other modern conveniences. I've lived here all my life, except for four years at Harvard and two years down the road at Kellogg for business school, but today it suddenly seems too much. I want to get up on this park bench and scream and tell everyone that they should stop pretending to be characters in Pleasantville or *Leave it to Beaver*, or whatever it is that makes everyone so happy and perfect all the time! But I know it's not fair, and I know that's not true; and of course, I would never actually get up on a bench and yell anything because I'm Jennifer Summer, and that's not what I do. So I get in my car and drive four blocks to the lawyer's office to find out what he has to tell me about my dad that he absolutely can't say over the phone.

Chapter Four
Mark

The spot next to mine is empty as I pull into a vast lot of the Deerfield office park, home to the headquarters of Summer Risk Management. Although there are no officially reserved spots, it was always understood that David got the parking spot directly across the walkway from the front door to the right of the handicapped spots, and I parked right next to him. Though he retired a few years ago, he still came in almost every morning to poke his head into meetings and provide his two cents. The vacant rectangle of concrete is a stark reminder that he's gone, even before I get inside.

I told Jen that I had to come in today because I had been away from the office for too long, but I know no one would miss me if I stayed away for the rest of the week and maybe next week also. My legs are almost too heavy to get out of the car, and it has nothing to do with the miles I ran on the treadmill this morning and everything to do with a physical dread of entering that concrete and glass box full of analysts and actuarial tables. For a brief moment, I allow the fantasy of driving away and going somewhere else for the day. Somewhere I don't have to wear a suit and pretend to care about spreadsheets and sit through endless meetings. I close my eyes and see clear blue skies, dotted with clouds, and the turf's vivid artificial green, and I hear.

"Mr. Olsen, are you okay?" a female voice says while rapping her knuckles loudly on my window.

"Yes, I'm fine," I reply, grabbing my bag off the passenger seat and opening my door to join the concerned window-knocker in the parking lot. She looks quite familiar, and I vaguely remember sitting in an interview with her a few months ago, possibly for a Human Resources position, but I don't have a clue about her name.

"I'm so sorry about your father-in-law," she says, as we walk together toward the building and through the automatic glass doors.

"Thanks, we're all quite shocked by this," I reply, as I've said dozens and dozens of times over the past few days.

We approach the elevator, and I push the "up" button and wonder if my unknown companion works on the same floor. When the elevator arrives and both get in, she pushes the button for two and three, presumably two for her and three for me. That's the problem with being the CEO, everyone knows who you are and everything about you, and I don't know anything about them. Summer Risk Management has one hundred thirty-four employees at the headquarters office and then another hundred or so out in the field, and I can't keep track of any of them. I swear I know about twenty people here, and the rest of the time, I smile and nod and pretend to engage. David knew everyone. Even on an intern's first day, David seemed to know them already. But then again, he was a natural at everything: good at sales, good with numbers, good with marketing.

"Glad to have you back," Kayla says, eyeing me sympathetically as I approach her desk, the one that sits right outside my corner office. I know Kayla was at David's funeral, but I don't remember if I even spoke to her that day; it was all such a blur.

"Thanks, Kayla," I say. "Do I have anything scheduled this morning? I didn't see anything on my calendar."

"No, I kept your morning free so that you could catch up, and your afternoon is pretty light too," she informs me.

"Thanks so much," I say, as I disappear into an office that is far larger than necessary for the work that actually gets done in here – I probably need less space than the analysts in the second-floor cubes with their giant monitors, charts, and files, but big title equals big office. I slowly approach my desk and play a little guessing game with myself – how many emails will be waiting in my inbox? I know I should have looked through emails while I was out, but it didn't seem right. I'm likely only cc'd on most of them anyway. There will be a handful directly to my attention, but I'll have to comb through all of them just in case there is a shred of pertinent information in one of the other emails. David taught me that lesson early on; to "Cover My Ass," especially as I got more senior in the company. He joked that the only reason anyone ever included him on an email was so he or she could claim that they ran it by him; it wasn't that they actually wanted his input. But he was wrong about that. Everyone wanted David's opinion, no matter the topic. However, I'm confident that the only reason *I'm* cc'd on these emails is for ass-covering.

Seven hundred thirty-nine is the tally of emails for the past three days. I was guessing eight hundred, so I suppose I should be happy, but the prospect of reading, or even skimming, these emails fills me with dread. And of course, new emails will continue to pile up as I sort through these; it reminds me of a Greek tragedy I read about in college, someone rolling a stone up a hill, but I wasn't paying much attention – I think that class was during the fall semester - football season.

I crank through the first seventy-five emails in twenty minutes and either delete or file them; as expected, almost all of them are cc'd, and nothing needs an immediate response. I have to start a folder for condolence emails, and I'm sure that will continue to grow as I work my way down the list. I'll eventually need to respond, but I'm confident there is an extended time period allowed for that sort of thing. Most of the sympathy letters mention Jen in some capacity, and I wonder if I should give her a call to check in and see how her day is going? She was going to go to the store and then stop by the lawyer's office, and she'll be without the kids for the first time in a few days; I should probably give her a call and let her know I'm thinking about her. But as soon as I pick up the overly complicated office phone to dial out, Kayla buzzes the intercom.

"I'm sorry to bother you, Mark, but Tracy is out here, and she says they need you in the conference room."

"Okay, I'll be right there," I reply with a sigh that I hope isn't audible.

Tracy is the Chief Risk Officer, highly independent and does not have a flair for the dramatics, so if she says I need to be in a meeting, then I'm sure she means it. As I make the short walk down the tan carpeted hallway to the fishbowl of a conference room, I wonder what I'll be able to add to the meeting that the rest of our senior team cannot. But when I see who's inside the conference room, I understand precisely why I was summoned.

Chapter Five
Lynn

I park my rental Ford Focus in the center of downtown Winnetka and marvel at what's changed since I was last here and since high school – the addition of numerous trendy shops, salons, and restaurants. But at the same time, it still looks pretty much the same – as if the town came straight off a set in Hollywood.

I stare out the undersized car window at Jen's shop across the street, and a gaggle of women has just come out with three shopping bags each, looking smug and satisfied. Although I imagine it's Jen, who should be looking smug and satisfied after selling them all that stuff, they can't possibly need. When I woke up this morning, the idea of coming to see Jen at her store seemed like a good one, but now that I'm here, I'm not so sure. She didn't want anything to do with me at the funeral or the reception, and she made no effort to ask how long I was staying, so I can't imagine she'll be thrilled if I surprise her at work.

I start the ignition, and my sad little car putters to life. As I'm about to back out of the space, I see Jen out of the corner of my eye, walking down the street. Her eyes are red and puffy like she's been crying, and it almost looks as if she's lost from the way she's wandering down the street. Even though we are practically strangers at this point in our lives, seeing her like this brings tears to my eyes, and before I know it, the car is back in park, and I'm on my feet, crossing Chestnut Street heading toward her.

"Are you okay?" I ask when I'm about eight feet away from Jen.

As strange as it seems, Jen doesn't appear remotely surprised to see me. I was slightly concerned that I would scare her, especially given her current state. On the contrary, she gives me a brief head nod when she sees me, almost as if she expected me to turn up unannounced in the middle of the street in downtown Winnetka.

"I've been better," Jen says, with a sad little laugh.

"Right, of course," I reply, trying to apologize for my dumb question, as usual.

"Do you want to get some coffee?" Jen asks.

For a moment, I'm not sure how to respond. I'm wondering what the catch is? Maybe it's just because she's sad or lost in grief, and I happen to be here. Or perhaps she's finally starting to lose it like Mom did, and she doesn't remember that she hates spending time with me. I take a quick glance over my shoulder to make sure she's talking to *me* before responding. "Sure," I reply.

"There's a Peet's right up here," Jen says, as she starts walking a few feet in front of me, which is more like it.

There is no more conversation until we are settled at a small table in the corner with our drinks, a chai latte for Jen, and an espresso for me.

I take a small sip of the bitter liquid, and Jen wraps her hands around her mug before bringing the milky drink to her lips, and I imagine she is deeply regretting her impulsive invitation.

"I just came from a meeting with Dad's lawyer," Jen says, pursing her lips the way she does when she's upset. It seems like she's about to say something else, but then she stops and takes a sip of her drink.

"I thought we were meeting with him later this week to go over the will?" I question.

"We are," Jen replies, without providing any additional clues.

"So, why did you meet with him today?" I ask her. It feels like I am pulling teeth, which, although painful, feels more like our usual pattern.

"He called me last night and asked if I could come by his office today," Jen replies, although that doesn't answer my question.

"So, what did he say?" I ask, my curiosity is piqued, and I wish she would just spit it out.

"Oh God, there's Brianna," Jen says and slumps visibly lower into her seat.

"What?" I ask, trying to follow the non sequitur, as I glance over my shoulder.

Before she can respond, a petite woman bounces right up to our table and begins talking – I can only assume this is Brianna. "Jen, I was so, so sorry to hear about your dad," she gushes. "And I'm so sorry I couldn't come to the funeral. We were up at the lake house, and you know how I try to stay off of my phone while I'm there, right?" she asks, but she doesn't wait for an answer before she plows ahead. "I didn't even find

29

out until I got back yesterday. But I just feel terrible that I couldn't be there. Is there anything you need? Is there anything that I can do for you? Or for Mark?" she adds, and I may be imagining it, but I swear I see Brianna lick her lips the tiniest bit before she says Mark's name, although I'm sure it's just a coincidence.

Only after she finishes her monologue does Brianna even seem to realize that there is someone else sitting at the table, and she turns her compact frame in my direction. "I don't believe we've met," she says, stating the obvious. "I'm Brianna," she says, sticking out a child-sized hand that is covered in diamond and sapphire rings (I can only imagine what her left hand looks like if this is how many carats she has on her right.)

"I'm Lynn, Jen's sister," I reply, shaking her hand, and trying not to crush it with my massive paw that is oversize even for my five-foot-ten-inch frame. I never thought twice about my hands until I met Trevor, and he pointed out my gigantic hands. At first, I thought he was joking, but clearly, he wasn't, and I've been self-conscious ever since – just one of the many gifts Trevor gave me.

"Oh! My! God! I had no idea Jen had a sister! You guys don't look *anything* alike!" Brianna screams. Although it's unclear which of us she is accusing of this crime of nondisclosure and identity theft, we certainly have the attention of the coffee drinkers at all of the surrounding tables.

I should be surprised, but somehow, I'm not at all shocked that Jen's friends don't know about me. In fact, she's probably gone out of her way to tell elaborate stories about her glorious childhood as an only child. Jen looks back and forth between Brianna and me as if she's trying to figure out which conversation will be less awkward. Not surprisingly, she settles on Brianna. "Lynn has been living out in California since college. It's hard to come back to the Chicago weather once you've lived in LA," she says, trying to make a joke.

"I love LA!" Brianna says. "What do you do out there?" she asks me.

Before I have a chance to answer, Jen replies for me, "Lynn used to be a model. And now she's an actress," she says.

"Are you in anything I would have seen?" Brianna asks, watching me intently.

"Um, well, I haven't been in anything in a little while. I don't think so," I reply, and I can feel my cheeks start to flush as I prepare for the array of inevitable follow-up questions where Brianna grills me on my resume until she lands on a show she recognizes. I'm not sure if Jen knew that this would happen, but I wouldn't put it past her to tell Brianna about my acting work, only so she can watch me suffer.

Unfortunately, this plays out exactly as I knew it would, and Brianna forces me to recap a long list of terrible shows and pilots that she's never heard of, where I played minuscule roles. Finally, I remember the walk-on I had in CSI: New York, and Brianna is thrilled that she recognizes the name and has the audacity to say, "I actually think I recognize you from that," which given my forty seconds of airtime hiding behind Gary Sinise, is virtually impossible.

"We really have to get going," Jen says, guzzling over half of her latte in one gulp and pushing her chair back from the table.

"Oh, of course," Brianna says. "Well, good to meet you," she says to me and, "See you soon!" she calls to Jen.

I take another quick sip of my espresso, but it wasn't that good to begin with, and I'm certainly not going to choke on it just because Jen says it's time to go. "Nice to meet you too," I say to Brianna, excusing myself from the table and following Jen to the door.

As I walk outside, I think I hear her say, "Will I see you again? How long are you in town?" But I pretend not to have heard and let the door close behind me – this doesn't seem like the time or place to have that conversation with Jen anymore.

Jen is already ahead of me when I get outside, but it only takes a couple of steps for me to catch up with my long legs. I want to make a funny comment about Brianna, but she'll probably take it the wrong way and accuse me of insulting her friend. We walk down the street in frosty silence, and whatever sisterly moment we had earlier feels like a distant memory. In fact, I'm starting to wonder if I imagined the whole thing. It's so out of character for Jen to be crying and vulnerable; it was most likely a jet lag induced hallucination.

"I'm going to go check in at the store before I head home; I'll see you later," Jen says, veering off to cross the street as soon as we hit the corner.

As I watch her walk away, I realize that not only did she fail to say goodbye after she dismissed me, but she never told me what the lawyer said to her. I'm sure it's not that big of a deal, but at the same time, she was upset by something, and if there is information about Dad, then it involves me too. I contemplate running after her to demand that she finish her story, but I know that won't end well. Instead, I get in my car and head south on Green Bay Road, back toward my lonely apartment in Evanston, because I have nothing else to do and nowhere else to be.

Chapter Six
Jennifer

"Momma, is everything okay?" Harper asks in her most grown-up voice.

"Yes, of course, sweetie," I reply, forcing a smile onto my face and leaning over to nuzzle her curly blonde locks. "Why would you ask me that?" I question.

"You didn't drink your juice, and you stopped reading the story," Harper replies.

I glance at my untouched glass of wine and marvel at how perceptive she is. As much as I love Ryan, there isn't a chance in hell that he would make that observation or even connect it to a mood or feeling. To almost everyone's delight, Ryan is taking after Mark. Although he's only six-years-old, he excels at every sport he's ever tried; the pee-wee football coach is already desperate to get Ryan on his team, even though that's more than three years away. Although I know part of that is because they hope Mark will be part of the package.

I lie through my teeth and say, "Momma's fine, I'm just a little bit tired."

"That's okay, we don't have to read anything," Harper says, putting *The Day The Crayons Quit* back on the table and climbing into my lap.

I try to ignore the pit in my stomach as I cuddle with Harper. I wonder what she would think of her mom if she knew what a bitch I had been to her aunt today. I know it isn't Lynn's fault, but hearing Brianna's shock that I could share my DNA with someone as breathtaking as Lynn, brought back the countless comparisons that have been made over the years, and today of all days, I just couldn't take it.

Sometimes, when I'm feeling entirely rational or maybe just magnanimous, I realize that it isn't Lynn's *fault; she* was blessed with height, boobs, a crazy metabolism, perfect skin, toothpaste-commercial teeth, and hair that looks sun-kissed and "beachy" without any effort. She didn't get to decide how the genes were split, so why should I be upset with her for looking like a model since the age of nine?

When we were little, our dad used to joke to people that I got the brains, and Lynn got the beauty. As much as I adored him, I also froze when he said that and hoped that in my silence and tight lips, he would realize how mean it sounded (to both of his daughters), but he laughed at his own joke and never realized the pain he caused with that simple comment.

My first week at Harvard was the first time in my life that I realized I wasn't actually ugly. Lynn arrived shortly after my third birthday and was naturally the most beautiful baby anyone had ever seen, and from that point onward, I was the ugly duckling to her swan. But after an icebreaker at our dorm, one of the guys asked if I wanted to go to a party with him, and once I recovered from the shock of being asked, I said yes. I'll never forget getting ready to go out that night and my roommate complaining about her tight jeans and blemishes and telling me that she wished she looked like me. I laughed so hard; it was more of a cackle, but then Lori started listing all of my assets, and when I looked in the mirror, it was like I was looking at myself for the first time.

Obviously, I didn't miraculously turn into Lynn while I was in Cambridge, but over four years, I learned how to maximize my best qualities and gained self-confidence that I had never had before. It didn't hurt that my dad was right about me having the brains, and I graduated with a 3.8 GPA and a member of Phi Beta Kappa.

Lynn had already disappeared to California when I came home from college. Although most people in town still knew us as the 'Summer Sisters,' I was working at my dad's office while applying to business school, and the feeling of inadequacy didn't feel as overpowering as it did when I was growing up.

There was a resurgence of "Lynn-Mania" when I was in my second year at Kellogg, and she had graduated from USC and landed a job as a model. I made the mistake of telling a few classmates that she was my sister when she made her first magazine ad (no shock to me, it was a toothpaste ad). Once word was out that my sister was the one in the Colgate ads, I could feel them looking at me and trying to figure out how the five-foot-three better-than-average-looking brunette could possibly be related to the toothpaste goddess.

Lucky for me, Lynn rarely came back from California, and even when she did a few more print ads, and eventually a string of terrible TV shows, I stopped telling anyone that we were related or that I even knew who she was because I had learned my lesson years ago.

I don't regret my decision to keep her in the shadows as far as my day-to-day life. Still, I do regret that Lynn saw it so acutely today *and* that it upset me so much that I ran away from her without even saying goodbye or telling her the shocking news from the lawyer.

***

"How was your day?" I ask Mark. The kids are both in bed, and although it's only eight o'clock, it feels more like midnight. Thanks to Rose, we are each staring at a beautiful plate of butter-roasted halibut with asparagus and olives. I used to feel guilty about Rose making dinner for us. Once Mom was gone, and I was in high school, Dad brought in someone to take care of the house and cook and clean for us because he was always at work, and he certainly wasn't going to be making our dinner. But that felt different because it wasn't like my mom could cook the meals and let someone else do it for her. However, once Harper was born, I gave up. I'm not a great cook anyway, and Mark is much happier eating the meals Rose makes than whatever I can cobble together. I rationalize that this gives me more time with the kids and at the store, but it doesn't mean I don't feel guilty when Rose is making my dinner before she goes home for the night, where I know she still has to cook for her own family.

"My day was okay, good to get back in the office," he replies, after clearing his palette with a sip of Chablis.

We take another few bites in silence, although I'm not particularly hungry. The events of the day have killed most of my appetite, and I would prefer to be eating popcorn in fuzzy sweatpants in front of the TV, but Mark likes to have a "real meal" when he comes home from work.

"What was the atmosphere like in the office?" I ask.

"It was good," Mark replies and then catches himself when he sees my face. "I mean, it was surreal to be there and see your dad's office in the corner, looking the same way it did the last time he stopped by. But I think people were glad that I was there today. Kind of lets everyone know that it's going to be okay," he tells me, gently nodding his head.

36

I want to scream that, "It's definitely not going to be okay!" but I know it doesn't solve anything, so I nod along with him. "I saw Lynn today," I say instead.

"Oh, really? Where did you see her?" Mark asks.

"She just showed up downtown as I was walking down the street. I was so distracted, I forgot even to ask what she was doing there," I tell Mark at the same time I realize it for myself.

"So, what happened?" Mark asks as he crosses the knife and fork on his almost spotless white china plate and pushes it away.

"We went for coffee. And we ran into Brianna," I say and wait for his reaction.

"How awful! She must have been falling all over Lynn, what a joke!" Mark says, pawing at the air as he mocks one of our fellow country club members.

At this moment, I am reminded of one of the things I love most about my husband – he doesn't think there's anything special about Lynn. And it's not just that he feels that way now after years of getting used to her (or the *idea* of her); he *never* cared about her.

Mark and I met at an insurance conference in St. Louis. He was eight months into his new life as an insurance broker at a rival firm, after his forced retirement from football, and I was there to represent our massive family firm. Only four years out of business school, my official title was Senior Vice President of Sales, but everyone knew my dad was grooming me to take over as CEO. Mark's celebrity status at the conference was so crazy that it was disruptive to the speakers and break-out groups, and people were falling all over themselves to get pictures with him and autographs. I was equally star-struck, but somehow watching grown men and women make complete jackasses of themselves was such a turnoff that I wanted no part of it. On the second night of the conference, Mark had come down to the hotel bar late at night and ducked into a corner booth for privacy and didn't notice that I was already sitting in the booth when he slid in and practically sat in my lap. He was embarrassed and apologized profusely, and I managed the perfect show of indifference to capture his attention. When I tell the story, I say that we didn't officially start dating until a few weeks later, after we'd exchanged several flirty emails, and he took me to dinner at Gibson's Steakhouse. But when Mark tells it, he says that we've been together since that night in the booth.

It took me two months to muster up the courage to tell him about Lynn. I was sure when I told him about her or showed him a picture, he would make an inappropriate comment or stare at her for a second too long or do any of the things my previous boyfriends had done to piss me off and ultimately end the relationship. But I figured I should get it over with before I got too attached to him. Even though Lynn was married to Trevor by this point and had a three-year-old son, it didn't matter. It wasn't that I thought Mark was going to up and leave me for Lynn; it was that he was going to *wish* that he could – to wonder why he got stuck with the lesser sister – and I couldn't handle that.

But to my ultimate surprise, Mark took one look at the first photo I showed him of Lynn, and his exact words were, "She's nothing special. She looks fake," he added, and he almost sounded bitter. Although I was thrilled, I couldn't be satisfied with his initial response, and I felt like he might be placating me, so I showed him dozens more photos and ads that I had stashed away, and he honestly didn't seem impressed. Then he took it a step further and told me how beautiful and smart and sexy I was, followed by the most mind-blowing shower sex imaginable, where Mark reinforced his admiration of my entire body.

I smile at Mark now as I recall that night and remember the feeling of confidence and security that came from finally finding someone who thought *I* was the best.

"She was awful," I reply. "It was painful watching her try and find a connection to Lynn," I relay, although I don't tell him that I'm responsible for initiating that conversation.

"That's because Lynn's never been in anything that anyone has ever heard of," Mark laughs, his dark blue eyes sparkling at me.

"That's not entirely true," I say, suddenly feeling defensive, even though I have no right. "Lynn was on CSI," I remind him.

"That was years ago, and you could barely see her," he says. "Look, I don't claim to understand what they do out there in la-la land," Mark says, holding up his humongous hands in mock surrender. "We all know Trevor's a dick, but they seem to work together, and he clearly makes enough coin that she doesn't have to do anything, so if she wants to keep saying she's an *actress*, why should I care?" Mark says.

I've had this same thought numerous times, but it sounds particularly cold when it's said out loud.

"Don't you think it's bizarre that Trevor and Declan didn't come for the funeral?" I ask, realizing this is the first time we've had the chance to talk about it, with all the chaos of the past few days.

"It's not just bizarre; it's completely disrespectful. I never liked Trevor, and you know your dad didn't either, so maybe he wouldn't have minded too much, but for his own grandson not to be here? That's just too much," Mark says, shaking his head. "And Lynn really didn't say anything about it?" he asks.

"I only saw her for a few minutes today. And then at the funeral, I barely spoke to her," I remind him.

"She's a piece of work," Mark says, more to himself than to me. "She's just going to disappear back to LA as soon as the will is read, and I doubt we'll ever hear from her again," he says, pushing back from the table and clearing both of our plates in one swift motion. "I've got some work to do; I'll be up in a bit," Mark says, putting the dishes by the farmhouse sink and making his way down the hall to his "office" – a thousand square feet dedicated to Bears memorabilia, multiple gaming consoles, a pinball machine, an eighty-inch TV and a desk somewhere back in the corner.

Once I'm alone at the sink washing the few dishes that Rose didn't get to, it occurs to me that I didn't tell Mark about the meeting with the lawyer either. I should have told Lynn right away, but Brianna threw me off. And I had every intention of telling Mark at dinner, but we got caught up talking about Lynn, and amazingly I forgot about it for a few minutes, or more likely, my mind still couldn't grasp the awful truth, so it created temporary amnesia. I'm sure that isn't something that actually happens, but it sounds like it could be possible, and considering my family history with memory loss, it seems plausible enough.

Then the idea floats over me, and I can't believe I'm considering it, but if I had to suffer the shock today with this news directly from Dad's lawyer – why should I cushion the blow for anyone else? After all, it's Dad's secret; I shouldn't have to do his dirty work. I'm sick and tired of being the oldest and the most responsible and always doing what I'm supposed to do to make everyone else happy.

Chapter Seven
Lynn

Since the divorce, my life has been in this crazy kind of limbo. Without Trevor and Declan, I no longer have any real responsibilities, and I stopped going on auditions even before the divorce, so it's not like I have to worry about work. Trevor pays for my car and my condo and gives me an allowance each month, but it isn't enough money to be frivolous. It's the exact amount that I need to support my pathetic lifestyle. Trevor is a total scumbag and, unfortunately, the best divorce lawyer in LA. He found every possible loophole while making sure my bargain basement attorney couldn't challenge him on a single thing.

I lost most of our "couple friends" during the divorce and most of Declan's friends' moms; so, the only friends that were left were from my acting days. But either I had already burned those bridges during my time with Trevor, or they're busy with work and can't hang out with me during my endless days of yoga classes and happy hours. I suppose I could have looked for a job after the divorce, but I was done with acting, too old to model, and it seemed pathetic to look for an entry-level job with my USC communications degree at the age of thirty-four.

But now I realize my life in LA these last two years have been somewhat vibrant compared to *this*. It's two o'clock in the afternoon, and I glance around at my current situation and sigh loudly, even though there's no one to hear me. I'm stretched out on the cheap, distressed leather couch in the living room, in red and blue flannel pajama pants and a faded sorority t-shirt touting a Kappa luau date party from 2003. My stomach starts to rumble, which reminds me that I have yet to eat breakfast or lunch because I haven't bothered to buy any food since arriving from California. I did a cursory check of the cabinets last night to see if the previous tenants left behind a box of crackers or cereal, but for better or worse, someone had cleaned everything out, including the crumbs.

I think back to my conversation with Ali and decide I need to give Trevor a call to tell him about my dad. I would rather just call Declan and leave Trevor out of it, but I assume he'll ignore my texts, and my calls will go straight to voicemail. I can't begin to imagine the terrible things Trevor has told our son about me; well, maybe I *can* imagine it, and that's what's so scary.

One of the many reasons he is such a successful attorney is that he can get people to believe everything he says. Although he has gotten slimier with age, I can't blame others for getting sucked in because I fell for his bullshit as a naïve college freshman. Five years older and a second-year law student, everything about Trevor was powerful and sexy. I never thought of myself as one of those girls who had "Daddy-issues" or needed to find a controlling older man to feel secure, but the day Trevor set his sights on me, I was a goner. Back then, his confidence was charming, and his admiration of my looks and desire to promote my modeling and acting career felt genuine and flattering. I'm sure some of it actually was authentic initially, and when I concentrate, I can look back and remember how much fun we had at the beginning. But then it changed, and maybe he didn't even change that much, perhaps he'd always been that way, like a wolf wearing a sheep costume, and over time he removed a furry glove, or tail and then one day the cute sheep mask came off, and I realized I was married to a naked wolf with razor-sharp teeth, but it was too late to do anything about it.

When Trevor picks up the phone, I actually imagine him wearing a wolf's head. It's so incongruous because I can picture the rest of him. He is wearing an immaculate Zegna suit (probably navy blue), with a custom-made white dress shirt, open at the collar, a four hundred dollar silk tie meticulously folded and resting inside his breast pocket in case he has to go to court, hand-made Italian leather shoes that take five months to make and cost more than some people make in a month, and to complete the look, an ostentatious watch (one of many from his vast collection) just to let everyone know exactly how much money he has, in case they didn't already.

"What is it?" Trevor says. His curt greeting lets me know that he already knows it's me calling, even though I refused to give my name to his secretary.

"I need to talk to Declan," I say, not wasting any time on pleasantries.

"He's at school," Trevor replies, his patience already gone.

"I *know* he's at school. It's the middle of the morning your time," I reply snidely.

"What do you mean, *my time*?" Trevor asks. "Where are you?" he questions, although I find it hard to believe that he cares.

Although I knew I would have to tell him to even have a chance of talking to Declan, I still prickle at the thought of talking to him about my dad. I can't fathom that he would be enough of a monster to say something terrible about my deceased father, but the two of them hated each other, and

Trevor is deplorable, so anything is possible. "I'm in Winnetka. My dad died," I say simply.

"Oh," Trevor responds.

"Yes. So, I would like to speak with Declan to tell him that his grandfather died," I say to Trevor, suddenly rising from the sofa and beginning to pace around the small living room as if movement will give me additional strength. Also, I know that Trevor is standing in his office right now, and it feels like I'm not on equal footing if I continue to lie here on the couch. Of course, he has me on speakerphone, and he's walking back and forth across his plush oriental carpet as he surveys the streets of Century City thirty stories below his floor-to-ceiling glass windows, but still, at least we're both standing up.

"When's the funeral?" Trevor asks, not even pretending to offer his sympathies.

"It was two days ago," I respond without thinking.

"What the fuck, Lynn. Don't you think Declan should have been at the funeral?" he shouts.

I'm so shocked by his response that I don't know what to say, which just gives Trevor more time to yell. "Why would you call now? You just want to tell him his grandpa died and that you couldn't be bothered to tell him about the funeral? Have you been drinking again, or is this your natural stupidity?" Trevor jeers.

"What? No, I haven't been drinking," I reply, which isn't what I mean to say at all. I don't need to defend myself, but as usual, Trevor has me so flustered that I forget what I want to say. "I tried to text Declan last week, but he didn't reply," I stammer.

"You were going to send him a text that his grandfather died? What the fuck is wrong with you?" Trevor yells at me.

"I asked him to call me; I didn't say anything about my dad in the text," I say lamely.

"So, your twelve-year-old son didn't reply to your text, and you decided that he didn't deserve to go to the funeral?" Trevor says.

"No, of course not!" I scream, and then I take a breath and try to compose myself. "I flew out to Chicago as soon as Jennifer called me and told me he died, and then I texted Declan once I got here. The funeral was held right away because that's how Jewish funerals work," I tell him. Although Trevor always knew I was Jewish, he used to say things like, "You're not really that Jewish" and "It barely counts because you certainly don't look Jewish." I'm mortified that I used to laugh along with him when he said those things, but now I wonder if he even remembers that tidbit about my family.

"Why didn't you call *me*?" Trevor asks harshly. "I mean, you're calling me now, and I picked up right away, so you can't say that I would have ignored you," he argues.

"I knew you wouldn't let me bring Declan with me to Winnetka, so I didn't even bother," I say to him. Although there is a lot of truth in this statement, I know that isn't the only reason I didn't tell him last week, but it doesn't make it feel any better right now.

"How do *you* know what I would have done?" Trevor scoffs.

"You wouldn't even let me have dinner with him a few months ago," I dispute.

"That's because Declan didn't want to have dinner with you. But this is different. I obviously would have come with him to Chicago for the funeral," Trevor says, making it all sound so easy, twisting my words and reality like he always does.

45

"That's easy for you to say *now*," I respond. I'm furious with myself for letting Trevor get to me, and also that he has additional ammunition.

"I guess we'll never know," Trevor sneers, and I can tell he is smiling. I used to think his Cheshire cat smirk was so sexy, but now I know better.

"Can you please have Declan call me after school? Or can you tell him to pick up his phone when I call?" I ask, trying to return to the initial purpose of the call.

"Why don't I pass along the message, and then he can decide if he wants to reach out?" Trevor offers.

I clench my free hand into a fist so tight that my nails leave tiny half-moon indentations in my palm. I know if I scream at him or tell him how evil he is, that he will throw it right back in my face as further proof of why I can't see Declan on my own or why my situation is what it is at present. "Trevor. Please let me be the one to tell Declan about his grandfather," I ask, in the calmest voice I can muster.

"I'll see about having him call you," Trevor says. "I have to go, Lynn; this has taken up enough of my day already." And with that, he hangs up the phone.

***

I remember driving by this bar a hundred times during high school, and I always imagined what it would look like inside. I envisioned it as dark and smoky, with a sticky wooden dance floor in the middle of the bar and small rickety tables and chairs around the perimeter, littered with dirty ashtrays and empty pint glasses. I pictured three or four regular patrons sitting at the bar, no matter the time of day or night, and a drunken couple swaying on the dance floor, hours past the time they should have gone home.

Considering my grim vision for this establishment, it doesn't make much sense that it's the bar I've chosen to come to for a drink when there are numerous restaurants in bars one town over in Winnetka where I know exactly what to expect. But after that hellish conversation with Trevor, this seems like the perfect bar to hide in and drink away my troubles. And as an added bonus, I can see if it looks like I pictured it would when I was sixteen.

As I push open the heavy door, I realize it's much brighter than I expected it to be, and of course, there isn't a trace of smoke because that's been banned indoors for years. It's still a bit of a dive, but more the style of a cozy English pub than the dirty warehouse I always imagined. There are also quite a few people here for this early in the afternoon, but then I glance at my watch and realize it's already five o'clock.

"What can I get you?" the bartender asks as I get settled on the maroon pleather stool.

"I'll have a bourbon on the rocks," I tell him.

"You don't care what kind?" he asks, in a husky voice that sounds like he smokes three or four cigarettes every time he takes his break.

"I'll have Woodford," I say, absentmindedly playing with the cocktail napkin that he put in front of me when I sat down and beginning to reconsider the wisdom in my decision to come here in the first place.

"We don't have that," he says, staring straight at me with his smoldering grey eyes.

"Okay, I'll take Widow Jane," I reply, beginning to tear the edges off the paper napkin.

"We don't have that either," he says, although he doesn't sound annoyed, he just sounds like I should know better, which I probably should.

"Maker's Mark?" I suggest.

"We got that," he says, turning around to grab the amber bottle of liquid off the shelf. I sneak a quick glance as he turns around, and although he's not my type, he's not tough to look at. His black jeans are impossibly tight, so much so that I find myself wondering how he's able to bend down and grab my glass from underneath the bar. His black t-shirt is equally tight and straining across his chest as he reaches underneath the bar toward the massive bucket of ice. He probably only weighs a hundred and fifty-five pounds soaking wet, which is not the size guy I typically even notice, but in his skin-tight clothes, it's hard not to notice that although he's compact, his entire body is made of defined muscle. He's also at least ten years younger than I am, although maybe all the scruffy facial hair is throwing me off, and he's actually more like fifteen years younger. Out in LA, it's impossible to guess anyone's age because of all the cosmetic surgery, so I've simply stopped trying.

"Nine dollars," he says, placing the glass in front of me. There are at least three ounces of bourbon in there. Even for Wild Turkey, I would have paid twenty dollars for that much booze out in LA, so I am thrilled and somewhat disturbed by the Midwest pricing (although it may only be this crappy bar, I doubt the prices are equally low at more upscale establishments in the area).

I place a twenty on the bar, and he glances at it and then lets it sit there while he goes to pour a beer for an equally skinny, scruffy guy at the other end of the bar. My first sip is larger than I intend, and it burns the back of my throat as I swallow. Still, after a few more, I can feel my body begin to relax ever so slightly, and I know it won't be long before the familiar warmth spreads through my chest, and I can start to forget the terrible things Trevor said on the phone.

The sinewy bartender has been deep in conversation with a cute blonde girl a few stools down for the past fifteen minutes, but apparently, he was paying attention because as soon as I knock back the last swallow of my drink, he appears in front of me and asks what he can get me.

I desperately want another large glass of bourbon to continue to wash away my call with Trevor, but then remember that I drove here tonight. "I'll have a Miller Lite," I reply. "And a glass of water," I add."

"No problem," he says, seeming a little friendlier than before. He places an ice-cold bottle in front of me, and the veins bulge on his forearms as he takes off the cap. I slide the twenty-dollar bill closer to him, but he ignores it and returns to his conversation with the blonde, leaving me alone with my weak beer.

I start to pick at the beer label since I've already shredded my napkin, and I can't help but think what people used to say this meant – a clear sign of sexual frustration. Although I think it's completely bogus to connect label shredding with sex, I can barely remember the last time I touched a man.

As if the universe could read my thoughts, a few seconds later, I feel a large, warm hand on my shoulder. "Lynn, is that really you?" a deep voice asks.

For a second, I don't say anything, and I don't dare to turn around because I would know that voice anywhere. In fact, I have heard that voice in my dreams over and over again for the past eighteen years, but I never thought I would actually hear it again for real. I know this is just a hallucination from the bourbon or the trauma of Trevor or the past few days with Jen, so I close my eyes and try to hold on to the hope for just a little longer before I have to turn around and know that the spell will be broken.

But when I open my eyes and turn around, it isn't a dream. Justin is standing in front of me, exactly as I've imagined so many times since we said goodbye in my driveway the night before I left for college. He looks a little older than he did our senior year of high school, but if anything, time has just made him more handsome. Justin's shaggy blonde hair is cut more closely now, and it looks a bit darker, but that could just be the lighting in the bar. His nose is still the tiniest bit crooked, and his eyes are as green as ever, and he has a few lines at the corner of his mouth that he didn't have in high school, but if I didn't get monthly collagen injections, I'm sure I'd have those too. His impossibly broad shoulders are even bigger than they used to be, he's probably put on a few pounds since his all-state wrestling days, but it only serves to make him look like a gigantic hug.

"It's me," I say sheepishly, unable to control my smile or my ability to stare anywhere other than directly into his eyes.

"Wow!" Justin says, looking me over from head to toe. "You look amazing," he says, followed by a little whistle.

"Thanks," I reply, feeling myself blush slightly. "You look good too."

"Eh," Justin says, pulling out the stool next to me. "Can I join you?" he asks.

"Of course," I reply, still trying to grasp the turn of events.

Justin gets the bartender's attention and orders two beers, because apparently mine is empty, even though I don't remember finishing it. "Cheers!" Justin says, raising his bottle to toast it against mine.

"I'm really sorry about your dad," Justin says, catching me totally off guard. "I'm sure that's why you're home," he adds.

"How did you know?" I ask, utterly confused.

"I read the obituary in the paper. But it's still a small town, Lynn, and your dad was a pillar of the community. I think it would be impossible *not* to know," he tells me, nodding his head sadly.

"Right, of course," I say. "Thanks," I add. "It's so hard to believe. I talked to him the day before it happened, and he seemed fine. And then poof! He's gone, just like that!" I tell him.

"I'm so sorry, Lynn," Justin says. "I heard that it was an aneurysm; that's so terrible," he empathizes. "And to go through it all after already losing your mom," he adds. "I'm so sorry about your mom as well."

"Thanks. Hard to believe that was eight years ago. But you know that she hadn't had much of a life for a long time. At least Dad didn't suffer," I say, changing the topic and repeating what mourners said to me at the funeral.

"I always loved your dad," Justin says, a smile spreading across his face as if he's remembering something particularly kind my dad said to him.

"You know my dad felt the same way about you," I remind him. I'm not sure I realized how rare their relationship was at the time, but Justin and my dad always had a special connection, which is usually not the case for dads and their daughter's high school boyfriends. I know Dad thought I was foolish to break up with Justin when I went off to school, another odd move for a dad, but I wasn't smart enough to listen to him.

I have so many questions for him; I don't know where to start. We have so much time to cover, I'm not sure how we'll be able to cover all of it, but I guess we don't have to get to it all tonight. "How have you been?" I ask, for lack of a better opener.

"Good. Things are good," Justin says. "How about you? I mean other than the obvious," he says, looking embarrassed.

"Good," I reply. And then I realize that I am desperate to tell him the truth and not hide behind my smile and pretend that everything's fine. "Actually, things haven't been great," I tell him.

"I'm sorry, Lynn," Justin says, looking at me intently.

"I got divorced a couple of years ago. And I lost custody of my son," I tell him.

"That's terrible," Justin says sympathetically.

"Yeah, I definitely picked the wrong guy," I say, giving Justin a sideways glance, but he is looking straight ahead and doesn't see me.

"How old is your son?" Justin asks.

"He's twelve," I reply, thinking of Declan, and realizing that school in LA must be over by now, and I still haven't heard from him.

"I can't believe you have a twelve-year-old. That's crazy," Justin says. "I still think of you as eighteen," he says, smiling at me.

"Things would be so much easier if we were, wouldn't they?" I ask him.

"Hmmm, I don't think I would do it all again," Justin says and laughs, his green eyes twinkling.

"Come on; you wouldn't go back to senior year again if you could?" I ask, playfully nudging his arm and feeling a spark of electricity run through my entire body as a montage of old pictures flashes before my eyes, most of them involving Justin with his clothes off.

"As much fun as we had in high school, you couldn't pay me to go back," Justin says, and his words are a crushing blow, but I plaster a smile on my face and try not to show it. "I've worked really hard to get to where I am now since high school; I can't imagine having to do it all over again," he continues, taking a swig of his beer and placing it back on the pristine napkin in front of him.

"So, things are good?" I ask, trying to move the conversation along.

"Things are good," he confirms, running his fingers through his shaggy hair as if he's not quite used to the length.

"Are you still working for your dad?" I ask him.

"Not anymore," he says.

"Oh," I reply, wondering if this is a good or a bad thing, but before I can inquire further, he provides the answer.

"I bought the business from him a few years ago, and my parents retired to Florida," he says proudly.

"That's great," I say, happy that he seems happy. Even though we were too young to be thinking about the future, this

53

scenario was one of the things we fought about in high school. I wanted to go out to California and become a famous movie star, and he wanted to stay here and work for his dad's landscaping company. I thought it sounded so boring, and I told him he wasn't living up to his full potential. Selfishly, I was also embarrassed that he was going to be a gardener. Now, it seems he's the one that's happy with his life, even if it didn't bring him fame or fortune, and I'm right back where I started.

"How long are you in town?" Justin asks.

"I'm not sure," I reply. "Things haven't been going too well in LA recently, so I think I may stick around for a little bit," I tell him. Although this is far more information than I've shared with Jen. I'm still not able to admit that I've rented an apartment here and have no idea when, if ever, I'll be returning to California. But running into Justin here tonight may be a sign that coming home was the right thing to do – my chance for a fresh start with my first love.

The bartender clears away our empty beer bottles, and I raise my hand to signal that we'd like two more beers. "This round is on me," I say to Justin, tossing my long, blonde hair over my shoulder and flashing him a suggestive grin.

"I'm going to have to take a rain check," Justin says. "I'm meeting Devin for a drink," he says. And before I can ask who Devin is, a petite redhead appears at his side and leans in to kiss him squarely on the lips before she says, "Sorry I'm late."

"No problem! I actually ran into an old friend from high school, and we were catching up," Justin says, pointing in my direction. "Devin, this is my old friend Lynn. Lynn, this is my fiancé, Devin."

"Nice to meet you," Devin says, reaching out to shake my hand.

"Nice to meet you too," I muster.

"We're going to go sit down, but it was good to run into you!" Justin says. "Maybe I'll see you again while you're back here."

"Okay," I reply because my head is spinning too fast for me to think of anything else to say. I watch them walk across the bar, and he puts his arm around her shoulder and whispers something in her ear, and I honestly want to die. Before tonight, I hadn't thought about Justin for a million years. That's not exactly true; I thought about him all the time, but it was more like a dream, and I was sure he was married with four kids, and I would never see him again. But now he's thirty feet away and just as cute and funny and sexy as he was eighteen years ago, but he's with someone else – his fiancé. I wonder if they've been engaged for a while or if it's still new and perhaps unstable, but I feel terrible for thinking that.

The underfed bartender comes back with two beers and gives me a puzzled look as he looks around for the other beer drinker. "I'll take them both," I tell him, taking another bill out of my wallet and putting it down on the bar. He shrugs and pops of the tops and takes the money; it's clearly no concern to him who drinks the beer.

I glance over my shoulder to see Devin curled up under Justin's arm, practically in his lap, and I increase my drinking speed, so I won't have to encounter them on the way out or have to witness any further displays of affection.

As I stumble out to my car, I curse Trevor and Justin, and Devin and hold them all responsible for the number of drinks I had, since my initial intention was only to have one or two to relax, but the circumstances changed. I sigh and take out my phone to call an Uber and pray that my stupid rental car will be okay in this parking lot overnight.

Ron, my Uber driver, has the misfortune to ask if I had a nice evening, and I cry the entire ride home.

Chapter Eight
Jennifer

Mitchell Freeman has been Dad's lawyer for the past twenty years, and before that, his father, Marvin Freeman, had been Dad's lawyer since the day Dad sold his first insurance policy. Dad was exceedingly loyal to the Freemans and to all of his other business and personal contacts, which makes some of his other decisions difficult to understand, but I can't think about that right now.

Mitchell's office hasn't changed much since he took over from his dad. It still contains the heavy oriental carpets, dark wood, and oversized, uncomfortable furniture that are to be expected of upscale suburban law firms, but he did add some modern artwork and, thankfully, some office equipment that appears to be fairly new.

Mitchell, Mark, and I are gathered around the mahogany conference table, and the two men are busy discussing the outlook for the upcoming Bears game on Sunday while I scan through the messages on my phone to see if I missed anything from Lynn.

"Did she say she was running late?" Mark asks, glancing at his watch.

"I'm checking right now," I reply. "But I don't see anything," I tell him, annoyed at Lynn for being late and with Mark for assuming I would know *anything* about my sister's whereabouts.

"It's only ten past," Mitchell says, trying to diffuse the tension. "Can I get you any coffee?" he offers.

We both turn down the offer and return to our own devices while we wait in silence. Mitchell takes the opportunity to shuffle some papers in front of him, divides them into multiple piles, and scribbles notes on the copy closest to him. I always thought of Mitchell as young because he was so much younger than Marvin, but observing him now and doing the math, I realize he's probably close to fifty. His dark hair has started to turn gray at the temples, and the remainder is getting that salt and pepper effect that men can pull off so well and just makes women look old. He's average height, maybe five-ten, he's slightly overweight with a visible belly and traces of a double chin, but anyone who's known him for more than a few years knows what a miraculous change this is from his former appearance. After being disastrously overweight his entire life, Mitchell had gastric bypass surgery two years ago, and the transformation is staggering. No matter his size, his skin always has a healthy glow, like he does most of his work on the golf course in San Diego, rather than in conference rooms in the suburbs of Chicago. I've always suspected he's a frequent visitor to the tanning salon over in Wilmette, but maybe it's just his natural, ruddy complexion. Today I'm grateful for his easy smile, kind demeanor, and even the perma-tan because I don't think any of us could endure a stone-faced, aggressive attorney.

"I'm so sorry I'm late," Lynn says as she slips into the room and glides into the seat at the far end of the table. Her long hair is piled into a messy knot on top of her head, and she has yet to remove her dark sunglasses. I can't tell if she came straight from the gym at her hotel or if she worked out and then changed into a different set of workout clothes, but she's sporting skin-tight black leggings with cutouts on the side and a tight grey zip-up hoodie. It's only the four of us in here, but still, I would have thought she might have realized the unwritten dress-code of what to wear when coming to a lawyer's office for the reading of your father's will – and it isn't gym clothes. I cross my legs, clad in wool Max Mara pants, and glare at Lynn. "Whatever," I mutter under my breath.

"Let's get started," Mitchell says, shuffling his papers again.

"I've got a meeting at noon," Mark says, to no one in particular, and I swear I can feel Lynn rolling her eyes, even though she's still wearing those damn glasses.

Mitchell clears his throat to get our attention, and when we are all looking in his direction, he continues. "Although there are some slightly complicated aspects of David's estate, related to trusts that he left for the grandchildren, the majority of his assets have been divided equally," Mitchell says.

Out of the corner of my eye, I think I see a look of surprise on Lynn's face, and I wonder if she thought Dad would do otherwise, especially in light of her recent revelation that she's been in constant communication with him. Although maybe her surprise isn't that she's included equally, but rather that she isn't getting more? I don't know exactly how Mitchell is going to phrase it, but I know the gist of what he is about to share, and I feel guilty that I kept it to myself. I mostly feel guilty that I didn't tell Mark, but I even feel bad about Lynn. I have no justification for keeping it to myself, other than I didn't want to talk about it. Right after I met with Mitchell and I saw Lynn, I was all set to tell her, but then Brianna appeared, and I couldn't even bear to be around her. Then I was planning to tell Mark over dinner, but he didn't even ask about my urgent meeting with Mitchell, and so I stubbornly decided not to tell him either. Obviously, I should have found time over the past two days to tell them, but I chose to remain in a selfish state of denial, and so here we are.

"I'm sure you were all shocked by the news when Jen told you," Mitchell begins, throwing me under the bus, "but hopefully, you've had a little time to digest the news and try to make sense of it."

"What are you talking about?" Mark asks, looking back and forth between Mitchell and me, his gaze coming to rest squarely on me.

"What is the news?" Lynn asks, staring directly at Mitchell and finally taking off her sunglasses to reveal faintly bloodshot eyes and traces of under-eye circles on her usually unblemished face – I mentally withdraw my earlier question as I am now certain that she didn't go to the gym this morning.

Mitchell looks at me helplessly, as if to say, "How could you not have told them?" and I shrug and slink back in my seat, acknowledging my error but still unwilling to speak up.

"Okay, well then, I need to do things slightly differently than I had planned," Mitchell says, shuffling more papers and seeming more than a little bit flustered. I feel bad for putting him in this position because he's such a nice guy, but at the same time, I wonder why it was supposed to be my job to break the news?

"What's going on? Please tell us what's happening," Lynn demands, looking like she might be sick, although I'm not sure if it's the sudden uncertainty of the situation or her hangover causing her nausea.

Mitchell takes a deep breath and shifts slightly in his seat before addressing our group. "Your father was a great man," he begins, and the room remains eerily silent as everyone waits for Mitchell to say the word, "but."

"However, he hasn't had an easy time of things. Everything he went through with your mother took a toll on him," Mitchell says.

"And it didn't affect us?" Lynn asks, incredulous.

"No, no, that's not what I meant. Of course, it was hard for you too. I just want you to keep that in mind," he says.

"C'mon Mitchell, just tell us what's going on," Mark says, sounding frustrated. He leans forward in his seat and puts his enormous palms on the shiny wood table. For years their size was a tremendous asset, making sure Mark never lost his grip on the ball, but now they are almost a nuisance when he's trying to type or text or simply blend in with average humans.

"The majority of David's assets are divided equally," he begins, but I wait and watch the other two because I know what's coming. "There is money left to charity, and then, of course, the money for the grandchildren as I mentioned, but the bulk of it is divided into three equal parts..." Mitchell continues, and I see Mark sit up a little straighter, and Lynn opens her mouth like she's going to say something and then close it again.

"The bulk of the assets are split between Jennifer, Lynn, and Courtney Stewart."

"Who is Courtney Stewart?" Lynn sputters, at the exact same time Mark says, "Who the fuck is Courtney?"

This is exactly what I said when I sat here with Mitchell a couple of days ago, but now I know the answer, so I keep my mouth shut and wait for Mitchell to explain. "After your mother moved into the facility, your father had a brief relationship with a woman named Mary Brown; it was for a few months in 1998," Mitchell pauses, exhaling heavily as he delivers this initial piece of news and waits for it to sink in.

"Is this some kind of joke?" Lynn asks, enraged. "I was a junior in high school in 1998!"

"I'm sorry to be the one to have to reveal this," Mitchell says, catching my eye before I can stare down into my lap again, "But I assure you this isn't a joke. Let me finish explaining, and hopefully, I can answer your questions," he says.

"David was beside himself after your mother had to go away. As you both remember, her dementia had started years before that, and he had been caring for her since she was in her early forties. They were both only forty-eight when he couldn't take care of her anymore, and she had to go to the in-patient facility in Wisconsin for her own safety. It was heartbreaking," Mitchell retells.

I'm waiting for Lynn to make a snide comment, so I'm quite surprised when I look over and see that there are tears in her eyes, and her lips are sealed.

Mitchell continues, "I'm honestly not sure where he met Mary; that was never a part of the story, but I know that she is a nurse and was about ten years younger, and they were only together for a couple of months. Your father was so hurt and lost, and he said it just happened, but the guilt overwhelmed him, and he broke it off. However, it turns out that Mary got pregnant during their time together," Mitchell says, and he pauses again.

Lynn and Mark both gasp at the same time, and I find myself wondering how they hadn't figured that out yet, but I'm sure I had the same stunned reaction, and I've already blocked it out.

"Although your father never resumed his relationship with Mary, he promised to support the child in whatever way Mary wanted," Mitchell says.

"This is un-fucking-believable," Lynn says, and I find myself agreeing with her.

"Mary had a little girl in 1999 and named her Courtney. Mary got married about a year after that to a man named Brian Stewart, and they have raised Courtney together, but your father has always provided her with financial support. Mary was reluctant to accept much from your dad, but she did accept enough every year to make sure Courtney had money saved for college and for summer camp and other activities that they wouldn't have been able to afford," Mitchell finishes.

"So, you're telling us that we have a sister somewhere out there?" Lynn asks, befuddled.

"Yes. Technically a half-sister, but yes," Mitchell says.

"Can you tell us about her?" Mark asks, speaking up for the first time since Mitchell delivered the bombshell. Although it's not his sister, Mark and Dad were incredibly close, and the addition of a new sister-in-law certainly impacts him. However, I worry that what's going to trouble him most is coming to grips with Dad's infidelity from twenty-one years ago. Mark has always put him up on a pedestal in light of the experience he had with his own father.

"I can give you the basics. She's twenty years old now and a sophomore at Northwestern," Mitchell says, leaning forward and putting his elbows on the table.

"She lives right here?! In Evanston?!" Lynn exclaims.

"She grew up in Lake Forest, but yes, she currently lives in Evanston."

"Oh my God," Mark says.

"Wait, does she know about Dad? Does she know about us?" Lynn asks, thinking to ask the question that I've been wondering for the last few days.

"She does now," Mitchell says solemnly.

"Has she ever met him?" I ask, finally able to ask the question I've been dying to ask, and drawing a sneer from Lynn, but I choose to ignore it.

"I don't believe so. I guess she may have met him when she was a baby, but I don't have that information," Mitchell says. "I'm really sorry to be the one to give you all of this news," Mitchell says, and I try to avoid his glare. "I suggested repeatedly to your father that he should tell you about this while he was alive, but he said he wasn't ready, and it wasn't my place to tell you," he says.

"How could he do this to Mom?" Lynn asks, incredulous. "Why would he cheat on mom like that?!"

I'm beyond surprised to hear Mark clear his throat and start to speak, and Lynn immediately scowls but waits for him to continue. "I know I wasn't around twenty years ago, but just watching your dad suffer when your mom died and how it has weighed on him since then, I can't imagine what it would have been like to be in his shoes," Mark finishes, but he's already staring off into space, and I can see the pedestal he's kept my dad on all these years crumbling to pieces.

"But twenty years ago? Mom wasn't even that sick! How could he do that to her?" Lynn protests.

"Oh, come on, Lynn," I interrupt. "Mom barely remembered my name when I was in high school, and that was two years earlier," I remind her. I know I'm not being fair because I had the same reaction a couple of days ago, and only after I've thought it through, have I even begun to wrap my head around it.

"So, how does this work?" Lynn asks, the hurt and anger visible on her beautiful, tired face and solely directed at Mitchell.

I almost feel bad for Mitchell when I see the pained look on his face as he manages this impossible situation. It's Dad's fault for putting him in this shitty position. I'm sure he gets paid well, but I'm not sure he gets enough money to make up for this kind of debacle. When I was here the other day, Mitchell told me that he thought Dad was close to changing his mind and was likely going to tell us about Courtney soon, but he wasn't quite ready. But then he didn't wake up one morning, and he never got the chance.

"Again, I know this is a lot of information for you to digest all at once, but your dad was very clear about making sure that he continued to provide for Courtney when he was gone..." Mitchell trails off.

"Mitchell, can we just get on with this so that we can get out of here?" Mark asks, reaching out to take my hand, further emphasizing that Lynn won't be included in our subsequent discussion.

"I think that's a good idea," Mitchell says, looking somewhat relieved at the prospect of all of us leaving his office. "However, David had very specific instructions. Although the law doesn't require everyone to be gathered here for the will to be read, that's mostly something that happens in books and movies, David was explicit that he wanted a formal reading before probate, and he didn't want his will to be read until everyone is here," he explains, shuffling his papers again and refusing to meet anyone's eye.

"Are you saying Courtney needs to be here for this?" Lynn explodes, banging her hand on the table.

"Yes, that is correct," Mitchell says.

"So, is this a waste of our time today? Why are we even here?" Mark asks, sounding annoyed and angry and glancing at his stainless-steel Rolex.

Mitchell takes a deep breath, and I swear I know what he's going to say before the words come out of his mouth. "Courtney's here today. She's waiting in the other room," Mitchell admits sheepishly.

The three of us look around at each other, and I wait for Lynn's outburst, but surprisingly, she doesn't say anything; she just shakes her head and mumbles something under her breath that sounds like, "Jesus Christ."

"I'll go get her if that's okay with all of you, and then we can begin," Mitchell says, already pushing his chair back from the table and making his way out of the room to fetch our long-lost-sister from wherever he's been hiding her. In the brief moments that he's gone, I wonder if I should attempt to break the ice since there is so much to discuss; but ultimately, I decide to keep quiet.

When the door opens again, there is an attractive, petite woman in her fifties, with dyed blonde hair, and I instantly recognize her as the distraught woman from the back row at Dad's funeral. I almost say, "Ah-ha, at least that finally makes sense," but thankfully, I keep that in my inner monologue. Behind her is a young woman with shoulder-length brown hair who is about Lynn's height. She isn't striking like Lynn, but with a smattering of freckles across her button nose and an overall girl-next-door vibe, she looks cute and approachable in a way that Lynn never has.

"Hello, I'm Courtney," she says in a quiet voice as she takes her seat at the table.

Chapter Nine
Mark

Mary gives a polite smile to Jen and Lynn and then fixes her gaze firmly in her lap. I know why she is avoiding eye contact with me, and I'm grateful for it. When Jen first asked about her at the funeral, I couldn't remember where I knew her from and didn't give it much thought, but later that night, I realized that I had seen her at the office a couple of times over the past few months. I assumed she was a friend or perhaps a potential client because I couldn't imagine another scenario, but now it's all falling into place. I know I don't have any reason to feel guilty, but I have an overwhelming feeling of shame at keeping this from Jen, even though I didn't realize I was part of some sort of conspiracy, and this isn't the type of secret I ever would have kept for David.

In the midst of the awkward silence, while we all await Mitchell's guidance, my phone vibrates so forcefully on the table that it jumps almost two inches to the left. Lynn and Jen both scowl at me like I planned the disruption, and I quickly grab the offending device and put it in my lap. Before I put it in my pocket, I read the text from Kayla that asks if I'm going to be back for my meeting at eleven. I quickly type a reply and tell her that it seems unlikely and ask if she can push the meeting back to the afternoon, and then shove the phone in my pocket to appease my wife and sister-in-law.

I've never been to a will reading before. When my mom died, I got a bunch of papers in the mail telling me about the outstanding bills that had become my responsibility, and that was that. So, with all of this build-up, I'm not sure if Mitchell will actually read David's will to us, like a bedtime story, or if this is just another one of those high-brow things that is called one-thing and means something else. I've had a lot of experience with that in my time with the Summer family, and just as soon as I think I have everything figured out, they throw something new my way that we never learned about in the trailer parks of Missouri.

My question is soon answered when Mitchell hands us each a piece of paper and instructs us to read it. It doesn't take long to figure out that this single page of thick cream-colored paper isn't David's actual last will and testament, but rather a letter from David written to explain his will. I glance over to see Jen's reaction, but her eyes are glued to the paper, and the rest of her features are eerily frozen, so it's impossible to tell what she's thinking. Conversely, Lynn's clenching the paper in her fist, her eyes squinted into narrow slits, and her lips are pursed in such a way that it looks like she might spit right on the table. If the situation were different, I would whisper to Jen that Lynn looks like an evil villain from a Disney movie, and Jen would dissolve into fits of laughter, but I don't think she would appreciate it right now.

Although the process has felt somewhat official up to this point, the letter from David is a short, handwritten letter on his personal stationery, which Mitchell has photocopied, so there are enough for all of us to read. I assume the actual will is full of legal jargon and is a thick, complicated document, but this note couldn't be any more straightforward.

Dear Jen, Lynn, and Courtney,

If you are all together and reading this letter, then it means I'm gone. I'm sorry to put you in this situation, but I hope you can forgive me. The documents will provide all of the details, but I have a few last wishes that I ask you to honor.

1) *Jen & Lynn - I know it won't be easy, but please try to forgive me for what I did to your mother, although I have never been able to forgive myself. Please don't let this be all you remember about me.*

2) *Please do not blame Mary in any way for keeping this secret with me. We did what we felt was best for all of you at the time.*

3) *Use this as an opportunity to start fresh. Jennifer and Lynn, my wonderful girls, please put the past behind you and appreciate how lucky you are to have each other. And now that you have Courtney, you must bring her into the family and make sure you all realize how blessed you are to have each other.*

4) *Take care of each other. I am far from perfect but creating all of you was the best thing I've ever done.*

5) *The company is yours to share, but I know I can count on Mark to keep things running.*

All my Love,
David

Due to its meager length, it's obvious that we're all done reading, but the room remains silent for an uncomfortable amount of time. Unsurprisingly, Lynn is the first one to break the silence. "This is bullshit," she says, attempting to throw her letter on the table, but the single sheet of paper merely glides lazily toward the center of the glossy wood table, which does not have the desired effect. "I'm out of here," she announces, grabbing her bag from the back of the leather chair and storming out of the room.

Once she's gone, Jen addresses Courtney, "I'm sure this is a lot for you to take right now too, and I know this isn't *your* fault," she says, turning her petite frame to glare at Mary, "But I can't sit here and have a family reunion right now. I just can't," she says, exasperated.

70

Jen turns her attention to Mitchell, "What are we supposed to do with this?" she asks, clutching the paper tightly in her hand. "Is this some kind of joke? Dad was never the kind of guy to talk about his dying wishes or any nonsense like that, and now we have this letter – what am I supposed to do with this?" she asks again, in utter disbelief.

"I'm *really* sorry," Mitchell says, and the pained look on his face and beads of perspiration on his forehead back up the sentiment. "Your father has also named you the executor of his estate," he continues, "It's a big job, so if you would like my help, I'd be happy to assist you with those responsibilities, or you are welcome to hire your own attorney," Mitchell offers.

"Don't be ridiculous," Jen says, dismissing the idea with a wave of her hand. "*Of course,* I'm going to have you do it. Just because I'm pissed at my dad doesn't mean I'm upset with you," she explains.

At Jen's comment about being angry with David, I notice Mary flinch. Mary has been so quiet that I almost forgot she was in the room, or at least as much as you can forget about someone sitting nine feet away from you. It looks like she might finally say something to Jen, but then she reconsiders and directs her gaze back toward her lap.

"I have to go. I'll call you soon to follow up about this executor stuff," Jen says to Mitchell. She grabs her Burberry trench coat off the back of her chair and looks at me expectantly, never once looking in Mary's direction.

"Courtney, I'm not sure what to say. I still can't wrap my head around this, but I guess we should get together at some point?" Jen suggests lamely.

"Sure," Courtney says, shrugging her shoulders, her shiny hair swaying gently with the movement.

"I should get back to work as well," I say to Mitchell.

"Thanks for coming. I know this was...difficult," he says, finally finding an appropriate word, although I'm not sure that begins to describe the situation.

"Good-bye Mitchell, good-bye Courtney," Jen says, turning the handle of the conference room door.

It's now my turn to say good-bye, and it feels shameful to ignore Mary the way that Jen just did. Blatantly giving the cold shoulder to this older woman goes against everything I believe in, but I also risk Jen's wrath if I acknowledge Mary, and that might be worse. Finally, I settle for "bye," with a casual wave toward the room and hope that Mary feels included.

***

When I woke up this morning, I was looking forward to the day. I assumed the meeting with the lawyer would be short and sweet, and then during my follow up meeting with Tom, I was going to get up the nerve to ask about opportunities, but now that's impossible. I glide into my parking spot in the quietest car ever made, so quiet and efficient that it takes the joy out of driving, and I shuffle inside, forcing myself to put my shoulders back, and my head up after the third employee gives me a sideways glance.

"They're waiting for you in the conference room," Kayla says as I approach her desk. "We brought in lunch," she adds, and my stomach grumbles to remind me that it is well past lunchtime.

I see Tom and Tracy chatting through the glass wall, with an overflowing platter of gourmet sandwiches on the table in front of them, large enough to feed a dozen people. There are a few other people in the room who are likely there to take notes and provide key points of information on supplemental disability insurance, but I'm embarrassed to say I don't know their names.

"Sorry I'm late," I apologize as I enter the room.

"Not a problem, man," Tom says as he comes around the table and claps me on the back in a one-handed bro-hug.

"You won't be late for practice now, will you?" I ask, glancing at my watch and then back at Tom.

"I'm good. We're not back until five-thirty today," Tom says, referring to the second practice of the day for The Chicago Bears' starting running back.

"This is what we prepared for you based on our previous meeting," Tracy says, bypassing additional small talk and plowing ahead to the main event. She stretches her long arm, clad in a purple flowery blouse, across the table, and hands Tom a professionally bound presentation with the gold "Summer Risk Management" logo emblazoned on the first.

I know that I won't be able to add much to the conversation if it goes into a detailed risk discussion, so I decide to jump in early. David's letter is occupying ninety percent of the space in my head, and although the news about Courtney is mind-blowing, I'm most concerned with his unwavering faith in me and that I've lost my faith in him. "Tom, you know I know better than anyone what happens when you get hurt playing ball. The basic NFL policies aren't going to cover you, so you're smart to get as much coverage as you can. I wish I knew a lot more about supplemental disability insurance ten years ago," I tell him and then try to break the awkward moment with a laugh.

It's not fair to say that I was ever in Tom's shoes because Tom was a third-round draft pick out of Tennessee, and he is in his second year as a starting running back for The Bears with over a thousand yards rushing in his first year and on track to beat his numbers this year. I was a seventh-round draft pick out of Illinois and damn lucky to make it through the Combine, but I worked my ass off every year in the NFL, even though I never started in a single game, and I wouldn't trade a minute of it.

Although our positions aren't quite the same, I do believe I am the ideal person to advise Tom and the dozen or so other Bears' team members that we serve as clients – perhaps the only thing I do well here. When I first signed my contract in 2002, it was like a dream come true. I couldn't believe that someone was going to pay me to play football, and the amount of money was staggering at the time. It was the league minimum of $225,000 but compared to my mom's paycheck from Wal-Mart or my paltry student loan stipend, I might as well have been Warren Buffet. At the same time, they handed me all sorts of paperwork about my benefits, including health insurance, life insurance, a 401K, and so many other plans that I couldn't keep track of it all. As a twenty-two-year-old, I was on top of the world and invincible, or at least it seemed that way until I tore all the ligaments in my knee and was told I would never play again.

"Let me walk you through it," Tracy says, opening her copy of the folder and indicating that Tom should do the same. I've listened to this presentation countless times, and I still don't know all the details, but I hear numbers like fifteen million and twenty million thrown around, and I know that Tom is much savvier than I was at his age, or at least receiving far better advice.

I walk Tom out of the building, and he thanks me profusely for my help. I make a point to stand as straight as possible, and I'm embarrassed to admit, I'm flexing slightly because there's nothing that makes you feel quite as old as a twenty-four-year-old athlete in the prime of his career. "Hey, man, on the phone the other day, you mentioned you wanted to ask me something about the team, or the coaches, or something, right?" Tom asks as if it just hits him.

"Oh right," I say, trying to play dumb. "I just meant if you know anyone else on the team looking for some extra insurance, you can send them my way; we'll take care of them," I say, with a goofy smile.

"Alright, cool, if that's all it is. I'll let you know," he says as he lowers himself into the drivers' seat of his bright yellow Lamborghini and raises his hand in a salute before he peels out of the parking lot.

I must be imagining it because there's no way I could actually hear anything over the roar of the engine, but I swear before he drives away, I hear him say, "You'd have to kill me before I sold fucking insurance for a living."

Chapter Ten
Courtney

Mitchell apologized multiple times after everyone left his office, but I waved off his apology; it's not like it's his fault my entire family is full of liars and assholes. My mom is blessedly quiet on the way out of his office and for the first few minutes of the ride back to Evanston, but as we hit the curve on Sheridan Road, she feels the need to justify her actions yet again. We've been having this argument for the past four days, and I don't understand why she thinks I'm ever going to see it her way. "Someday when you have children of your own..." she begins, and I cut her off.

"Just stop, Mom," I say, turning my body to stare out the passenger window at the stately old homes.

"I'm only saying that I was just doing what I thought was best," she says in a soft voice that I found remarkably comforting up until a few days ago, and now it sounds like nails on a chalkboard.

I promised myself I wouldn't engage anymore after our blowout fight in the living room of my sorority house two days ago, but I can't help myself. "You seriously thought it was in my best interest to tell me that my birth father was dead when he lived thirty minutes away from me?!" I shout at her. "I missed out on the chance to meet my real dad because of you, and now he's dead. You honestly thought that was the best decision?!" I scream, unable to control the volume of my voice, as I feel myself starting to shake, and my cheeks grow hot.

"I'm so sorry," she says as her voice wobbles, and I can tell she is about to cry. I'm furious with her, but it's still heartbreaking to watch your mom cry.

"Please let me out here," I ask her as we pass through the northern part of the Northwestern campus.

"Don't you want to go back to your room?" she asks.

"I'm going to go to SPAC, some of the girls are training now, and I have clothes in my locker," I tell her, using the well-loved acronym to refer to the massive sports pavilion where I spend the majority of my free time training with the varsity women's basketball team.

"Okay," she sighs, pulling over at the stop sign on Sheridan in front of the tennis courts. I'm shocked she doesn't put up more of a fight or lecture me again about how hurtful it is to dismiss Brian as my *real* father – the only father I've ever known.

"Bye," I mutter as I get out of the car and slam the door behind me before she has time to reply. As I watch her sensible light gray Toyota Highlander drive away, I can't help but think what car my mom would have been driving if we grew up as the legitimate family of David Summer. These thoughts keep sneaking into my head, and it makes me feel greedy and selfish, but I can't stop them from coming. Growing up in Lake Forest, it was clear that we had less money than a lot of other families, but it never bothered me. My "dad" was the principal of the high school, and my mom was a neonatal intensive care nurse at Lake Forest Hospital. We lived in one of the smaller houses in town, but it's a beautiful house and perfect for three people. There was never a question of money when it came to vacations or fancy basketball camps, or even having enough money for college. But some of the pieces of that puzzle are coming together more clearly as I learned that David Summer gave my mom money each year to pay for things like sports camps and school trips to Paris, and he was the one who funded my entire college savings account.

I wander through the massive brick fraternity quads of north campus on my way to the gym and marvel at the relative quiet of the Thursday afternoon. In a few hours, this place will be filled with drunk coeds stumbling from one keg party to the next. But right now, students are walking back to their dorms from grueling lectures in the tech building or hurrying to make it down to south campus in time for a class that starts in ten minutes, and they still have almost a mile to go, all against the backdrop of a crisp fall day, the ground already covered in a blanket of colorful leaves.

Christina is waiting for me outside the main entrance, and I'm beyond happy to see her after my shitty morning. She's wearing a faded purple t-shirt with a small NU logo on the chest and a pair of minuscule black spandex shorts that make her muscular, espresso-colored legs look about a mile long. At five foot eight, I am one of the shortest players on the team. Christina is three inches taller than I am, making her only average for the basketball team, but it always feels like she towers over me, especially with her trademark cornrows piled on top of her head, adding at least another two inches.

"What took you so long?" she asks, as soon as I'm within earshot.

"I can't even begin to tell you how bad it was," I moan. "Sorry I'm late, but it was horrible," I say, resting my head on her shoulder as she pats me on the head like a puppy. "Where's everybody else?" I ask, realizing that of the four girls on the text chain, Christina is the only one here.

"They all had to go to some discussion group. I'm the only one nice enough to wait for your sorry ass," she says playfully.

"Thanks," I say awkwardly, suddenly aware that I told everyone I would be here an hour ago.

"Let's go," she says. "You can tell me all about your evil step-sisters while we're doing weights," she laughs, heading toward the shiny doors of the Henry Crown Sports Pavilion.

"It's evil *half-sisters*," I tell her, laughing for the first time all day.

"C'mon, I'll bench press twice as much as you, and then you'll feel like a loser and forget all about it," she jokes.

"God, let's hope so," I say with a smile, trying to clear my head and forget about this new reality, even if only for the next hour.

***

When I arrive at Norris Student Center a few hours later, Preston is already waiting for me at one of the round tables in the corner, with an enormous tray of french fries and chicken fingers in front of him. I slide into the white plastic chair, and he hands me a fry before he even says hello. I know I shouldn't take it, Coach would kill me if he saw me eating it, but Christina and I just had a killer work out, and as hard as I tried, I'm nowhere near forgetting my shitty morning.

"Thanks," I mumble as I munch the hot, greasy fry. He hands me another, and I shake my head, "Not all of us can eat like that in season," I remind him.

"You're only pre-season right now; I'm actually *in* season. And I had four hours of practice today, so I deserve this,"

79

Preston says, shoving an entire chicken finger into his mouth in one bite.

"Okay, you win," I laugh, shrugging my shoulders as I lean back in the white plastic chair and accept that I'm going to have to watch him eat the entire plate of fried food while I sip ice water from my Hydroflask.

"Besides, how am I supposed to keep up my fine physique if I eat protein shakes and salad and grilled chicken all the time like you," he teases, using his free hand to direct attention toward his two-hundred-and-thirty-pound frame.

Preston was on my floor in my freshman dorm, Bobb; we met the first day of class and have been friends ever since. The pressures of Big-Ten football and Women's basketball are admittedly different, but there is something about being a varsity student-athlete that ties us together when so many other students can't begin to understand it. Preston is from Houston; Christina calls him my southern beau, and she is convinced that we should be together. I am equally convinced he only sees me as a friend, and at this point, I couldn't imagine seeing him as anything else either – especially after watching him *date* half of our class.

I feel like everyone on campus knows Preston. He is the team's best defensive linebacker, and in addition to his outgoing personality and reputation with the girls on campus, he is six-foot-four, two hundred and thirty pounds and is a striking combination of his Kenyan father and Norwegian mother with light brown skin, hazel eyes, and hair that he alternates between dyed blonde and shaved bald. But even though everyone thinks they know Preston because they see him at a party or high five him on their walk to class, there are only a few people who really know Preston, and I'm one of them.

"How was it this morning?" Preston asks, grabbing another handful of fries and dipping them all in ranch dressing as one giant chunk.

"Worse than expected," I reply, sighing heavily. Christina and I talked about it briefly, but I told her I was trying to get my mind off of it, so she didn't push the topic. But now I find myself wanting to re-examine every little thing from that lawyer's office this morning, and there's no one I would rather do it with than Preston.

"It couldn't have been that bad," he says, finishing the last chicken finger, pushing the whole tray to the side, and wiping his greasy fingers on a series of tiny brown eco-friendly paper napkins that barely absorb anything but make us feel like environmental heroes.

"We got to the lawyer's office at ten-thirty this morning, which is when they told us to arrive, but apparently somebody got there late, and then they sat in the conference room for like an hour before we could come in. I don't know what they were talking about, although I assume it was me, but that left me sitting alone with my mom in this guy's office for that entire time!" I tell him, trying to convey just how bad it was.

"Did she tell you any more about your dad? Or anything else about why she lied to you?" he asks.

Thankfully, Preston knows all the details, and he's the kind of friend that remembers everything because as soon as my mom came to visit me last week and broke the news about David's death and her lifetime of lies, I went straight to Preston's apartment to tell him everything. I threw myself on his bed and poured out the whole saga that my mother had just unloaded onto me. She had a brief relationship with a married man, whose wife already had bad Alzheimer's even though she was only in her forties, so although he was cheating on her, it was supposed to be somehow more excusable. Then they broke up, and she found out she was pregnant. Apparently, he offered to pay to raise me but wasn't interested in actually being a father, and she said she was happy with that. And then, when I was eleven months old, she met Brian, and they got married, and he essentially became my dad. When I turned six, she explained that Brian wasn't my biological dad and told me that my dad had died when she was pregnant. Brian was the only dad I ever knew, and I was fine with that until the day she turned up at my sorority house and informed me that my real dad *had* been alive for the past twenty years, living only a few towns away, but now he was dead.

Fortunately, I don't need to fill Preston in on any of this; I can just pick up with what happened this morning, which is a relief because I don't think I have the energy or patience to go through it again. "She had the same lame excuses as she did the other day. She said that they were trying to protect me, and she thought it would ruin both of our families if she told me the truth," I say while leaning back in my chair and stretching my arms over my head in an unsuccessful attempt to loosen my triceps.

"Man, that's harsh. I'm so sorry, Court," Preston says, in his comforting southern drawl. "What are you going to do?" he asks.

"There's nothing *to* do," I whine, wallowing in self-pity. "My dad is already dead. It's not like I can turn back time and have the rest of my childhood to spend with him," I complain.

"So, that's it?" Preston asks.

"What do you mean? My mom and my dad, or I guess I should just call him Brian now, lied to me my whole life and then dump this in my lap. I have no interest in listening to them try to defend themselves, and there's nothing else for me to do. I've got two more years here, and then I'll get as far away from the north shore of Chicago as I can get and never come back," I say triumphantly.

"That's one way to do it," Preston says, sounding skeptical.

"What's wrong with it?" I say, not loving the smirk on his handsome face.

"It sucks that your parents lied to you, and it really sucks that you never got to meet your dad, but you have two sisters now. I don't know why you're totally giving up on them; it's not like it's their fault," he reasons.

"Ha! You should have seen them today. Neither of them wanted anything to do with me! They hate me!" I tell him, feeling even sorrier for myself.

"They don't even know you. And you have to give them a little time. It sounds like they just found out about you, the same way you found out about them – that's a lot for all ya'll to figure out," Preston says, giving me the smug look he gives when he knows he's winning an argument.

"So, does that mean I'm supposed to invite them to lunch or something, or maybe see if we can all go get our nails done together?" I ask sarcastically. I'm trying to visualize the three of us at the nail place in downtown Evanston and finding it very funny.

"I'm just saying you should be patient. I know you're pissed at your mom right now. Hell, I don't know what I'd do if I were in your shoes. But I don't think you should write off the rest of your family so quickly," Preston says, sounding so much wiser and thoughtful than a twenty-year-old should.

Before I can reply, I feel my phone vibrate, and although I'm sure it's another annoying message from my mom, I take it out of my pocket just to see what she has to say. But it isn't from my mom; it's from an unfamiliar 847 number.

Hey, it's Jennifer. I got your number from Mitchell. I'm sorry about how things went this morning. I know that none of this is your fault. Let me know if you want to talk.

Although I know his ego doesn't need any more inflating, I turned my phone around to show it to Preston.

"Looks like I was right," he smiles, flashing me his megawatt smile and then reaching over to grab me in a headlock and ruffle my hair with his knuckles.

Chapter Eleven
Lynn

The drive back to Evanston was a complete blur. Thank God the traffic was light because I barely registered the other cars on the road, and I know I ran at least one stop sign, possibly more. The angry honking was what jolted me out of my stupor when I realized I ran through the four-way stop on Central Ave. I attempted a lame wave to apologize, but the irate baby boomer was having none of it, and I distinctly heard, "dumb, blonde, bimbo!" as I drove away.

Looking out the small living room window onto the quiet suburban street lined with oak trees, I am acutely aware of how much I miss the beach, palm trees, and what I used to think of as a boring life. After leaving the lawyer's office, I didn't want to come back here, but in the middle of the afternoon on a Thursday, there's nowhere else for me to go. It's not likely that Ali will be free to talk right now, but I decide to give her a call anyway, and my day improves slightly when she picks up on the second ring.

"I've been worried about you!" she begins as soon as she answers the phone. "How are you?"

"I've been better," I admit. "Today was a crazy day; you would not believe what happened this morning at the will reading," I tell her. "Wait, do you have time to talk?" I ask, wanting to confirm before I dive into my story.

"I actually have tons of time!" Ali says excitedly. I just dropped the kids at school, and I'm driving to Burbank, which at this hour is going to take ages," she laughs, and her carefree joy is evident in the sound that rings loud and clear into my living room.

"What's in Burbank?" I ask, my curiosity getting the better of me. Ali lives near the beach in Santa Monica and rarely ventures much further away from that area unless she's visiting friends in Brentwood or Bel Air, but that's not too far either.

There's a pause before she says anything, and I wonder if there's an issue with the connection or if Ali is actually hesitating before she answers. "It's not a big deal, but I'm heading to Warner Brothers," Ali says, trying to sound nonchalant.

"Why are you going to the studio?" I question, sounding more accusatory than I intend.

"I'm doing a bit of voice-over work; it's really not a big deal," Ali says. "Tell me about your crazy day," she requests.

"What kind of voice-over work? I didn't even know you had been auditioning," I say, feeling hurt.

"It's just a small part on this new animated series, really not much to talk about," Ali assures me.

"Ali, just because I stopped auditioning doesn't mean I don't want to hear about what you're doing. C'mon, tell me about it," I urge her.

"It's a Flintstones remake," Ali says.

"That's great. What's the part?" I ask.

"It's Wilma!" Ali says, struggling to hide her excitement.

"Oh. Wow. Um, that's great," I say, trying to hide my surprise at the key role and my own disappointment. I'm about to say that I was never interested in voice-over work anyway since it isn't really acting, but somehow, I'm able to stop myself before I ruin a friendship out of jealousy.

"Please, tell me about your morning. Have you heard any more from Trevor? Tell me everything," Ali requests, and so I do. Thirty minutes later, I've filled her in on my call with Trevor, my run-in with Justin, and the incredible news that I have a twenty-year-old half-sister named Courtney who lives in the same small town where I'm renting an apartment! Ali is appropriately shocked at all of my news and says all the right things. She doesn't have any magical answers for me, but it's good to have someone who listens and is on my side. By the time Ali arrives in Burbank and has to go, I feel slightly better about the situation.

I'm not one for notetaking, but during the call, I scribbled a few thoughts on one of the papers from Mitchell's office this morning; Ali brought up a few points, and I wanted to think more about them later.
1) Text Declan or Trevor?
2) Call Courtney?
3) Call Justin?
They all seemed like good ideas when Ali mentioned them, but now that I'm looking at this paltry list, it seems laughable. I know that I need to contact Trevor, even if it's just to make sure he doesn't do something crazy, like stop paying the mortgage on my condo. But I also need to find a way to convince him to let me talk to Declan; if I were back in LA, I would wait for him outside after school and try to talk some

sense into him. I've only tried this tactic once before, and Trevor gave me hell for it, but now that he's at the new campus for the middle school, I feel like I would have a better chance. However, after this morning's disaster, I'm too fragile to handle any more stress, so I'll have to wait on this one.

Reaching out to Courtney is an interesting idea, and although I didn't show it this morning, I know that she bears no responsibility for what's happened. I actually feel really sorry for her. She's barely out of her teens, and she just realized that her mom is a total liar, and she never knew her real dad. That would be hard to handle at any age! It might be nice to have someone to commiserate with, and Jen doesn't seem to have any interest in playing that role, so maybe my new half-sister would be perfect. Although I would have to ask Mitchell for her phone number, and at the moment, I'm not too proud of how I handled myself this morning, so that call will have to wait too.

That leaves Justin. He's engaged to someone else, and I don't know how to reach him, but I know that if I could find him, he would be the perfect person to talk to all of this. He's known my family forever, and he would be able to understand - I just know it. A glance at my watch tells me that it's only four o'clock, but by the time I shower and change and get to the bar, it would be a reasonable time to get a drink on a Thursday evening. I know it's crazy to assume that Justin will be at the bar again tonight, but it feels like my best option.

***

By the time my Uber arrives at the bar, it is close to six. I didn't intend to get so done up, but once I started with my hair and makeup, I decided to go all out and use the flat iron on my hair, create a full smoky eye, and put on false eyelashes. Now that I'm here, I realize that I'm way too overdressed and made up for this midwestern neighborhood tavern, and I feel absurd. I take the first seat at the bar and hope that sitting down will make me less conspicuous, although I can still feel everyone's eyes on me and hear hushed voices saying, "Did you see her?" and "Where does she think she is?"

The lean bartender is here from the other night, and he slides a cardboard coaster in front of me and asks for my order, totally unfazed or unimpressed by my appearance. I learned my lesson and don't attempt to order anything fancy this time. "Jack and Diet," I say, and throw in a "please," as he's walking away.

It's more crowded than it was the other night, but there are still a few empty tables, and except for the two twenty-something girls at the far end of the bar, I'm all alone up here. Once the bartender brings my drink, I try to casually survey my surroundings to see if there is any chance I missed Justin when I walked in. The tables and booths are mostly comprised of groups of four or five, men and women drinking and laughing, enjoying their happy hours, and making plans for the upcoming weekend. Unless I stand up and walk onto the dance floor, I can't see the tables on the outskirts of the room, but showing off my skintight jeans, black cropped sweater, and knee-high boots again doesn't seem to be worth it.

I swivel back around to stare at the wall of liquor bottles and contemplate the rest of my evening when I see the reflection of a man coming up directly behind me in the bar's mirror. I'm sure it's just a coincidence that he's coming so close to me, but there is a familiar tightness in my chest and overall unease, for which I have Trevor to thank. I stare into the remaining ice cubes in my glass and pray that the tall black-haired man will order his drink and go away, but in the middle of my prayer, he pulls out the stool next to me and sits down. Not surprisingly, my luck continues to be shitty; it serves me right for trying to find Justin and for wearing this ridiculous outfit.

I'm staring so intently into my glass that I can feel my eyes start to burn, and the muscles stiffen in my neck and back, but I refuse to turn even a centimeter to the right and acknowledge his presence – eventually, he will have to get the hint. I listen as he orders a Moscow mule, and I have to suppress a giggle because it's not at all what I expected. I wait patiently while I'm sure the bartender will deny him, but I'm surprised yet again when he says the drink is, "Coming up."

I'm debating between getting up and moving to a table by myself or simply throwing money on the bar so I can leave when the Moscow mule-drinker taps me on the shoulder; for the third time in as many minutes, I'm caught off guard.

"You're Jen Summer's little sister, right?" he asks.

"What?" I reply, unprepared for the question.

"Sorry. I didn't mean to scare you. I'm Nick Lee. I was friends with Jen back in high school. We did student government and debate club and other really lame activities together," he jokes, and the corners crinkle next to his dark eyes, and he looks a lot less menacing than he did a minute ago.

"Yes, I'm Lynn Summer. She's Jen Olsen now, but she's my sister," I tell him, turning my body ever so slightly to face him.

"You were a freshman our senior year, but it would be hard to forget you," he says, and then a hint of a blush starts to creep into his smooth tawny cheeks, and I feel myself relax.

"You were treasurer or something like that?" I ask, a flashback coming to me of Jen as class president on the stage for some assembly with Nick standing next to her. However, it looks like he was a late bloomer because my fuzzy memory of him when I was fifteen was that he was shy, short, and skinny with glasses and a smattering of acne on his forehead. But the man sitting next to me now is tall and broad with a clear complexion and a ton of self-confidence.

"You remembered," he says, and he blushes again but looks pleased. "I held the coveted position of student body treasurer as well as president of the math club and vice president of the debate team," he tells me with a grin, and I can tell it's the type of thing that might have embarrassed him at one point, but he realizes now it just means he was smarter than everyone else in high school and probably still is.

"That's why you and my sister were friends; the nerds like to stick together," I tease him and playfully punch his shoulder, pleased to discover how solid it feels underneath his suit jacket.

"It was quite the exclusive club," he replies, and he casually signals to the bartender for a refill of both of our drinks as he says it.

"Let me guess. You went somewhere like Harvard, like Jen did, for school, and now you're a lawyer or a banker?" I tease him, although I'm pretty sure I'm right.

"Actually, I didn't get into Harvard; thanks for rubbing it in," he laughs. "I went to the University of Illinois because they gave me a full scholarship. And I'm a statistician for a healthcare company, not nearly as exciting as being a banker or lawyer," he says.

"That sounds a lot more interesting," I say honestly. "There is *nothing* exciting about lawyers."

"You may be the first person to say that statistics is interesting," Nick jokes. "So, what do you do? And how is this the first time I'm seeing you since high school? I would definitely remember if I saw you in here before," he adds.

"I live in LA. Well, I *lived* in LA. I've been back here for a week or so, and I think I may be staying," I divulge. "It's complicated," I sigh and take a swig from my drink.

"What brought you back here last week?" Nick asks, staring at me intently.

"I came back for my father's funeral," I say sadly.

"I'm so sorry," Nick says sincerely.

"Thank you. It's been pretty shitty," I admit.

"Is the rest of your family still here?" he asks.

I'm not sure if he remembers about my mom or not. Her condition was relatively well known in high school, but that doesn't mean he remembers, and of course, he wouldn't know that she passed away. This poor guy thought he was going to try and hit on me, and now he's going to end up in an impromptu therapy session.

"My sister and her husband live in Winnetka with their kids, and my mom was sick and passed away several years ago. Oh, and it looks like I have a half-sister who I just found out about this morning who lives here in Evanston," I say before I realize the words are out of my mouth. The look on Nick's face is priceless, and although I feel terrible for dumping this on him, it's almost worth it to watch him try to figure out how to respond.

"Wow! I feel like I should have some sort of intelligent response, but I can't think of anything," Nick says, the adorable blush creeping back into his cheeks.

"I'm so sorry! I didn't even mean to say that. I've had quite a day," I say.

"Sounds like it," he replies.

"It's almost too crazy to be true, but unless this is an elaborate prank involving attorneys and wills and forged documents, it seems to be real. But I definitely didn't mean to blurt it out to a stranger," I apologize.

"Don't worry about it. And we're hardly strangers. I was friends with your sister *and*, you and I *did* go to high school together for one year, so it's more like we're getting reacquainted," he says, smiling at me with his perfectly proportioned lips and pearly white teeth.

"When you put it that way, it's totally okay," I return his smile and then laugh, feeling a sense of levity that I haven't felt in days, maybe longer.

"Are you staying with Jen while you're here?" Nick asks.

My initial reaction is to tell him that neither of us would survive that visit, but I realize he has no way to know that, so instead, I say, "She's got her hands full with the kids, so I rented an apartment in Evanston for a few months while I figure out what I'm going to do next."

"I actually just bought a house in Evanston," Nick says, looking slightly embarrassed. "But my old place was close to this bar, and I'm kind of a creature of habit," Nick shares.

"Lucky for me, I guess," I say and give him my best smile.

"I think I'm the one who's lucky," Nick says, and we are now in full-on flirt territory. I've slept with a handful of guys since my divorce, but they've all been booty calls or worse. This conversation is the first time I've actually enjoyed talking and flirting with a potentially nice, normal guy since Trevor dumped me – it's only a matter of time until I fuck this up too.

Chapter Twelve
Jennifer

"How was the rest of your day?" I ask Mark, trying to make conversation at the dinner table. We haven't seen each other since we left Mitchell's office, and there is so much to discuss, but we are having a family dinner tonight, and I don't want to mention anything in front of Harper and Ryan.

"It was okay," Mark says, sounding pre-occupied and taking another bite of meatloaf.

"Mommy, this chicken tastes funny," Harper says. Smelling the food on her fork and looking at it quizzically.

"That's because it isn't chicken," Ryan says wisely, taking a bite of mashed potatoes and relishing his role as the older brother.

"What is it?" Harper asks, looking around the table suspiciously and scrunching up her adorable little face.

"It's meatloaf," Ryan says, sticking out his tongue as he lets her in on the big secret.

"Ewww," Harper says, "I hate meatloaf," and she pushes her pink melamine plate away from her.

"You've never had meatloaf before," Mark says, sounding annoyed.

"And I never want to have it again," Ryan adds.

"Watch it," Mark snaps, raising his voice and staring at Harper and Ryan. "Rose worked hard to make this dinner, and you should be thankful and eat every bite of it!"

I don't know if the kids or I am more surprised by Mark's outburst, but none of us move as we digest Mark's flare-up. Although some might assume Mark has a temper or is prone to anger because of his size and news they've heard on ESPN about irate football players, but Mark can best be described as a gentle giant. He rarely gets upset, and when he does, it is usually for a very good reason – not because his kids don't want to eat their dinner.

"It's actually not *that* bad," Ryan says, taking another bite. I wait to see how Mark will react since I imagine this statement isn't what he was hoping for, but it seems to be enough of a concession that he doesn't respond.

Following suit and blessedly able to read the room at such a young age, Harper takes another bite of her meatloaf and then exclaims in a loud and exaggerated voice, "This chicken is yummy now!" Mark and I both burst out laughing, and the tension disappears from the kitchen as quickly as it arrived.

***

After the kids are asleep and the kitchen is cleaned up, I wander down the hall to Mark's office to check in on him. The door to his office is mostly closed, but since it isn't shut, I take that as a sign that I can enter as long as I knock at the same time to alert him of my presence.

"Knock, knock," I call out as I rap my knuckles on the door and push it open.

"Hey," Mark says, looking up from the iPad in his lap. He's sitting on the navy leather couch, with his long legs stretched out in front of him on the matching ottoman. He bought that furniture after he received his first NFL paycheck, and no matter how worn it gets or how badly it clashes with the rest of the décor in the house, he'll never get rid of it.

"Are you going to go up to bed soon?" I inquire.

"What time is it?" he asks.

"It's only nine-thirty, but I'm exhausted from today. I don't know if I'll actually be able to sleep, but I feel like I can barely hold my head up," I say as I take a seat on the end of the well-loved couch.

"I'll be up in a few; I just want to finish watching this," he says, indicating the screen in his lap.

"What are you watching?"

"It's game footage of Tom Turner – he's a running back for the Bears," he tells me.

"I know who he is," I reply, somewhat indignant that he doesn't think I would know this, considering every weekly Bears' game is an event in our house. "Why are you watching him?" I ask.

"We signed him today for supplemental disability insurance; it's a big policy," he says.

"That's fantastic," I reply, feeling like this is the first good news I've heard in a long time.

"Yeah, it's good. But I'm watching the tape from his last game, and he really needs to work on following his blockers and running his routes. He's doing fine, but he could be so much more effective," Mark says, seeming quite distressed.

"How does that impact his policy? Is he more likely to get hurt?" I ask, trying to understand Mark's concerns.

"No, nothing like that," he says. "It just makes me wonder about the offensive coaching…" Mark says, trailing off.

"Oh," I reply, unsure what to say. "Who's the coach again?" I ask, now questioning if I actually pay attention on game day, although I'm pretty sure I've heard Mark yelling at him on the TV for the past several years.

"It's Coach Reyes, he was the offensive coordinator when I was there, but I think he's lost his touch," Mark laments.

"Hmmm," I respond.

Mark continues, "The Bears could really have a shot this year, but not if they can't optimize the skills of their best players, like Turner. And don't get me started on what's going on with the new wide receiver," Mark says, getting worked up.

"Good thing you got Turner signed," I say, trying to turn the conversation around. "Maybe you could sign the new wide receiver too – hell, it seems like you should have the whole team," I say, getting up to stretch my legs and leave Mark alone to watch his game reruns.

"Yeah, I guess that should be my priority," Mark says, sounding suddenly deflated. He shuts off his iPad and throws it down on the couch. "I'll come up with you; I'm pretty tired too."

As Mark follows me up the stairs, I can't help but wonder if we'll have sex tonight. It's an odd thing to wonder about since it can be entirely within my control. I know that if I initiate or even hint at it - it will happen, and the same with him; neither of us ever says no, but that doesn't mean we have a particularly active sex life. When I was in high school, or even college, the idea of sleeping in bed with a man every night would have automatically meant having sex every night since I couldn't imagine why anyone would have the opportunity and choose not to do anything about it. But that was before c-sections and midnight potty training and early mornings and responsibilities and love handles.

We conduct our bathroom routines in companionable silence – washing, brushing, and flossing. The first year Mark and I dated, I used to wait until he was asleep and then sneak back into the bathroom at his apartment to painstakingly manage my evening rituals of creams and gels; I couldn't imagine ever letting him see me without makeup or tweezing a stray eyebrow! I can't pinpoint exactly when it happened because it was a gradual slide. On our honeymoon, it was evident that I was going to have to go without makeup at some point - two weeks sharing a suite in Hawaii doesn't leave a lot of options. Then I broke my wrist, and I needed help showering and shaving, and not in a sexy way. And after Ryan was born and I had mastitis and an infection in my c-section incision, it was all over. I'll admit that there's something comforting about not having to hide or pretend, but I certainly feel like an old married couple when I'm standing at the sink using a Waterpik in my cotton robe, and Mark doesn't even flinch.

Mark is propped up and shirtless, resting against the hand-carved wood and linen headboard, with an issue of Sports Illustrated in his lap. One look at his smooth, muscled chest makes me pull my robe a little tighter around my waist as I slide into the crisp cotton sheets and grab my unfinished copy of The Economist from my nightstand. I'm trying to focus on this article about trade in Latin America, but my mind is wandering. I'm pretty sure we had sex one night last week, but it can't be a good sign that I don't quite remember. I actually feel a familiar tingling between my legs and contemplate extending my leg ever-so-slightly to rub against his bare leg and give him a signal. I'm still feeling a bit bloated from dinner, and the small strain against the waistband of my pajama bottoms reminds me that I need to do more sit-ups, but the growing sensation underneath the lace of my underwear is winning the battle as I decide my body could definitely use a distraction after today's events and I choose to put aside my body issues for some pleasure. I reach over and rub Mark's arm, letting him know I'm game. I start to undo the belt of my robe, and I'm about to stretch my hand out to the waistband of his boxer briefs when he says, "Good night hon, I can't even keep my eyes open to finish this article," and he rolls onto his side and is lightly snoring within seconds.

I know I didn't overtly suggest anything, and I'm sure he didn't mean anything by it, but still, I'm emotionally hurt and physically frustrated. I lie there and stare up at the ceiling, and the first thought that pops into my head is to wonder what Lynn would do in this situation. But then again, I'm sure Lynn has never found herself in this situation. There's never been a man within thirty feet of her that didn't want to sleep with her and certainly one who wouldn't jump at the chance, even after a slight arm rub. I remind myself that Mark is the exception in this scenario, and I feel slightly better. I can hear Lynn's voice in my head, and her message is loud and clear – I'm a grown woman, and if I want an orgasm, I can take care of it myself. Of course, she's right. It's not like I don't know how to do that, but it feels wrong to do it while Mark's in bed next to me. Now I hear Lynn saying what a prude I am, but I try to block that out as well, and instead, I grab my phone off the nightstand and hope for distraction instead. I have one new text, and it's from Courtney!

Hi Jennifer. Thanks for your text. This is all so weird. I'd like to talk sometime if you want.

I start writing back to her before I even think about what I want to say.

Hi Courtney! So happy you wrote back. I hope this isn't too much, but how would you feel about meeting up? I could come to campus, and we could grab coffee? This is weird for all of us, but it shouldn't keep us from getting to know each other. Let me know what you think!

I press send before I can analyze and overthink my message and then regret it as soon as it's sent. It's probably too pushy and will likely scare her away. I'll be lucky if she ever writes back. But before I know it, I see the three blinking dots, and then her message appears.

How about this Sunday afternoon?

I reply immediately:

I would love that! Pick the place and the time and I'll be there!

Her response arrives just as quickly:

I'll text you on Sunday – see you then.

And just like that, it looks like I could be on the way to a relationship with my half-sister.

Chapter Thirteen
Courtney

"Are you sure this looks okay?" I ask Christina. She's lying on my extra-long twin bed, still in her warm-ups, paging through an old copy of The Daily Northwestern.

"I told you it looks good," she replies, lifting her head slightly off my pillow to give me a once-over.

I take another look at the full-length mirror on the back of my closet door. I'm trying to assess if this really is the right outfit for coffee with my newly discovered half-sister, but I'm not sure there is a *right* outfit for that. September in Evanston usually means the beginning of beautiful fall weather, but it's just over seventy degrees today, so I opt for a pair of white jean shorts, a black flowy top, and I'll bring a denim jacket in case I get cold. It's much more casual than the dress my mom insisted I wear to the lawyer's office, but I see no reason to get fancy for this and try to look like something I'm not. Although I did put some extra effort into blow drying my hair, so it turns under at the bottom, instead of letting it air dry and throwing it into a ponytail like usual. And I also put on a tiny bit of mascara and lip gloss, but I'm still debating if I should wipe it off.

"I promise you look great. But you need to leave now, or you're going to be late," Christina warns.

"Are you going to stay here?" I ask.

"I might, is that okay? That awful guy my roommate is dating was just coming over when I left, and I really don't want to go back until I'm sure he's gone," she says, making a face that shows how much she dislikes him.

"That should be fine," I reply. "Kerry probably won't be back for a while. She went to study," I say, referring to my roommate.

"That's fine. I can leave when she comes back," Christina says, "Or maybe we'll hang out and do each other's nails and gossip," she says, laughing.

"Be nice," I warn her, shooting her a look. I'm still not sure what possessed me to join a sorority freshman year, although I'm glad that I did. But it's resulted in two very distinct friend groups. I have the girls from the basketball team and then my sorority sisters. Most of them get along fine with each other, but they certainly wouldn't choose to hang out together if it wasn't for me. Kerry and Christina tolerate each other, but that's about it. Kerry and I bonded during freshman rush and then chose to room together. She's not my best friend in the house, but we're both neat freaks, we don't like to party too much, and she respects that I need to get up early to train. I respect her crazy pre-med study hours, and it just works for us. I think Christina can't get past Kerry's Georgia debutante exterior, but once you get to know her and negotiate the massive drawl, big blonde hair, and nail extensions, she's super smart and quite sweet.

***

102

We are meeting at the Unicorn Café at four o'clock. I picked it because it's my favorite coffee shop in town and it's also not where I go to study with my friends, it's where I go to study by myself, so although it might be packed, the chances of running into someone I know are hopefully slim.

I see Jennifer immediately when I walk in the door. She has secured a table by the wall and has angled her chair to face the door; I guess she didn't want to miss me when I came in. She looks more relaxed and also more anxious than she did the other day, which seems difficult to pull off. Maybe it's that she looks less angry than she did at the lawyer's office, but she's certainly on high alert. She's perched on the edge of her chair, and her driving moccasin is tapping so rapidly, I'm worried she's going to burn through those silly rubber dots they put on the soles. She's dressed more modestly as well, but certainly not as casual as I am. Not surprisingly, she sticks out like a sore thumb in here. Not only because she's almost twenty years older than everyone else, but also in her linen slacks and short-sleeved sweater with diamonds sparkling on her wrists, ears, and fingers, she has no chance of blending in with the Sunday afternoon still-hungover college crowd.

She stands up when I approach the table, and we both consider our potential greeting options, and it's as if we simultaneously decide that nothing would be appropriate, so we sit down without so much as saying hello.

"I ordered a latte and an iced tea," she says, as I notice the two drinks in front of her. "It was probably dumb, but I thought maybe you would want one of these, and I'll have the one you don't want. But of course, you can get whatever you want..." she rambles on.

"I'd love the iced tea. Thanks," I say as I reach across the table and take the glass.

"Perfect. That's great. I'm so glad," she stammers, and it's clear that no matter how uncomfortable I am right now, she's at least ten times that, and that makes me feel oddly more at ease.

"What should we talk about?' I joke, trying to break the ice.

"This is just so crazy. I'm sorry, I feel like I should be more prepared - I'm always prepared, but this is pretty hard to prepare for," Jennifer says. "Let's start with you, is that okay? Tell me something about you? About school?" she offers.

"Okay, sure. I just started my sophomore year at Northwestern. I guess you know that already. I'm double majoring in women's studies and economics. I'm on the varsity basketball team," I say, and she interrupts me as soon as the words are out of my mouth.

"Wow! That's so impressive! You clearly didn't get that from our side of the family," and then she clasps her hand over her mouth. "I'm so sorry, I didn't mean to say it like that, I just meant that no one in our family plays basketball, even though my dad and Lynn are both really tall like you are," and then Jennifer bites her lip as if she's made another error.

"It's okay, don't worry about it. Isn't that why we're here? To talk about things like this?" I ask.

"I guess so. I mean, of course, you're right; it's just still so new," she says. "Tell me something else. Do you like school? What else do you like to do?" she inquires, pausing to take a sip of her latte from the glass mug.

"I really like school. It's a lot of work, but it's not too bad. Basketball takes up a lot of my time, but it's my favorite thing. Most of my friends are on the team, and then some of my other friends are from my sorority house," I tell her.

"Oh, you're in a sorority?" she asks, sounding surprised.

"Yeah, I'm in Kappa. I think it's different here than it is at a lot of schools. I spend most of my time with the team, but it's nice to have a different group of friends too, and they're nice girls, well most of them," I say, laughing.

"Do you have a boyfriend?" she asks. "Or a girlfriend?" she quickly follows, clearly more enlightened than I had given her credit for.

"I don't have either," I reply, "But it would be a boyfriend if I did have one. One of my best friends at school is a guy; his name is Preston. Some people think we're a couple, but we're just friends," I say, trailing off, not sure why I told her any of that. "So, tell me about you?" I ask, putting her on the spot. I feel a little awkward turning the tables since she is so much older, but I also don't really care given the absurd nature of our circumstances.

She takes one more sip of her latte, as if for fortification, and then puts it down with a heavy exhale before she begins. "I'll try to give you the quick version," she says.

"I don't want the quick version," I reply immediately.

"Fair enough. I live in Winnetka with my husband, Mark. I guess that makes him your brother-in-law. Anyhow, we have two kids, Ryan is six and Harper is four," she says, smiling in spite of herself as she says their names.

"Which would make me an aunt?" I ask, trying to absorb this new information.

"I guess it would," she laughs. "I know I'm biased, but they're pretty great," she says. "Mark runs our family insurance company, Summer Risk Management, the one my dad started over forty years ago. I guess it's the one *our* dad started," Jennifer says, shaking her head. "God, this is so weird."

"No shit," I reply and then shrug as if to apologize for my language.

"So, Mark runs that now," she says, and a trace of what looks like annoyance crosses over her face. "And I have a little boutique in downtown Winnetka that sells scarves, jewelry and handbags and other things you couldn't possibly live without," she says. "It's just what I thought I would do with my Harvard undergraduate degree and MBA from Kellogg," Jennifer exclaims, rolling her eyes.

Now it's my turn to be impressed. "Wow!" I almost say, "What happened?" because it seems like a waste of her expensive education, but thankfully I stop myself.

"Just kidding," she says as if she realizes she's done something wrong. "It's a great little shop, and I have more time to spend with the kids this way."

"When did you open the store?" I ask, making conversation.

"A few years ago. I worked at the company with my dad after business school, and then I worked there for a couple of years after we got married, but Mark was also working there, and once I had Ryan, it didn't make sense anymore," she trails off.

"Oh, so you met Mark at work?" I ask.

"Not quite. He actually played football professionally; I don't know if you know that. I'm sure you're way too young to know who he is, but he got hurt and had to retire. He got a job selling insurance, and I met him at a convention where I was speaking; then, we started dating, and not too long after that, my dad offered him a job. It sounds a little weird now, but it all made sense at the time," she says, waving her hand like she's swatting away insignificant details.

I nod my head, but the story doesn't sound quite like the happily-ever-after she's making it out to be.

"What can you tell me about your dad?" I ask, not feeling ready yet to refer to him as "my dad or our dad."

"Of course," she sighs. "Up until a few days ago, I thought I knew him pretty well, but I guess that's all changed now," she says. "It's hard to tell you about Dad without telling you at least a little bit about my mom," Jennifer says. "Are you okay with that?" she asks.

"Sure, that's fine," I say, although I'm not sure if I mean it. I'm actually not sure about any of this right now, and I wish I were back in my room with Christina or watching a movie with Preston in the smelly living room of his Noyes Street apartment, but here I am.

"I don't know if you know any of this, but my mom got sick shortly after she turned forty. I was in fifth grade, and Lynn was in second grade when it started. At first, she would just forget little things, and it was kind of funny, and my dad would tease her about being forgetful, but then when I was in middle school, it got worse. She was at the grocery store once and forgot how to get home. And she had a habit of leaving the stove on, and she started a small fire in the kitchen; luckily, my dad was home to put it out. By the time I was in high school, it had gotten pretty bad, and she had started to see doctors for early-onset Alzheimer's. I was a teenager, so I mostly focused on how it impacted my life, but even as a self-centered brat, I saw that it was really hard for my dad. He tried to take care of her and still go to work, but it got to the point where she couldn't really be alone," she tells me.

"That sounds awful," I sympathize, wishing that my mom had shared some of this with me as preparation.

"It sucked. The year I left for college, my dad had to put her into a facility full-time because he couldn't take care of her anymore. He tried getting live-in help, but none of it worked, and she used to wander out of the house, and the police would end up bringing her home, but not before we had spent hours looking for her. And once I left, I guess it was just Lynn and my dad doing that," Jennifer says, shaking her head sadly.

"I'm so sorry," I say, trying to alter the image I've had in my head all week of David Summer's perfect family.

"Thanks," Jen offers. "My dad was always able to put on a good face, and most people didn't know how bad it was at home. He continued to expand his company, growing it to one of the largest insurance companies in the Midwest, and he found time to play golf with clients. Most people would probably describe him as big-hearted and charismatic. He also volunteered with Big Brothers Big Sisters and donated a lot of time and money to them over the past fifteen years. And he was a wonderful grandpa. My kids adored him," she says sadly.

I nod along, but it seems like she has more to say, so I don't interrupt her.

"It's somewhat ironic because I planned to say a lot of this last week during the eulogy, but then I didn't end up saying any of it. And now, with this news, I just don't know what to think anymore. It changes everything," she says, resting her forehead on her fingertips and staring down at the table.

"Thanks for telling me that," I say. "I wish I'd had the chance to meet him," slips out of my mouth before I can stop it. I don't know how Jennifer will respond, but I see her flinch as I say it and hope she isn't too upset.

"I don't understand any of it, actually. Maybe I get why he had to keep it a secret at first, but my mom's been gone for six years now…" she says, trailing off.

"It was probably my mom's fault," I offer quietly, although the conversation has dwindled, and we are both thinking aloud more than anything else. "I should probably go. I've got studying to do," I say, sensing that Jennifer's ready to leave and feeling the urge myself.

"Right, of course," she says, snapping to attention. "I'm sure Mark's ready for me to come back too. Harper's stopped taking naps, so the afternoons are very long," she says, plastering on a smile.

We both get up and walk side-by-side to the door to put our glasses on the tray table meant for dirty dishes, and it feels like the end of a mediocre date. I wonder if I should offer to call her, or if that's her role as the older sister. Or perhaps her curiosity has been sated, and she doesn't even want to see me again.

But before my mind can wander any further, she interrupts my thoughts. "I'd love to have you come over and meet Mark and the kids some time if you would want to do that," she suggests.

"I'd like that," I reply. I have no interest in talking to my mom or Brian, and I'm still angry at the dad I'll never meet for just about everything, but I don't hold any of this against her. "Jennifer, could you also give me Lynn's number? I'd love to talk to her, too," I say.

"Call me Jen," she says casually and then adds. "I can give you her number, but I can't promise you what you'll get," she says cooly.

"What do you mean by that?" I ask.

"She is less than reliable. In fact, it's possible she's already back in LA by now and didn't even tell anyone," Jen says, rolling her eyes.

"Oh, wow, okay. Well, I'll still give her a try if that's okay," I say.

"Suit yourself," Jen says, not unkindly, as she flashes me an entry for Lynn on her phone that contains a mobile number and nothing else.

"I'll talk to you soon," I say after I enter Lynn's number into my phone.

"I'd like that," she says, and she leans toward me and stands on her tiptoes to give me a hug.

Chapter Fourteen
Lynn

Today is the fourth day in a row that I'm up before ten and the third day that I've gone for a run. I'm no closer to having a job or finding a solution to my issues with Trevor, and I haven't heard from Declan, but at least I'm no longer lying on the couch in my pajamas all day long. My phone buzzes in my armband as I'm finishing my post-run stretch outside the steps to my apartment building. I smile in anticipation of reading it. Nick and I have been exchanging flirty texts multiple times a day since we met at the bar the other night, and I'm waiting for a reply to the one I sent to him right before my run. But as I release my phone from the Velcro pocket, I'm surprised and disappointed to see that it's not from Nick; in fact, it's from an unknown number, and I'm about to delete it without even reading it when I see who it's from.

Hi Lynn. It's Courtney. I got your number from Jen. I don't know if you are still in town, but if you are, would you be free to meet up sometime?

My emotions are all over the place as I try to digest this development. I'm excited to hear from her. I've been trying to get up the nerve to call Mitchell for the past few days to get her number, and now that's been taken care of, and it seems like she wants to see me as well! But at the same time, I'm embarrassed that *she's* the one who reached out even though she's still in college. And then I'm furious that she's already met with Jen. Of course, Jen jumped on this first. She always has to do everything first and everything better, and I'm sure she already told her all about me, so I'm already starting off as second best.

While I'm figuring out how to reply, the text I was waiting for from Nick pops up on my screen.

Sorry, data emergency ☺ Any chance you are free tonight or tomorrow night for a drink or maybe dinner?

I desperately want to reply that I'm free tonight, so I only have to wait seven or eight hours until I see him, but it feels like I'll sound too available if I tell him I don't have plans tonight. I'd also love his advice on how to reply to Courtney, but I'm just going to have to figure that out on my own.

Can't tonight, but dinner tomorrow is good.

His reply is instantaneous, and I love that he doesn't leave me hanging like Trevor always does – cutting out in the middle of a text exchange without warning and never saying goodbye.

Sounds great! I'll make a reservation. If that's okay?

I reply that it sounds perfect, and Nick says something nerdy about needing to get back to his numbers, but it's nerdy in a cute way. Instead of going back inside the building, I sit on the brick wall next to the steps and tell myself I'm not going in until I reply to Courtney. I also want to send Jen a text giving her a piece of my mind for stealing Courtney, and I want to check on the status of Dad's will, but I know neither of those will go well. I think for a minute and decide that a simple response is best; there's no need to overthink it.

Hi Courtney. Sorry, I didn't reach out sooner, but I'm so glad you did! I'm still here, and I would love to meet up. My schedule is pretty free, so let me know what works for you.

She starts typing almost as soon as I hit send, and I watch the little dots wiggle on my screen as I wait to hear what she has to say.

Can you have lunch tomorrow? I have a break from 12-2. Would you be able to come to Evanston?

I laugh out loud at this last part, as my living arrangements are apparently still a secret. I know that I never told Jen where I'm living or how long I'm staying, but she also never bothered to ask! Who knew when I decided to rent an apartment in Evanston that I would be living this close to my secret half-sister? The universe works in mysterious ways. I decide not to tell Courtney too much over text because it will be easier in person, and I also want to find out what Jen's said to her already.

Of course! I can be there at 12 and anywhere in Evanston is good for me – whatever is best for you.

Let's meet at Clarke's at 12. Courtney writes.

It's probably killing this poor kid to have to text me in complete sentences when she must be used to using emojis and weird acronyms. I know from texting Declan (when he used to text me) that he hated having to write so I could read his messages, but I insisted – I wonder if Courtney's mom insists on the same from her? Then it hits me that I might be closer in age to her mom than I am to her, or at least halfway in between – I shudder at the thought.

See you then! I write back. It looks like I have two dates tomorrow.

***

I arrive early at Clarke's and sit outside the diner to wait for Courtney to arrive. It's a beautiful fall day in Evanston, one of the few days where I prefer the weather in the Midwest to California. There's a slight chill in the air, enough that I need a light sweater, jeans, and boots, but with the sun shining on me, I don't even need to wear the jacket that I grabbed on my way out the door. The sky is a brilliant shade of blue, and the trees are almost on fire in hues of red, orange, and yellow. I never miss the bitter winters or the icy wind whipping off Lake Michigan, but as much as I love palm trees, they don't hold a candle to fall foliage in the Chicago suburbs.

There are students walking past me in groups and pairs and some on their own, furiously texting away on their phones. I'm the only one that seems to be appreciating this beautiful fall day, but I'm sure I didn't appreciate nature much when I was their age. I do get a couple of glances from some of the young male students, and although they are way too young for me, I'd be lying if I didn't acknowledge that it's a much-needed ego boost to get looks of appreciation from guys almost twenty years younger.

It's still only eleven forty-five, which means fifteen minutes before Courtney is due to arrive and means it's before nine in LA. Declan's classes start at nine, but he usually gets dropped off at school around eight forty. I know it's a long shot, but I wonder if he would pick up if I tried calling him when Trevor wasn't around. I call before I lose my nerve.

"Hello?" Declan asks when he picks up the phone on the first ring.

"Hi," I manage in a whisper, shocked to be talking to him for the first time in over two months.

"Who's this?" he asks, and I can feel my heart break into a million tiny pieces.

"It's me. Your mom," I offer, trying not to cry.

"Oh. Hey. Dad took your number out of my phone, so you didn't show up on my caller ID," he says, somewhat awkwardly.

I let this sink in for a second, and although my initial instinct is to scream and tell him that his father is an asshole and he isn't allowed to do that, I take a deep breath and decide to save my tirade for Trevor and leave Declan out of it. "It's so good to hear your voice. I miss you," I tell him.

"Where are you?" he asks bluntly.

"I'm in Evanston. That's right near Winnetka, where Aunt Jen lives and where Grandpa used to live," I say.

"Did he move?" Declan asks.

I'm stunned at his question, and then my blood boils as I realize the continued depths of Trevor's cruelty. I hadn't given much thought to the nature of my conversation with Declan today; in fact, I didn't really think that he would pick up, but I certainly hadn't planned on having to inform him of his grandfather's death in the ten-minute window before he went to first period. Based on our phone call, it seemed clear that Trevor was going to convey the news since he wouldn't let me do it – or at least that's what I thought. Declan wasn't close to his grandfather the way that most kids are. Due to Trevor's intense dislike of my family and unwillingness to ever let us go back to visit, one could argue that he barely knew him. But until the divorce two years ago, Declan would join me almost every week when I called Dad, and the last several years, those calls turned into FaceTime visits, so Declan did get to know him in his own special way even though the last time he saw him in person was eight years ago at Jen and Mark's wedding.

"I'm so sorry to tell you this, but Grandpa died," I tell him. "I thought your dad told you," I add.

"What? When did he die? What happened?" Declan asks, sounding flustered and much younger than he did only a moment ago.

"He died last week; he had an aneurism. It was all very sudden," I try to explain.

"Were you ever going to tell me? When's his funeral?" Declan asks, his voice shifting to sound a little angrier.

"Of course, I was going to tell you. I called your dad several times to try to get in touch with you, and I tried texting you," I say, but it sounds so lame when I hear the words come out of my mouth.

"I never got any texts," Declan declares.

I want to argue with him and insist that I *did* text him, and something must have happened with the messages, or maybe Trevor deleted them! But as the adult, I know that I can't do that. "I'm so sorry. I don't know what happened," I reply sadly.

"So, when's the funeral?" Declan asks again. Over the years, he would occasionally ask why we never visited Grandpa, and he barely knew enough about Jen and the kids to even ask about his aunt and cousins, but I always had a reason why we didn't go see them. Trevor would happily take us for a beach vacation in Maui or skiing in Jackson Hole, but he made it clear that Winnetka wasn't an option, and I knew better than to argue with him.

"The funeral was this past Monday," I tell him, feeling the bile start to rise in my throat as I deliver the news and realize their implications.

"Are you shitting me?" Declan asks. I don't even think of correcting his language as he parrots one of Trevor's favorite phrases.

"It was a Jewish funeral, so they had to do it really quickly. Jen made the decision on the timing. *I* barely had time to fly out to be here for it," I tell him, reaching for excuses. "I didn't think your dad would have even let you come with me," I say, and I regret it as soon as I say it.

"Have you been drinking again?" Declan asks.

"What did you say?" I ask, stunned at the question from my twelve-year-old son.

"Dad says that you start to say and do crazy things when you drink, and that's why we can't trust you. It sounds like maybe he's right," Declan says.

"Declan, that's a terrible thing to say," I tell him, trying pathetically to chastise him.

"Whatever. I've got to get to class," he says, and he ends the call. I think he's hurt and angry, even though he's trying to sound like he doesn't care, but I'm not even sure I know him enough anymore to know what that sounds like.

I wasn't even on the phone for ten minutes, but nothing feels the same when I hang up. It's still a beautiful autumn day, students are still milling around on their way to and from class and into downtown Evanston to meet friends or go shopping, but everything seems different now. I'd been holding out hope to get in touch with Declan, and when it finally happened, it exploded in my face. I want to blame Trevor for all of it, but I know that I'm partially at fault for fucking it all up, and that makes it even worse! I'm already pounding out an angry email to Trevor and thinking about how I can possibly rectify this situation when I feel a gentle tap on my arm.

"Hi, Lynn. Sorry, I was trying to get your attention, but you seemed really focused. Hope I'm not bothering you," Courtney says, giving me a shy smile.

"Oh my God, of course not!" I say, and I shove my phone in my back pocket as I jump to my feet. "Sorry about that," I tell her. I'm about to say that I'm writing a nasty email to my ex-husband when I change my mind. Right now, Trevor and Declan are the last things that I want to talk about. I don't know what Jen told her, but since I haven't even mustered the courage yet to tell Jen that I'm divorced or that I've lost custody of my only son, she can't have said much. At the moment, I really want to leave all of that in California and start fresh, without baggage – or at least only with the currently required baggage from my dad's secret lovechild.

Without thinking, I give her a hug and then take a step back as I feel her body tense under my embrace. I was such a bitch when we met the other day that I'd like to make amends with a gregarious greeting, but I can't expect Courtney to interpret my inner monologue. "I haven't been here in forever," I say, as we open the door and the familiar smell of grease and coffee wafts over us.

"You've been here?" Courtney asks, seeming surprised.

"We used to come here in high school," I tell her.

"Really?" she asks, turning around to stare at me as the ridiculously young-looking hostess leads us to a booth at the back of the restaurant.

"Seems funny now, but we would take the El here from Winnetka and walk around town and eat here and then go back. I had a boyfriend, but my friends were always looking for college guys," I laugh, remembering how silly we must have seemed but how grown-up we felt.

Courtney slides her long, athletic frame into the booth, and I slide in across from her on the worn vinyl; and she looks at me for a minute as if considering her reply. "When was that?" she asks.

"When was I in high school? I graduated in 2000, so probably 1998 and 1999," I reply, reaching over to grab the spiral-bound menu from the edge of the table where the hostess left it, but not opening it.

"I was born in 1999," Courtney says as if trying to put the pieces of a puzzle together.

"It's surreal, right? How are you doing with all of this? It's got to be a lot," I say as if suddenly realizing how much more significant this news is for Courtney than it is for either me or Jen. We may have found out that our dad had a brief affair and that we have a half-sister, but she learned startling news about her birth father and that she would never get to meet him!

"Honestly, I don't know," Courtney admits, running her fingers through her shiny hair. Her hair color is somewhere between mine and Jen's, potentially best described as very dirty blonde or really light brown. However, now that I'm sitting across from her, I realize that we share the same delicate nose and full lips, while her light green eyes look exactly like Jen's. I'm tempted to point out the similarities, but I don't sense that this is the right time.

Courtney takes a sip of ice water from the giant plastic tumbler in front of her and then continues. "Sometimes, I almost forget about it. I get busy with homework or basketball or something else for an hour or two, and then it comes back, and I can't believe that my whole life has been a lie," she says, shaking her head.

"I can't imagine," I tell her. "I've had one picture in my head of my dad this whole time, but now that's changed. Although I was really angry when I first found out. And I know I was a total bitch at the lawyer's office," I say, slipping that in there as a tiny apology. "But now that I've had a few days to think about it, I'm not quite as upset anymore. I mean, I wish I could ask him about it and understand why he had to keep it secret; but I think there was a lot I probably never really knew about him and my mom and how he had to handle that, and maybe it's not my place to judge him," I ponder aloud.

"Jen told me about your mom," Courtney says tentatively.

"I figured as much. I'm sure she told you lots of things," I say, trying to keep the edge out of my voice.

"I can see how it happened in the first place; that kind of thing happens all the time," Courtney says, waving her hand away at the idea of an affair. "But I can't accept that they hid it from me. My mom lied to me and kept me from meeting my sisters and my real dad! I can never forgive her for that," Courtney says indignantly.

"I'm so sorry," I tell her and reach across the table to cover her hand with mine.

"Not your fault," Courtney says as she shrugs and then shakes her head and exhales like she is freeing herself of the topic. "Hey, do you want to split an order of fries? I really shouldn't, but I'll run extra today," she adds, giving me a smile that looks like what I see in the mirror every day.

"I'd love to," I tell her, smiling right back.

Chapter Fifteen
Mark

As the big boss, it's rare that I get invited for drinks after work, and even rarer that I actually join, but when James stopped by at five-thirty and asked if I wanted to grab a beer, it was just the escape I'd been searching for. James joined the company a few years ago and is roughly my age. David hired him away from Chubb to be our general counsel when the previous attorney, a fraternity brother of David's, finally retired. Coming into the company as Jen's fiancé and then quickly being promoted as David's son-in-law and eventually taking over the firm, it's not a surprise that I never made any friends at work – I sure as hell wouldn't have been friends with me. But James already came in as a big-shot attorney with an Ivy league resume, and he never seemed to care about my title or relationship with David. I think he knows we are lucky to have him, and he could leave at any time – his relocation package, annual salary, and bonus speak to that as well. This leaves him as the only employee at Summer Risk Management who is comfortable hanging out with me, and vice versa.

I pull into the parking lot of the local beer and burger joint where we agreed to meet and marvel at how packed it already is before six o'clock on Monday night, but then again, maybe everyone's had a long Monday. As I walk into the pub and see the big screens blaring with pre-game coverage, I'm appalled with myself for failing to connect the crowd with tonight's football game.

"Big game tonight," Tony says to me from behind the bar, as he puts a pint of Bud Light in front of me. "Sure is," I reply, handing him a ten-dollar bill and continuing toward the empty maroon vinyl stool at the end of the bar next to James.

"How can you drink that shit?" James says laughing, as his way of a greeting.

"I could say the same to you," I reply, motioning toward the rich amber liquid in his pint glass – four hundred calories of some heavy ale. We both laugh and clink glasses to acknowledge a continued truce to our beverage disagreement.

We sit in silence for a reasonable amount of time. James reads through messages on his phone, and I stare intently at the screen in front of me where former NFL players in two thousand-dollar suits stand around a television studio and make jokes and projections about the Bears' and the Packers' chances in the game later tonight. "So, what do you think?" James asks, raising his eyes toward the television where everyone's just put odds on the Packers victory.

"I wish they were wrong," I reply. "But I don't think we have it together yet. It could happen later this season," I say, trailing off.

"Don't you go to all the home games?" James asks, making conversation.

"I gave my tickets for tonight's game to a friend. Last week's game too. It didn't feel right to go with everything that's going on. I don't want to leave Jen home all night," I say, just as I realize that I forgot to tell her I was going to stop and get a drink on the way home.

"How's she doing?" James asks.

"She seems to be doing okay, but it's hard to tell – it's a lot to handle," I say. Jen and I haven't discussed what we're telling people about Courtney's existence, but I get the feeling that she doesn't want me telling other employees and having it spread like wildfire through the company, so I'll have to leave it at that.

"They found a spot on my dad's lung last year, but we were lucky that they found it so early. It was a tough year for him and for my mom, but it looks like he should be okay. It was rough for us to imagine losing him. I can't imagine what Jen is going through," James volunteers, and I'm momentarily speechless at his revelation. I've known him for at least two years now, and he did not mention his dad once; but I guess it's fair to say that until now, our conversations have been about work, football, or fishing.

"I'm glad he's going to be okay," I tell him, simultaneously raising my hand to let Tony know that we need another round.

"How's your old man?" James asks casually, draining his beer.

If it wasn't obvious before, it is now apparent that James and I have never shared much with each other. I've answered this question in a multitude of ways in the past, but I've only been truthful with a handful of people. However, something seems to snap inside my head, and the short, pathetic story flows out. "I have no idea *how* he is. Because I don't know *who* he is," I say, glancing over at James to gauge his reaction. If James is shocked, he doesn't show it, so I continue on. "My mom was twenty-one when she got pregnant. She wasn't from the kind of family that would go to college, but she had moved away from home and was waitressing and living with a roommate outside of St. Louis. She met my dad one night when he came into the bar. They were together until sometime around my

123

first birthday, and then he started cheating on her with a few other women in town. My mom said she gave him an ultimatum, and he just walked out one day, and we never heard from him again. I was too young to even remember him, but she swore we were better off without him. When I was old enough to start asking questions, and she reluctantly gave me some details, it was too late – it was like he had disappeared. There was no trace of the guy with the name he had given her. I hired a private investigator a while ago, once I finally had some money, and they found a few loose ends, but essentially this asshole vanished in the early eighties," I tell him, relieved to tell my tale without any embellishments.

"Wow," James says, shaking his head back and forth as he tries to absorb my story. Based on what I have achieved and where I am today, this is not how anyone imagines my beginnings.

"Yup," I respond, staring back at the television as they highlight footage of the Packers' new quarterback.

"So, it was just you and your mom?" James asks, clearly trying to get an image of my youth.

He's going to be sorry he asked, but there's no reason to detour from the truth at this point. "She died nine years ago of cirrhosis of the liver," I say.

"Oh man, I'm so sorry," he says, looking shaken.

"Thanks. This is going to sound terrible, but it was almost a miracle she even made it to fifty-two considering how much she drank." I feel bad once I say it, especially once I see the look on James's face, but part of me feels like it's my right to say things like this; it may not be kind or respectful, but after what I went through growing up in her house, I feel like I've earned it.

"David was almost like a father to me," I blurt out, trying to ease the tension, but I realize that I'm probably making it worse. "I just mean that David took me under his wing, and I owe him everything, even though he was far from perfect," I say. I'm fumbling for the right words as I try to voice my inner struggle over the new revelations about my father-in-law and reconcile them with all my feelings about David and my own father up until last week – I can feel the conversation sliding downhill quickly.

"I wish I'd gotten to know him better, but he was pretty impressive from what I saw. It must be really hard for you to lose him," James says, throwing me a desperately needed lifeline.

"Thanks," I reply, hoping this one word captures everything I'm trying to tell him. Thank you for listening, thank you for understanding, and most importantly, thank you for never bringing this up again.

***

James and I stayed at the bar for a while, and although I should have left when he did, I decided to remain to watch the game and eventually texted Jen to let her know I would be home late.

When I walk in the house at ten thirty, all the lights are off, with the exception of the light in the mudroom, which Jen must have left on just for me. The only sounds are the quiet hum of the dishwasher and the annoying tick of the wall clock, and while I'm sad to have missed seeing the kids, silence is exactly what I need right now.

I flip on a light in the kitchen, so I can get a glass of water and notice that Jen has left a note for me on the island. It's on a small lined yellow sheet of paper, and for a moment, a terrible thought crosses my mind, and I envision a scene from a movie where the husband comes home to find that his wife has left him, and all she leaves behind is a "Dear John" note on the counter. Things may not be at their absolute best with Jen right now - everything I do seems to annoy her, but I can't imagine she would actually leave me. I shake my head as I pick up the paper and wonder why I would even think that, and if my subconscious is trying to tell me things are worse than I think.

Mark,
Mitchell called with a couple of questions about probate for dad's will. We need to find a time to call him tomorrow.
Also need to call Lynn to get some info from her about how she is going to want her money, etc. Would you take care of that? Please? xoxo
And I invited Courtney to dinner on Thursday night. Hope you had fun watching the game.

My first thought is pure relief. This note is as close to normal as we've been in weeks, and I'm filled with a sense of elation as I realize how much I've missed these small marital interactions. But then I re-read the part where she asks me to take care of talking to Lynn, and a new sense of dread takes over. It's no secret between us that I don't particularly like Lynn, but Jen has always assumed it's purely out of an allegiance to her. It has seemed easier to let this theory stand, especially with Lynn out in California and barely a part of our lives, but seeing her again and facing the potential of having to engage with her on a more frequent basis makes it much more difficult.

I can still picture exactly how she looked the first night we met. Even through the heavy makeup, overly highlighted hair, and dress so tight and small that it looked more like a scarf than a dress, she was stunning and looked far too young to be at the party. We had just beat the 49ers and were celebrating in a suite at the Westin St. Francis. Lynn had arrived with a group of models, they were in town for a shoot, and it didn't take her long to go through the majority of a bottle of vodka and get friendly with many of my teammates.

I was single at the time, and I couldn't deny how beautiful she was, but something about her immaturity and recklessness seemed more trouble than it was worth. However, it wasn't an issue for several of the other guys on the team, and she flirted with them all night, kissing several, before going back to Tim's room in the adjoining suite. The next day Tim regaled us all with tales of the barely legal model he had screwed (which was a bit of an exaggeration, considering she was twenty-three) and further bragged that his conquest was even better because the girl was engaged.

I saw her a couple of times later that season at after-parties when we had games on the West Coast, and I didn't think much of it, other than feeling sorry for the shmuck she was engaged to, when I watched Tim pick her up and carry her back to his room in her tiny skirt, with her high price engagement ring hanging on her finger for everyone to see. I had forgotten all about her until I met Jen four years later, and she showed me a picture of her younger sister with her husband and three-year-old son.

Chapter Sixteen
Jennifer

As I rush around the kitchen to prepare for Courtney's arrival, I wonder for the millionth time if this is really a good idea. It seemed perfect when I texted her on Monday afternoon, but seventy-two hours later, it doesn't feel quite as clever. I dump the assorted Whole Foods containers of salads into our blue and green Villeroy & Boch bowls, and I question why I'm bothering with this charade. It's not like anyone is going to believe that I made five different kinds of salads to accompany our steak dinner. But Courtney doesn't know me yet. Even though I wouldn't want to be the type of person who stays home all-day roasting quinoa or whatever you do to cook it, I want her to know that I put careful consideration into her visit. If spending more than an hour agonizing over which salads and desserts and type of meat to get at Whole Foods counts as careful preparation, then I get a big check, but I hardly think I can tell her that.

Mark promised he would be home by six since Courtney is coming at six-thirty. I have no reason to doubt him, but I start to get nervous as the minutes tick by on the annoyingly loud kitchen wall clock. It was an impromptu purchase after a few beers at a local craft fair when we were engaged. We should have gotten rid of it as soon as we got home and realized how loud it was without the sounds of a Dave Mathews cover band, but it was one of the first things we bought together, and as much as I hate it, I can't bear to part with it.

At five fifty-five, I've set the table, put out appetizers in the living room, and gotten everything ready for dinner, except for the steak, which is sitting in the marinade and waiting to go on the grill. I'm in the middle of writing a text to Mark to passively-aggressively remind him that he promised to be home in five minutes when he walks through the door. I feel my body relax at the familiar sight of his handsome face and broad chest in a wrinkled light blue button-down – his tie and jacket likely on the backseat of his car, or possibly still in his office. I chastise myself for thinking he would be late and silently apologize to him for the argument I was starting in my head. I'm not sure what to say, but I know that I've been bitchy the past few weeks, and although he's not perfect, I know he's tried to be supportive, and I should find a way to tell him.

"How was your day?" Mark asks as he grabs a bottle of bud light from the fridge.

"It was fine, I guess," I reply. "Yours?"

"It was okay," he says, sounding a little defeated. I want to ask if he heard back from any of the other players or how the new HR director is working out, but his response doesn't make it sound like he wants to talk about work. "Where are the kids?" he asks.

"Upstairs with Liliana. She stayed a little late to give them a bath so I could get ready," I say.

"Get ready for what?" Mark asks, taking a long swig from the bottle.

"You don't remember?" I ask, as my generous feelings from moments ago quickly disappear.

Mark's look says it all. He *doesn't* remember, but he is in no mood to play the game where he is made to guess what it is that he forgot.

"Courtney is coming for dinner," I tell him, trying not to sound as annoyed as I feel.

"Right," Mark says, glancing over at the dreaded clock. "What time is she coming again?" he asks.

"She should be here in half an hour," I say through clenched teeth.

"How long do you think dinner will last?" Mark asks, taking another sip of his beer.

"Is there somewhere *else* you need to be?" I ask him, no longer bothering to hide my anger.

"It's nothing. This is fine," Mark says, shaking his head.

I should let it go because Mark *is* home in plenty of time to help, and he's staying for dinner, and everything is fine, but I just can't leave things alone. Even as I start to speak, I know I should stop talking, but I can't help myself. "You forgot about dinner with my new half-sister, and you came home early for some other reason, and you can't even tell me what it is?" I ask him, and I hate myself more with every word I utter.

"It's not a big deal. I'm here, aren't I?" Mark asks, raising his voice ever so slightly, but it's a rhetorical question. "I told Hank I would stop by and help Logan with some routes, but I'll just text him I'll have to do it some other time," Mark says.

"Hank? From the club?" I ask, totally confused.

"Yeah. I ran into him the other night, and he asked if I could give Logan a little help. His son is a junior on the New Trier varsity team and plays mostly wide receiver. Hank thinks he's pretty good and might have a shot at playing in college, but Hank doesn't know much about the game," Mark says earnestly.

I'm not sure how to respond. I'm annoyed, but I'm really not sure why. Am I upset that he was going to come home early to go help some stranger play football instead of seeing his own kids? Maybe...but it's not like he doesn't see the kids most nights, and I was happy to have the house to myself on Monday night. Am I upset because he forgot that Courtney was coming over? Perhaps...although he's here now. So, what is it? And why can't I figure it out and have a normal reaction?!

"I'm going to go get changed and check on the kids," Mark says, after a moment of silence when it seems clear, I'm not going to respond.

***

I peek through the living room window when I hear tires crunch over the leaves on the circular driveway. Courtney exits from the backseat of a Honda civic that is probably as old as she is, and instantly I wish I had insisted on coming to campus to pick her up instead of letting her take an Uber. The old car putters off, and I watch as Courtney assesses the house before walking to the front door. I don't know what she's thinking, but my guess is she thinks that our seven thousand square foot brick McMansion is more than slightly ostentatious. There are many things I do love about the house, and sometimes I forget just how grand it is, but whenever I look at it through an outsider's eyes, I groan inwardly.

The doorbell rings, and I attempt to calm my nerves and remind myself that we did meet for coffee only a few days earlier and that went quite well, so this should be good too. I open the front door, and Courtney is holding a small bouquet of daisies and wearing a black sundress with a jean jacket thrown over her shoulders; she's wearing more makeup than she was the other day, and there's something about her that makes me think of Lynn for a second, but I try to shake it off and pretend I didn't see it.

"Welcome!" I say, a little too effusively, and throw my arms open because I can't decide if I should hug her or not, so instead, I end up looking like a scarecrow. "I'm so glad you could make it; come on in!"

"Thanks for inviting me," Courtney says, stepping into the imposing two-story foyer while glancing up at the enormous chandelier above her head.

"Is she here? Is that her?" Harper squeals as she comes flying down the wide staircase, fresh from the bath in her pink unicorn pajamas, blonde hair dripping on her tiny shoulders.

Courtney studies the small child on the stairs and seems to instantly relax as she smiles at her. "I'm Courtney. What's your name?" she asks Harper, in a soft, friendly tone, as she casually bends down, so her tall body is close to Harper's height. Her move is a signature of any good babysitter, and from the looks of it, she probably did a lot babysitting in high school. I have a fleeting thought that she should have been here babysitting for Ryan and Harper these past six years, and not just meeting them now, but then I let it go.

"I'm Harper," my little girl tells her, "and you're my Aunt Courtney," she says boldly.

Courtney looks at me for a moment, and I shrug an apology, but she takes it in stride. "I guess I am," Courtney says, smiling.

"Do you want to see my room?" Harper asks, pulling Courtney's hand back toward the direction of the stairs.

"Sweetie, why don't we let her get settled and get something to eat and drink, and then you can show her around," I say, trying to buy a few minutes.

"Okay, fine," Harper says, defeated, but she doesn't let go of Courtney's hand as we make our way into the living room.

I agonized for days over how to tell Harper and Ryan about Courtney. How could we explain that they had an aunt that we never knew about? What would they think of their grandpa? Would they understand that she had a different mother than I did? Luckily, I stopped overanalyzing every detail and realized that at the ages of four and six, they really wouldn't care or even think to ask all of those questions, and I was exactly right.

Harper is lovingly making up a messy plate of carrots and cheese for Courtney when Mark and Ryan enter the room. Mark has changed into a light green polo shirt with khaki pants, and Ryan is attached to Mark's back, wearing dinosaur pajamas. Before I can make any re-introductions, Courtney stands up, and Mark extends his arm across the back of the couch to shake her hand, "So glad you could make it," Mark says warmly, and Courtney grins. As always, everyone is drawn to Mark's charm. My mind wanders again, and I wonder what my dad would think if he could see this tableau. One of the things he loved best about Mark was his charisma and his ability to put others at ease with a simple smile – however, I'm not sure he ever envisioned this scenario.

***

Two hours have flown by, and I am clearing the dishes while Mark and Courtney chat happily at the kitchen table; Harper and Ryan finally went up to bed, but after the evening's excitement, I wouldn't be shocked if they aren't yet asleep.

133

Mark and Courtney both offered to clean up, but they are bonding over shared experiences as collegiate athletes, and I don't have much to add, so I insisted they leave me to it. I'm listening to most of the conversation, although not following it intently when I notice that Courtney has stopped talking about basketball at school and moved on to her friend who plays football.

"Preston would love to meet you," Courtney says. "Would you ever want to come to watch a home game?" she offers. "You could all come," she adds, looking over at me, "The kids would love it."

"That would be great!" Mark adds quickly. "I've been following a few guys on the team, and Preston could go pro," Mark says knowingly.

"Seriously?" Courtney asks, sounding surprised. "I'll tell him you said that," she says. "I'm sure he'd love to meet you as well sometime," she adds.

"Of course," Mark says. "I could even stop by practice one day," Mark says, sounding excited. "I'd be happy to talk to him, or any of the other guys about their options, or the Bears, or anything really!" he says eagerly.

"Don't they practice during the day?" I ask, clearly interrupting the conversation. "I mean, wouldn't you be at work?" I add as if I wasn't clear before.

"Right, of course. It probably wouldn't work," Mark says, sounding deflated. "I'll check out the schedule and see if there's a game we could make," Mark adds.

"Great," Courtney says, but the enthusiasm is gone from her voice as well.

I wish I could hit the rewind button, so I wasn't the one who sucked the joy out of the room, but these days it seems to be my specialty.

Chapter Seventeen
Lynn

"Tell me more about him," Ali probes from almost two thousand miles away.

"He's really cute, and he's *really* smart. He was a total nerd in high school – friends with Jen, unfortunately, but I guess I can forgive him for that," I laugh. "He works in statistics or something. I'm not entirely sure what he does, but at least he isn't a lawyer!" I exclaim. "What do you think of this?" I ask Ali as I hold the phone as far away from my body as possible to give her a full view of my outfit.

"I love it," she cheers. "It's sexy, but not at all slutty, the perfect combo," Ali declares.

I glance down at my clingy, burgundy wrap dress and black stilettos and decide that Ali is correct. The dress hugs in all the right places and shows a bit of cleavage, but it isn't too short, and it's even long-sleeved, so it can't be that bad – perfect for a second date.

"What does he look like?" Ali asks.

"He has black hair and super dark eyes. He's pretty tall too, definitely above six feet, and he's in good shape. I think he would naturally be pretty skinny, but he works out. Not the kind of guy who could ever be fat, even if he wanted to," I add. "Did I mention that he's Korean?" I ask.

"You didn't," Ali says. "Does it matter?" she asks.

"No, of course not," I backpedal. "I don't think I even mentioned it because it doesn't matter, but then somehow it seems weird *not* to mention it. I've lived in LA for too long; I feel like I'm being racially insensitive no matter what I do," I complain.

"I think you're fine," Ali says, trying to placate me. "Where are you going for dinner?" she asks.

"He asked if sushi was okay, and I told him I loved it, so I assume that's where we're going, but I have no idea which restaurant. He should be here in twenty minutes, though, so I better go finish touching up my makeup," I announce.

"He's picking you up?" Ali asks, raising her voice in excitement. "That's adorable! Can you imagine anyone in LA ever offering to pick anyone else up?" she questions.

"He lives close by, so he said it would be silly if we both drove. I can't remember the last time I got picked up on a date, although there was that one awful time last year where the guy picked me up in his Uber pool. Do you remember that?" I ask, cringing as I recall the horrific evening that ensued.

"You only have yourself to blame," she laughs. "I still can't believe you got in the car!" she accuses.

"I felt like it would have been rude otherwise," I say, defending myself. "Okay, I have to go. Need to fix my mascara and reapply lipstick," I tell her.

"You look gorgeous! You don't have to do anything. Stop being so nervous," she advises. "He'll love you for who you are."

"Woah! I think love is getting a bit ahead of things," I warn her.

"You know what I mean," she says playfully. "Okay, have fun, and call me tomorrow!"

"Thanks," I say as I end the call and wait nervously for Nick to appear. I attempt to take Ali's advice and refrain from applying a fourth coat of mascara.

***

I simply cannot believe it when the waiter brings a check and gestures to the empty tables around us. I glance at my watch and am stunned to discover it's ten fifty-five; we've been sitting here since seven, and the entire evening flew by. I don't know if I've ever had a dinner where the conversation was as seamless or the jokes as funny, and between the two of us, we only drank one bottle of wine.

"I think they're trying to tell us something," Nick laughs, as he takes the black leather folio from the waiter and slips his Amex inside without even looking at the bill.

"Can you believe we've been sitting here for four hours?" I ask him, desperate to know if he feels the same way that I do about the impossible passage of time I've just experienced.

"I had no idea," he says, smiling directly at me. "I barely remember ordering and eating. I feel like we just got here," he marvels. "I don't think we stopped talking the entire time. Is that possible?" Nick asks, looking for confirmation.

"Oh my God! That reminds me of this dinner I went to in San Diego," I say excitedly, as I launch into yet another story. Suddenly, I can feel the presence of the waiter over my left shoulder, and I am certain he wishes terrible things upon both of us, as his co-workers have already cleaned their stations and left for the night and he is still stuck here. I'm sure Nick is a good tipper, but I send a silent prayer out into the universe as he's signing the bill that my instinct is correct. "Never mind, I'll tell you later," I say, and I swear I can hear the waiter mumble "thank God" under his breath.

The banter continues on the short drive home, and I'm feeling great until Nick pulls up outside my apartment building and drives into the open parking spot directly in front of the front steps. He turns off the engine, and there is silence and awkward tension for the first time all night. On our first date last week, we grabbed lunch in downtown Evanston and then took a walk around campus by the lake. When we got to North campus, and it was time to part ways, I gave him a quick hug and a kiss on the cheek, and that was it. We were on a street corner in the middle of the afternoon – it didn't feel like there were any tough choices to make. But now it's eleven o'clock at night, and we're sitting in a dark car only a few feet from my apartment, after a couple of glasses of wine – there are so many ways to fuck this up.

My usual move would be to invite him up for a drink, then we'd have sex, and I'd either kick him out shortly thereafter or first thing in the morning. But I really like Nick, and for the first time, I don't want it to be like that. But if I don't invite him up, will he think I'm not into him? Or that I'm a prude and not worth his time? And if I do invite him up, will he think I'm a slut? Is it possible for him to come upstairs and actually just have a drink?

My mind is racing with these thoughts, and I must have a crazy look on my face because Nick interrupts my inner struggles by asking, "Is everything okay?"

139

"Yes, yes, I'm fine," I try to reassure him with a coy smile.

"I had a great time tonight," Nick says, his dark eyes looking directly into mine.

"Me too," I reply, trying to anticipate what he's going to say next.

"I'd love to see you again," he says.

"Me too," I reply.

"Would you think it was crazy if I asked if I could see you tomorrow?" he asks, and I can see the adorable faint blush spread across his cheeks, even in the dim light inside the car.

I don't want to be cynical, but I begin to wonder if this is his crafty way of asking if he can spend the night because then he could also see me in the morning. I want to believe that he's different than most of the other guys I've met, but a line like this is quickly putting him right back in the herd.

"I don't know," I hesitate.

"Oh," he says, his disappointment so tangible it fills the entire car. "Okay."

He looks like a lost puppy, and his sadness is hard to take. "Maybe," I offer, trying to make it better without doing a complete one-eighty.

"No, it's okay, I get it," Nick says, staring straight out the front windshield across Sheridan Road.

"No, that's not it," I say, trying to explain. "I really want to see you again too. I was just taken by surprise," I say.

"Don't worry about it," Nick says, but the excitement and energy from a few minutes ago are gone.

"What about the day after tomorrow?" I ask. "Sunday?" suddenly desperate to see him again.

"I'll call you," Nick says, and he leans over and pecks me on the cheek, which I read loud and clear as my signal to get out of the car.

"Thanks for dinner. I really had a great time," I yell to him as I'm closing the door. As I watch his red taillights pull away into the night, I'm not even surprised that I messed things up; I'm only surprised that it took me until the second date.

Chapter Eighteen
Courtney

I never attended a single football game in high school. It seemed pointless to sit in the bleachers on Friday nights or Saturday afternoons to watch mediocre athletes pile on top of each other and do ridiculous dances in the endzone on the off chance that they happened to score. On the other hand, the Lake Forest girls' and boys' basketball teams were both state champions, and if I wasn't playing in a game, I was in the gym cheering on the boys' team. Everything about basketball was more interesting and more exciting than football, and I couldn't imagine that I would ever find myself at a football game, let alone eager to attend one. But the energy of college football, and Big Ten football, is entirely different. It also helps that one of my best friends is on the team, and he would kill me if I didn't come watch him play.

It's a perfect early October day. There isn't a single cloud in the robin's egg blue sky, and the crisp temperature and sunshine are perfect for jeans and my oversized purple sweatshirt with the giant N on the front. The game has flown by in a bit of a blur, which is likely a result of the pre-game tailgating Christina and I partook in this morning. A glance at the scoreboard shows we are beating Purdue by fourteen points, and there are only three minutes left in the fourth quarter, so victory seems certain.

"What are you doing after the game?" Christina asks, draping her impossibly long arm around my shoulders.

"I promised Preston I would wait for him," I tell her, starting to feel the onset of a slight hangover as my hard seltzer buzz wears off. "Can I have some of your water?" I ask, staring longingly at Christina's Hydroflask and kicking myself for leaving mine at home.

"Sure," she says, handing it to me. "But seriously, Preston needs you to wait for him?" she says, pursing her lips and squinting her eyes. "I told you he was into you," she chides.

"We're just friends," I protest.

"Whatever," Christina says, holding out her hand to take back her water bottle. "I'm gonna walk back with some of the girls, and then we might go over to SPAC if you want to meet us there," she offers.

"Sounds good. Just text me. I may try and get some studying done," I tell her.

"You gonna *study* at Preston's?" she asks, giving me a knowing look.

"Oh, stop!" I tell her. As if to punctuate my complaint, the signal blares announcing the end of the game, and the student section around us erupts into cheers. The majority of the students start to rush down the bleachers, even though the security guards with their folded arms and matching jackets will not let anyone past them – rushing the field is a thing of the past. Christina and I weave against traffic as we walk up the bleachers and make our way through the dark tunnel into the closed concession area. Christina turns right, and I turn left to walk to the north end of the field and wait for Preston outside the locker room.

As I approach the dated building, which houses the locker room and training facilities, or at least dated compared to the brand new outrageously expensive fieldhouse on main campus, I notice a familiar-looking man, but it takes me a minute to place him. Then I realize it's Mark! He's talking to one of the coaches, and I don't want to interrupt, but I think it would be weird if I don't at least say, "Hi!" When I'm only about ten steps away, it occurs to me that it's far weirder that Jen didn't let me know she was coming to the game. They were here for the whole game and were going to leave without telling me! I'm about to turn around when Mark calls my name.

"Courtney! Hi!" Mark says as he says goodbye to the beefy coach and heads straight for me.

"Hey," I say, staring down at my sneakers and feeling awkward.

"I'm glad I ran into you. This ended up being last minute," he says, reaching out his massive arms to indicate our surroundings, "And I came to the game by myself, but then realized I probably wouldn't find you," he acknowledges.

"Oh, so Jen and the kids aren't here?" I ask, although his statement doesn't require much clarification.

He hesitates before answering. "She wanted to come but decided it would be too much for the kids. And I rarely miss a chance to see any game," he adds with a grin.

"It was a good game," I say.

"Your friend Preston had a great game," he says, nodding his head in approval.

"Yeah, he's going to be pretty happy," I say, feeling myself swell with pride as though I am somehow responsible for his performance on the field. "How do you know that guy you were talking to?" I ask, changing the subject.

Mark looks perplexed for a second and rubs his slightly stubbly square jaw before the proverbial light goes off, and he figures out what I'm asking him. "Oh, Charlie? We were on the team together the first year I played. He had already been playing for a long time by then. He was traded to Atlanta after that and then retired shortly thereafter. He's the new head defensive coach here," Mark tells me, although I already know that.

"Charlie is Preston's favorite coach," I tell Mark, oddly pleased at being able to share this insight.

"Charlie's a great guy," Mark says knowingly. "Preston's in good hands."

"How am I good hands?" Preston says, appearing suddenly behind me and enclosing me in a bear hug.

"Great game!" I attempt to say, although it comes out somewhat muffled with Preston's fleece partially over my mouth.

"Excellent game, man," Mark says, extending his hand to Preston.

"Thanks," Preston says, removing his arms from my shoulders to shake Mark's hand.

"Preston, this is Mark Olsen, Jen's husband," I start to say, but Preston interrupts me.

"I know who he is," Preston says, giving me a look to indicate that I'm crazy. "Did you see the whole game?" Preston asks Mark.

"I missed the first few minutes but caught the rest of it. I saw all four sacks," Mark says, and Preston beams with pride.

"Are you still here?" Charlie says to Mark, coming over to clap Preston on the back and give me a quick kiss on the cheek. "I see you've met my star player?" Charlie says, putting his meaty paws possessively on Preston's shoulders, looking at the three of us with a hint of confusion.

"I just introduced them," I inform Charlie.

"How do you and Mark know each other?" Charlie asks me, looking genuinely baffled.

"She's my niece," Mark says before I can answer.

Charlie looks back and forth between the two of us a few times before replying, "you're shitting me."

"It's a long story," Mark tells him, giving me a conspiratorial look that quickly puts him on the top of my new family list.

"Want to grab a beer and tell me about it? We could finish up that other issue too," Charlie says.

"I'd love to, but I have to get home," Mark says, regretfully looking at his watch. "Raincheck?"

"Sure," Charlie says, already backing away toward the locker room. "Great work today, Preston – go party, but not too much," he laughs. "Courtney, keep an eye on him," he yells to me.

"I'll try," I call back. As we say good-bye to Mark and start the walk back to campus, I try to listen to Preston's play-by-play of the game, especially since I wasn't at my best for most of it, but the more he talks about the parties he wants to hit tonight

146

and how much he wants to celebrate, the more I want to stay home so at least I won't have to watch.

***

The Kappa dining room is as blissfully quiet at ten on Sunday morning as it was two hours ago when I came downstairs, and I am grateful for the continued silence. While all of my *sisters* sleep off their hangovers upstairs, I have finished my econ homework, and I'm halfway done with my calc problem set. My phone buzzes for the fifth time this morning on the table next to my mug of tea, and I command myself not to pick it up, but my self-restraint is no longer strong enough. There are four texts from Christina and one from Preston.

Preston: Where did you go last night? You okay?

And the string of texts from Christina gets progressively more demanding:

You disappeared last night, what happened?
Where did you go?
Are you okay?
You better text me back!!

I knew that Christina would realize I left the house party shortly after we got there, but I'm shocked Preston noticed. It's not that I care, but when I showed up, he was already surrounded by about twenty shiny-haired freshmen, all pawing at him, and the whole thing was just gross. Christina was hanging out with some of the girls from the team and this volleyball player that I know she likes, so I didn't think she would care if I left either.

Courtney: I'm fine. I wasn't feeling well. I went home and went to bed

Christina: Really? And that's the only reason you left?

147

Courtney: Yes, really. I feel great now. Got up early and have already done two hours of work. I bet I feel a lot better than you do…

Christina: I feel like ass. But last night was awesome, you missed a great party

My fingers waver above my keyboard as I contemplate whether I want to know more, but I decide against it, and three little dots let me know she isn't waiting for my reply.

Christina: I'm gonna go back to sleep. Lunch later?

Courtney: I can't – I'm meeting my sister…

Christina: Jen?

Courtney: Nope – Lynn

Christina: Okay – have fun – I'll talk to you later

I'm supposed to meet Lynn for a run at eleven, so I might actually be back in time for lunch, but I'm not really in the mood to hear about the party and deal with Christina's questions; although I *am* curious if she hooked up with Bella, the volleyball player she's been stalking for the past month.

The second half of the problem set proves too tough to finish in the time I have left, so I pack up my books and head back upstairs, passing many bleary-eyed, pajama-clad girls on my way. Kerry is still asleep when I get back to the room, which isn't totally abnormal for a Sunday, although it's not because she was out late partying, it's because she was up studying. I feel around in the dark to grab my running clothes and the shoes from under the bed and get dressed in the enormous communal bathroom.

It would be far more direct to run up Sheridan Road to meet Lynn at the designated spot outside her building, but the run through campus and past a bit of the lake is so much prettier, even if it's out of the way. Luckily, I have extra time, and I missed training yesterday, so I could use the additional miles.

When I reach the corner of Sheridan and Noyes, Lynn is standing outside looking far more glamorous than anyone should look to go running. She's wearing skintight black capri leggings and a tiny black cropped tank top that reveals about two inches of her flat belly. Lynn's blonde hair is pulled back into a high ponytail that falls effortlessly down to her shoulders, and she has oversized designer sunglasses perched on the top of her head. One look down at my gray Nike running shorts and faded purple Wille the Wildcat shirt, and I have the ridiculous feeling that I am underdressed for a jog around my own college campus.

"Hi!" Lynn says excitedly, leaning over to kiss me on the cheek. "I'm never going to be able to keep up with you! You have to promise to take it easy on me," she pleads, with a gorgeous smile.

"I bet you'll be fine," I reply. "Which way do you want to go?" I ask her.

"I don't care. You lead the way; this is your territory," she says, giving her hamstring one final stretch.

"I was going to run back through campus, but let's run north. We can run up to the Baha'i Temple," I decide. "And there are some great homes we can run past," I say, and then wish I hadn't. I love running past the gigantic homes on the lake, but I'm sure it sounds weird to someone like Lynn, who grew up in a mansion.

"That sounds perfect," Lynn replies, and we begin our jog up Sheridan Road.

We're both quiet at the beginning, and although it's clear that Lynn is in good shape, it's also clear that I'm in far better

149

shape, which I *should* be, but that still makes me feel good. Between breaths, she asks questions about school and classes, and everything stays pretty casual until she asks about Jen.

"I didn't realize you'd been to her house," Lynn says, somewhat clumsily. "How many times have you seen Jen?"

"It wasn't a big deal. We had coffee, and then I just went for dinner last week," I say. "Oh, and Mark came to the football game, but Jen and the kids didn't come."

Lynn doesn't say anything and even quickens her pace a bit, but it's easy for me to match her stride and keep up. "Why don't you come for dinner this week?" I offer, "I'm going there on Wednesday. It would be fun for us to all be together," I add.

"I don't think Jen *or* Mark would like that," Lynn says, with a dry laugh.

Before I have a chance to ask her for more information, we both hear someone calling her name from across the street.

Lynn gives a quick wave as if she intends to keep running, but the man jogs across the street, and we have no choice but to stop. "Who's that?" I ask quickly, as he stops to wait for a car to pass.

"It's Nick. We went on a couple of dates, and I thought it went well, but then I messed it up," she says simply.

Nick doesn't miss a beat, and he pulls her in for a hug as soon as he reaches us. "What a coincidence! I just texted you to see if you wanted to have dinner tomorrow night," Nick says. Lynn glances at her watch to check the text as if she isn't sure she should believe him.

"I'm Courtney," I offer, sticking out my hand to shake his.

150

"Oh, wow! So nice to meet you," Nick says, and it's obvious by his response that he knows our crazy family story already.

"So, dinner?" Nick asks, looking at Courtney.

"Sure, that'd be good," she replies, sounding happy and confused at the same time.

"Great! Enjoy your run! Nice to meet you, Courtney. I'll text you later," he says to Lynn as he jogs back across the street.

"Doesn't seem like you messed things up to me," I say to Lynn as we pick up the pace.

"I guess not," she says with a grin.

It doesn't seem like the right time to bring up the topic of Jen or Mark again, but I decide I'll find a good way to get the three of us together soon.

Chapter Nineteen
Mark

I never used to understand why people hated Mondays as much as they did. For me, it usually meant a day off from practice because we had a game over the weekend, or we were getting ready to play that night. If we had a home game, I used to sleep late on Monday, then go for a long run by the lake and end up at this hole in the wall diner near my apartment that served the best omelets in the city. But now I finally understand the deal with Mondays, and I despise them just like everyone else. I'm sure Jen is sad when the weekend is over as well, but her mood is always pretty chipper in the morning (at least until recently). I guess she looks forward to going into the shop.

My calendar is light for the day, thanks to Kayla's management, but that doesn't do much to improve my mood. I glance at the legal pad where I took notes at Friday's executive team meeting, and the list of tasks that I personally need to complete is almost nonexistent, or at least they all seem fairly menial. David always said that the key to management was delegation, but recently it feels like everyone is taking everything off my plate before I even have a chance to assign. It's hard to tell if everyone feels bad for me, or if they no longer trust me now that David's gone, or maybe I'm just paranoid. After nine years here, and several of them shadowing David, I have a good sense of what needs to be done, but I've never had the passion that David did, and in his absence, I continuously doubt everything he seemed to see in me. That doubt is certainly reinforced by my colleagues' recent behavior, or at least that's how I see it. I try to remember what Jen said last week about using Tom to recruit other players or creating multiple packages to offer directly to the NFL, or maybe it was to individual teams; I can't remember specifically, and as much as I don't really want to get started on my "busywork," I'm not too eager to develop a proposal either.

As if reading my mind, Kayla buzzes my phone to let me know that Tom Turner is on the phone. "Put him on," I direct her as I grab a company pen and my legal pad and prepare to take notes.

"Hey Tom, how's it going?" I ask as soon as I hear the line click over.

"It's good. You?" he questions.

"Can't complain," I reply, keeping up the banter. "What can I do for you today?" I ask him. "Everything okay with the policy? I think the final paperwork was supposed to be there last week," I tell him.

"Yeah, yeah, that's all fine," Tom says. "I was actually calling about something else," he says.

"Oh, okay. What is it?" I ask, slightly nervous, although I don't think I have any reason to be.

"I overheard one of the coaches talking the other day, and it looks like the wide receiver coaching position might be opening up," Tom says.

I use my left hand to cover my gaping mouth and then slowly rub my chin as I try to think about my possible response, but Tom speaks again before I have a chance.

"You've just been really great, and I thought I might be able to help you out," he says, faltering a bit. "I know you didn't actually say it, but I know that's what you were fishing for when you asked me about coaching info a few weeks ago, and then Bam! I heard this at practice the other day and wanted to let you know before word hit the street," Tom says, and I can almost hear the high-voltage smile in his voice.

"I really appreciate you thinking of me, but I'm not looking for a coaching position. I love football, but insurance is my game now," I tell him, and I wince as the bullshit words leave my mouth, and I'm grateful that we're on the phone, so I don't have to see him roll his eyes or give me whatever look it is that I deserve.

"Alright," Tom says with a fair amount of disbelief.

"Thanks again for letting me know," I say.

"No problem," he says, "See you around," and I hear a loud click, indicating the call is over, but what it really sounds like is "Your loss, coward."

***

Earlier today, I wasn't sure how I was going fill my day, but somehow the hours and meetings and phone calls all blurred together, and somehow, now it's six-thirty, and the office has practically emptied out. I decide to take the long way home because as much as I want to see Jen and the kids, I still need a little more time before I need to be the fun, happy dad that's expected when I walk through the door.

I don't expect anything unusual on my detour through Wilmette; I'm only hoping for an additional ten minutes to clear my head with the slight chill of the autumn evening whooshing in through the open car windows. But stopped at the corner at Lake and Ridge, I get far more than I bargained

154

for. Lynn is impossible to miss getting out of the passenger side of a silver Audi in tight jeans and red silk shirt, slipping casually off one of her shoulders. Her blonde hair glows under the streetlights, and she tosses it to the side as she waits patiently by the car door for the driver. I shake my head as I sit with my foot on the brake to watch the scene play out, and I quickly check my rear-view mirror to ensure no one is behind me. A tall, good-looking Asian guy unfolds himself from the sports car, and I commiserate with him for a second, but I don't feel too bad for him and his orange TTS. I know what's about to happen, but I'm still a little outraged when the guy walks around the back of the sports car and puts his arm around Lynn and plants a kiss firmly on her lips, and she smiles up at him as they turn to walk into a nearby Italian restaurant. When they are out of sight, I lift my foot off the brake and begin the rest of my journey home; however, now my thoughts are filled with loathing for Lynn.

I never liked Trevor, and it's clear that he wants nothing to do with us, but still, the fact that Lynn continues to cheat on him pisses me off. I know that it has little, if any, impact on my life, but I just can't stand it; it's just one more way that she's pretending to be something she isn't.

As I weave through the suburban streets, passing a mix of warmly lit large Tudors, colonials, and Victorian homes, I wonder if I should tell Jen about what I just saw, and what I saw last year at the conference in Vegas, and then, of course, there's the first time I ever laid eyes on Lynn, but that seems like ancient history at this point, and way past the point of being able to say anything.

I've tried to forget it, but I can still easily picture Lynn in a silver dress in the lobby of the Bellagio Hotel last spring. I knew she hadn't seen me earlier that evening in the casino, but when she walked, or rather wobbled, away from her table toward the elevator, I decided to follow and see where she was going. I don't know what I expected to find, but when a short, stocky guy in a lime green polo shirt left the VIP check-in desk with his black roller bag and made a beeline for her at the elevator and buried his face in her cleavage, I knew she wasn't in Vegas with Trevor. On the way to my conference the following morning, I saw her at the pool with her gentleman friend, and from the way he was judiciously applying sunscreen to the areas not covered by her thong, it was quite apparent that they were not merely friends.

By the time I pull into the driveway, I've forgotten almost entirely about my tedious day at work, and the shame of the call with Tom has even started to fade a bit. The only thing I can focus on is my illogical anger with Lynn. I know it's wrapped up in Jen's feelings toward her, and what happened over twelve years ago and with Declan – I should just let it go, but I can't. I take a few deep breaths and determine to try to put it out of my mind for the night. Jen is waiting for me in the kitchen when I walk inside.

"How was your day?" Jen asks while loading the kids' brightly colored plastic plates into the dishwasher.

I hesitate for a moment, so I can consider my response. "It was okay. Not great, but it was fine," I reply – a vague answer that provides no real information, but I know it will suffice. "How was yours?" I ask.

"Mostly fine," Jen replies, equally vague. "But I did get a call from Mitchell, and he says we need to make a few decisions before we can finish things up." Jen closes the gleaming stainless dishwasher and leans against it with folded arms as if the next part of the conversation requires proper footing.

"What do we need to decide?" I ask, feeling perspiration start to form on my forehead and under my arms with the uncertainty.

"Mitchell said that everything has been divided three ways, although Courtney's share will go into a trust until she graduates from college. But that includes the company. Even though you're still the CEO, technically Courtney and Lynn would each own a third of it," Jen says, without trying to conceal her disgust.

"Would they be on the board? Would they have any decision-making power?" I inquire, unclear if this is upsetting news or not.

"It doesn't seem that way, but still, I can't stand the idea of Lynn owning part of the firm. You know that won't go well," Jen says as she uncrosses her arms and runs her fingers through the loose strands of hair that have escaped her messy ponytail.

I wouldn't have been thrilled with the idea of Lynn having any piece of the business before, but after today, I just want to be done with her. I want her to take her money and get the hell back to California to her cuckold husband and mysterious son and never return. "So, what can we do about it?" I ask Jen.

"Mitchell suggested that we could offer to buy them out," Jen says. "Lynn is my bigger concern, but we just met Courtney – how well do we really know her? I think it would be simplest to buy them both out," she says resolutely.

There's a part of me that wants to suggest we ask them to buy *us* out and they can take over the exciting world of insurance, but no matter how I feel about David's infidelity, I know that I could never do that to David, and Jen certainly wouldn't go for it. "Let's do it," I agree, trying to muster an appropriate amount of enthusiasm.

"Great!" she exclaims. "I'll talk to Courtney, but I can't handle talking to Lynn. "Can you do it? Please?" she pleads.

Chapter Twenty
Jennifer

Mark stands there for a minute, and his face twists into a pained scowl as if he can't figure out how to answer the question. I know Mark isn't a big fan of Lynn's, but he knows how hard it's been for me to talk to her recently, so I can't imagine he would deny me this request.

"There's something you have to know about Lynn," Mark explodes, "She's cheating on Trevor – I saw her," he says, the condemnation evident in the way he forms his words.

"What? When did you see her? Where did you see her?" I ask, trying to wrap my head around this.

"I just saw her tonight. I drove through Wilmette on the way home, and I saw her get out of the car with some guy, and then they kissed, and he put his arm around her before they walked into a restaurant. I can assure you; it wasn't platonic," he scoffs. Mark rubs his eyes and pulls out the kitchen stool to sit down as if he knows this isn't going to be a short conversation.

"Are you sure it was her?" I question, but the look Mark gives me makes us both cringe because there really isn't a chance of mistaking Lynn for anyone else.

I didn't learn the full story about Mark's parents until we had been dating for a few months, but once he told me, it was clear that he had a zero-tolerance policy for cheating. That happens to make the issue with Dad even *more* difficult, but he seems to be burying his emotions with that for the moment. I know I need to tread lightly with how I approach my questions about Lynn, but I still need some answers.

"So, let's say she is cheating on Trevor, or at least something is going on there…why does that change our approach to offer to buy her out of the business?" I ask him.

"This isn't the first time," Mark says quietly, using his fingers to trace the faint lines in the marble countertop.

"What do you mean?" I ask, unable to disguise the shock in my voice.

"I saw her with a guy a year or so ago when I was at a conference in Vegas," he says quietly.

"And you didn't tell me?!" I shout at him.

"I don't know," he says meekly, "I didn't want to upset you. And it didn't seem like it would make much of a difference. You weren't even really talking to her at the time. It just pissed me off more, but I didn't think it would help anything if I told you," Mark says, staring into the counter, unable to meet my gaze.

I want to be mad because it seems like that's the proper emotion, but I think he's right – it wouldn't have made much of a difference if I had known, only I might have felt a shred of sympathy for Trevor, and I'm not exactly devastated to have missed out on that.

I sigh and then ask, "Okay, so what does this mean now? Does it change anything?" I pull out the stool next to him to take a seat, silently wishing I had already changed into pajamas or at least yoga pants, so the waistband of my skinny jeans wasn't digging into my soft middle.

"I'm not sure. But she's still here, which seems weird. I would think she would be back in California by now, right?" Mark asks, but he keeps going without waiting for my response. "What if she's leaving Trevor and wants to stay here with this guy?" he postulates.

"She wouldn't do that to Declan...would she?" I question.

"Who knows? I think it's fair to say that we don't know much about her or their family. For Christ's sake, he was a baby the last time we saw him!" Mark fumes.

"Oh God," I groan. "What if she *is* back here because of the company? Maybe she's here because she wants a piece of it? She isn't going to just take her money and go home," I say, voicing my fears out loud.

"I can't imagine she would want anything but the money. And honestly, Trevor must pull in a few million a year, so I'm not sure she needs the money either," Mark says, but he doesn't sound very convincing.

"Who do you think the guy was? Did she just meet him? Or is it someone she already knew?" I wonder aloud. "I mean, she hasn't been here in forever..." I trail off.

"Does it really matter?" Mark asks, rising from his stool to grab a cold bottle of beer from the fridge. "Do you want one?" he asks me.

"I'd have a glass of wine if there's something cold," I reply, feeling a bit of nostalgia for evenings from the past when we would have drinks and talk about our days. It seems wrong to enjoy this conversation, but for the first time in way too long, it

160

feels like we are on the same team, trying to solve a problem together.

"I don't know if it matters," I reply, in answer to his question. "What if he's from another insurance firm? Or if he's a lawyer? Maybe she's getting outside legal advice?" I suggest.

Mark gives a deep throaty laugh, and I realize it's the first time I've heard him really laugh in weeks. "As much as I like the way you're thinking about this, I think you're giving her too much credit. It looked like sex, not subterfuge," Mark smiles, and his shoulders relax as he joins me back at the counter. This time his knees bump up against mine, and although we're talking about my sister's adulterous actions, all I can think about is that it's been way too long since I've had sex with my husband.

***

"I've missed that," Mark says as he plants kisses on my collarbone and disentangles himself from my lower limbs. I assume he is going to roll over to his side of the bed, and I'll hear his soft snoring within moments, but instead, he curves his body next to mine and wraps his arms around me. "I've missed *you*," Mark says. He uses his finger to trace slow circles around my nipple, and then his hand moves lower to rest on my soft belly. I try and shift my hips so I can lie face down on the mattress, but Mark places his free hand on my hip and whispers in my ear, "I love you so much." I curve my back into his chest and try to relax with Mark's hands exactly where they are.

***

Although nothing is resolved with Lynn, I still have a million questions for Dad that will never be answered, and every day at the store feels more mind-numbing than the last, but there is a renewed sense of ease with Mark that makes everything a little

161

better. Over breakfast yesterday morning, using our own little code so the kids wouldn't understand, we determined that it would make more sense for me to talk to Lynn about the will. As annoyed as I am with her at all times, she is *my* sister. And while it's my sister and Dad who cheated, I seem to have accepted it, but Mark is still trying to come to terms with Dad's transgression and Lynn's infidelity and suspected neglect of Declan, which stir up all sorts of issues for him.

Although I still think it's the right thing for me to talk to Lynn, I'm feeling less and less certain as I get closer to Evanston. I liked the idea of surprising her, but then I realized I had no idea where she was staying while she was in town. Considering how affluent the north shore suburbs are, it is surprising that there aren't better hotel options, and the best hotels are still all in Chicago. I assumed that Lynn would be at the Sheraton or Renaissance in Northbrook, as those are close to Winnetka, and she isn't going to do much better unless she goes into Chicago, but she merely suggested that she would be in Evanston for the day and we could meet here. I guess that could mean she is staying at the old Orrington, but it's more likely that means she is visiting Courtney, either before or after she sees me – I know from Courtney's texts that the two of them have also been getting together. Upon realizing we would all be in Evanston, I wondered if I should suggest that the three of us try to get together, even if only for a few minutes, but I immediately thought better of it.

I'm delighted to find a parking spot right across from the Unicorn Café on Sherman and wonder again if she picked this place because she is meeting Courtney here, and I already know it is one of Courtney's favorites. I've arrived ten minutes early, which isn't even that early for me, but instead of going inside and getting a table to wait for Lynn, which is what I would normally do, I decide to wait in the car and let her be the first one there; then I can stroll in a few minutes late. I completely accept that I am being juvenile or perhaps passive-aggressive, but it still makes me feel oddly smug.

162

The majority of the pedestrian traffic on the sidewalk is college students, either walking in groups or walking alone and glued to their phones, oblivious to the world around them. But then the unmistakable shiny, blonde ponytail emerges through a sea of unwashed millennial hair and ironic trucker hats. Even though it's been less than two weeks since I've laid eyes on her, it's as if I've forgotten just how striking she is, and I'm seeing her again for the first time. As annoyed as I get with her and as jealous as I am of her, there's always an odd feeling of pride that runs through me when I watch other people stop to look at Lynn. And somewhere deep inside, there is a part of me that wants to shout, "that's my sister!" And then I want to tell them that she's so much more than just a pretty face. But that thought is usually fleeting because jealousy or resentment takes over long before I can act on anything else.

At first, I just see Lynn. She's dressed in black leggings and a cropped black hoodie sweatshirt, looking identical to every model on the Lululemon website, but then I notice she is holding hands with a man! He steers her from the middle of the sidewalk toward the doorway to Unicorn Café, where he leans in, cups her chin with his hand, and kisses her for longer than I would consider appropriate in the middle of the day in front of a coffee shop. After that, he slips his hand away and waves as he crosses the street. I'm astounded by my good luck. It's not that I needed to confirm Mark's story with my own eyes, but still, somehow, seeing it for myself feels significant. I don't see it initially, but while I watch Lynn's mystery man cross the street and then pause on the sidewalk to listen to a message on his phone, I realize that he looks familiar. His face reminds me of someone, but I can't quite place him.

Lynn's already inside, so there's not much use waiting in the car at this point. As I come around the back of the Range Rover to pay for parking at the pay station, I hear Lynn's mystery man talking on his phone, and although I had trouble placing his voice, the voice is unmistakable – Lynn is having an affair with the class treasurer, Nick Lee – Holy Shit! I abandon the parking meter and get back in the car to grab my phone; there's no way I can sit across from Lynn drinking coffee and trying to persuade her to take her money and run back to California now that I know about Nick! I shoot Lynn a text telling her that something came up, and I need to cancel and quickly pull out of my auspicious parking spot and head north to figure out what all of this means.

Chapter Twenty-One
Lynn

I'm staring at Jen's text as I watch her shiny SUV drive away, and I can't figure out a logical explanation. I guess something could have come up with the kids, and she had to go, but why wouldn't she just say that? Instead, she sent a vague message that something came up and she could no longer make it, but in reality, she was already here and had been sitting in her parked car for ten minutes and then sped away. I reach for my sparkling water and desperately try to give her the benefit of the doubt, but it's almost impossible. And then I get even more pissed off as I realize I cut short my time with Nick in order to meet Jen, and I could still be with him right now. He did say that he had to get back to the office; he was only working from home this morning because of a dentist appointment, but I still feel cheated.

I'm also annoyed because Jen said she wanted to go through a few details in Dad's will, and that clearly isn't going to happen. I don't want to look too eager, but I'm going to need to find out what my share is and actually get money in the bank, especially since there is no way Trevor is going to give me anything if I don't go back to LA. Logic would say that he would be happy for me to be as far away as possible, especially as he continues to limit my exposure to Declan, but he sees it differently.

I leave my empty seltzer glass on the table and walk outside into the dreary October day. I can feel the heavy gaze of a short, dark-haired young man, who's clutching a laptop in one hand and a coffee mug in the other, and it seems selfish to keep the table when angsty college students need it far more than I do. I stop when I get a block from the café to assess what I'm going to do with my day. I wasn't necessarily looking forward to seeing Jen, but foolishly, as I always do, I thought this might be the day that we find common ground or that she stops hating me. Also, it gave me something to do, and now I have no plans for the rest of the day or tomorrow or even the day after that, and no more details about my financial situation.

I stop at the bench on the next corner to contemplate my afternoon. I can't imagine Courtney is free, it is the middle of the day on a school day, but it couldn't hurt to see if she's busy. Thinking back to my sophomore year at USC, I certainly didn't spend a lot of time in class or doing homework, although most of my time was occupied with Trevor once we started dating spring of my freshman year. I remember feeling so mature, dating a twenty-three-year-old law school student when all of my friends were going to date parties and bonfires on the beach – what would have happened if I listened to everyone who said he was too old for me and partied my way through college like my friends? I guess it's far too late to play that guessing game now.

Lynn: Hi there! Any chance you are free today? This afternoon?

The three little dots let me know that Courtney is writing back immediately, so at least I won't have to wait for her reply.

Courtney: Sorry! I'm swamped. I have class and then practice and a paper to write ☹

I can barely dribble a ball, and I hate writing, but I have a pang of envy as I read her text.

Lynn: Of course – no worries. Maybe this weekend?

Courtney: Sure! Gotta go

Lynn: Bye

I didn't expect it to work out, but I feel deflated anyway. I rest my phone on my thigh and tilt my face toward the sun to feel the warmth on my face. Every day here feels a couple degrees colder, and I don't know what I'll do when it finally gets cold and gray, and the sun barely comes out – my memory of the first eighteen years of life. I've gotten so used to the beautiful California weather; I may no longer be able to tolerate a Chicago winter. My phone vibrates in my pocket just as I'm finding a moment of inner peace, as my old yoga teacher used to say. I try to stay in the moment, but it's futile. I'm guessing it's an additional text from Courtney, but I can't help but hope it's from Nick (telling me he misses me already) or even from Jen with an actual explanation of why she blew me off. My heart sinks as I see Trevor's name and the words, "CALL ME NOW!" all in caps.

My head spins as I try to think about all of the reasons he could be upset, or more upset than usual. I haven't heard from him since my call with Declan last week, so that is the likely culprit, but it's weird that he didn't react sooner. I know from experience that he'll tell me what I've done wrong, but I also know that it's better to be prepared; that way, I can have my defense ready. Before I can finish thinking through other reasons, Trevor could be upset, my phone rings.

"I was about to call you," I say defensively, "You just sent that text about thirty seconds ago," I add.

"I don't like waiting," Trevor says; the slight echo in his voice lets me know that I'm on speakerphone in his office. I used to hate it when he did that, but I learned there were more important battles.

"What do you need to talk about?" I ask, chewing my lip as I wait for his response.

"When are you coming back?" he barks at me.

"I'm not sure," I reply, and then I add, "Why does it matter?"

"I got a call from your landlord this morning. He's fixing the air conditioning in the building, and he needs access to your apartment," Trevor says, sounding annoyed.

"Okay," I say, drawing out the last syllable. "Why did he call *you*?"

"He hasn't seen you in a few weeks, so he didn't know what happened to you. And the apartment is in *my* name. Because I own it and pay the mortgage," Trevor adds, as if he needs to remind me.

"I'll give him a call right now," I say, trying to reason with him since this seems like an easy fix.

"*And* he said your car needs to be moved because it is blocking access to something in the garage, and it's not like he has the keys to your car. What are you going to do about that?" Trevor challenges.

"I'll ask what the problem is when I call, but Ali has a spare set of keys. I'll ask her to come move the car," I respond, attempting to keep my voice level.

"I don't need to take care of this shit for you," Trevor explodes. "I have plenty to do without worrying about your problems," he chides.

I want to scream at him but sitting on this bench in the middle of town, surrounded by students, gives me the strength to channel my emotions. It also makes Trevor insane when I scream, and I know that won't help anything. "You don't have to do anything," I say carefully. "I'll call the landlord and straighten it all out. This is the last you'll hear of it," I promise him.

"Maybe I should call him and tell him to put that place on the market? Why am I even paying for you to have that place if you aren't going to live there? And the same goes for the car..." Trevor says, his words dripping with spite.

"That's not part of the settlement, and you know it," I say, no longer able to control the edge in my voice.

"But I drafted that agreement, and I'm sure it's based on you actually living in the apartment and driving the car," he counters.

"Trevor, all of my stuff is there! I'm here because my father died. I've only been gone a few weeks. I'll be back when I'm ready to come back – you don't need to be such an asshole about it!" I yell at him and then mouth an apology to the group of students standing a few feet away, as it's obvious my conversation is garnering attention.

"If you're not back in a few weeks, maybe I should see if Missy wants to use the apartment?" Trevor suggests.

There's a moment of silence as I attempt to absorb his comment and determine an appropriate response. Missy is the twenty-five-year-old aspiring actress that Trevor dumped me for and is now engaged to. At first glance, she looks like a

169

younger version of me; tall, blonde, with big boobs and a few modeling jobs on her resume. But from what I saw on her YouTube channel, she's much closer to an adult film star than anything else, which clearly explains Trevor's interest in her.

I take two deep breaths before I reply, and I can hear Trevor squeezing one of his many stress balls while he waits for me to speak. "What would Missy do with my apartment? Isn't she living with you?" I ask.

"She is, but she's got a lot of stuff. You know how much I hate having all that shit lying around. If I'm paying for your place and you aren't there, maybe Missy can keep some of her stuff there," he muses, as if telling his new fiancé to take her belongings to his ex-wife's apartment is perfectly normal.

"That's my apartment, and I'll be back soon," I assure him through clenched teeth.

"Don't forget to take care of your car!" Trevor barks.

"I'll make those calls as soon as we hang-up," I assure him, clenching my fingers into a fist on my free hand and wishing I could punch his pretty face.

"Oh, and don't bother calling Declan again; he doesn't want to talk to you," Trevor adds, and then the line goes dead.

***

The last few days are a bit hazy. I went straight home after the phone call with Trevor and closed all the blinds, took an Ambien, and got into bed. I slept away most of the afternoon and early evening, but when I got up around eight, I just felt worse, and then I knew I would be up for most of the night. I exchanged texts with Nick and Ali and Courtney, but mostly I've spent the days asleep and the nights binge-watching a bizarre mix of romcoms and true crime on Netflix with the last few bottles of wine that were in the apartment.

By mid-morning of day four, most of the pain from my call has subsided, and I'm now so disgusted with my slovenly state that I know it's time to get out of my slump. I have to admit that a big motivation for this turnaround is the text from Nick earlier this morning asking if I'm free for dinner tonight.

Three miles of running, one hour of cleaning, thirty minutes of showering, and over ninety minutes of blow-drying and primping, and I'm finally feeling human again. We didn't decide where we are going to go for dinner, but Nick said he would come by here at six and we could decide once he got here. Once I'm ready at five, I try to keep busy, but the minutes tick by slowly. I contemplate calling or texting Jen to ask what's going on with the will; I haven't heard from her since she ditched me the other day, and with Trevor's latest threats, it's increasingly more important to know where I stand financially. I pull up her name in my contacts, and my finger hovers over her cell phone number, but I decide not to risk it. The likelihood of the call going well is slim, and when it doesn't, I'll just be back in a bad mood when Nick arrives, and it's not worth it.

Nick's punctuality is a blessing, and he buzzes the apartment at six o'clock on the dot, putting me out of my misery. I give myself another once over in the mirror as he's on the way up the stairs and determine that it's impossible to tell I spent the last four days in bed.

"Hi!" I chirp as I open the door and see Nick's smiling face in the hallway. He's wearing a black leather jacket over an untucked light blue shirt and faded Levi's, and he's holding a bouquet of pink roses. Without a second thought, I grab him by the neck and kiss him full on the mouth before he even has a chance to enter the apartment.

"It's good to see you too," Nick chuckles after I release him from my death grip and close the door behind him.

"I missed you," I say candidly.

A slight flicker of confusion passes over Nick's face as if he's trying to process how I missed him when I just saw him a few days ago, but then he gives me a sexy grin and replies, "I missed you too. Where do you want to go for dinner?" he adds.

Looking at him casually perched against my sofa in his sexy leather jacket and shy grin, still holding my flowers, I'm overcome with desire. We've kissed a few times now, but after five dates, that's as far as it's gone, as we've always been out in public or at least in the car. But now alone in my apartment, and so many months since the last time I've had sex that I've stopped counting, it feels like I'll die if I have to wait any longer.

Feeling more brazen than I have on any of our previous dates, I whisper, "I'm not very hungry right now," and step toward him, carefully placing the roses on the counter and taking his hand to lead him toward the bedroom. Thankfully, Nick doesn't need any additional prodding, and he willingly follows my lead, kicking off his loafers as he goes.

Until two years ago, I had only slept with two men – my high school boyfriend Justin and then Trevor. Well, actually three if I'm being totally honest. There was that one football player that I slept with a few times when I was engaged to Trevor, but that was only after finding out Trevor had repeatedly been cheating on me with half a dozen paralegals. Sleeping with someone else to get back at him wasn't the answer. I should have called everything off as soon as I found out about his infidelity, but then I found out I was pregnant with Declan, and everything changed.

After seventeen years with Trevor, and the other guys, a distant memory from my youth, I didn't care much about sex. It was something that occasionally happened with Trevor; it was perfunctory and rarely satisfying. But a few months after our messy split, I ended up on a date with one of Ali's friends and remembered that sex could be pretty fucking amazing. Since then, I've decided to enjoy one of the few positives that have come from this divorce – safe, satisfying sex with no-strings-attached – or at least that's all I've been interested in until now.

Nick and I are both trying to go slowly, but the tension that's been building over the past few weeks is making it challenging. He finishes unbuttoning his own shirt because I'm struggling with the last two buttons, and as he pulls it over his head, I'm rewarded with soft skin and hard muscles, exactly as I pictured they would be. I slip my cashmere sweater over my head and consider leaving on my jeans for the thrill of letting Nick take them off of me, but I'm past the point of having that kind of patience. I roll on top of Nick, and even as he's murmuring in my ear, "We don't have to rush, I want to enjoy every minute of this," it's clear from the movement of his hips that his body has other ideas.

With no time to spare, I find a condom in the inner pocket of my cosmetic bag (conveniently lying on the night table), and Nick and I simultaneously fail on our attempt to take anything slowly. However, lying in the crook of his slightly sweaty arm, Nick says, "Don't worry, that was just a practice round," and kisses me softly on the temple.

Chapter Twenty-Two
Courtney

It feels like the quarter just started, and fall sports are barely mid-season, so we should still be working our way back into heavy practices. But as Coach reminded us yesterday, our first regular-season game is in four and a half weeks, *and* we have pre-season games starting in three, so it's time to start busting our asses. I'm reminding myself how much I love the game as I pack my gym bag and my backpack at six in the morning while Kerry sleeps peacefully in her bed. After conditioning this morning, I have a full day of classes and then practice this afternoon and won't be back to the house until dinnertime; I'm carrying so much stuff it feels like I'm moving out!

"Your mom called again," Kerry whispers in a sleepy voice.

"Sorry if I woke you up," I apologize in a hushed tone.

"Don't worry about it," she mutters, "I have to get up soon anyway; I have a bio midterm tomorrow. I have so much studying to do," she yawns as she stretches her thin arms over her head.

I don't question that Kerry will study every waking moment between now and her exam, but I do question whether she really needs to study that much. Kerry had a 4.0 GPA last year, and I'm pretty sure she has gotten an A on every test she's taken so far in college, which is saying a lot for pre-med. She says that it's because of how much she studies, but I know she is also naturally smart. She's convinced she won't get into Stanford Medical School without a perfect undergrad transcript, which seems crazy, but I think her future patients will be lucky to have her.

"What do you mean, my mom called?" I question. I've heard people talk about the phones that they used to have in dorm rooms and in the sorority houses. Roommates had to leave messages for each other and share time on the phone, and there are still empty phone jacks in the walls as proof, but it doesn't work that way today.

"Your mom called my cell," Kerry clarifies. "She called the other day too. I texted you, didn't you see my text?" she asks, still sounding slightly raspy.

"No, I must have missed it. The last few days have been insane," I say, shaking my head as I try to put the pieces together. I wouldn't even think my mom could call Kerry, but then I remember that I gave her the number in case of emergencies. "What did she say?" I ask Kerry.

"She wanted to see how you're doing. And she wants you to call her. She said you aren't returning any of her calls," Kerry trails off.

"I'm so sorry to get you involved in this," I apologize, getting more annoyed with my mom by the minute.

"It's not a big deal. I told her I would pass along the message, but I know what you told me, so I didn't make any promises about trying to get you to call her," she assures me.

"Thanks, Kerry," I say. "I don't want to talk to her, but I'll send her a text and tell her not to bother you anymore," I promise.

Kerry swings her long, thin legs over the side of the twin bed and stretches again; there are a few blonde hairs out of place, but as always, she braided her hair before she went to sleep, so it wouldn't be too unruly in the morning. I don't really want to spend the day studying for biology and going to an organic chem lab, but part of me is jealous. Kerry will hole herself up in the special section of Deering library that she likes for most of the day, and if she finally remembers to eat, she'll go get fruit salad or a smoothie at Norris, and then she'll talk to her twin sister after dinner for half an hour (she's a sophomore at the University of Georgia), and then she'll study some more and go to sleep. Right now, that looks simple and appealing.

"Don't worry about it," Kerry assures me. "I really don't mind."

"Okay," I reply quietly. "Have a good day. Good luck studying!"

"Thanks, you too!" Kerry echoes as I close the door behind me.

***

"I almost died," Christina gasps, still panting and chugging water from her water bottle as she collapses onto the locker room bench.

I haven't even caught my breath enough to be able to speak, so I simply nod and guzzle more water while I wait for the burning in my chest to subside and the flames on my cheeks to cool down. When I can speak, I reply, "I was doing okay with the stairs and even the sideline sprints, but the suicides were inhumane! Doesn't she realize this is our first day back?" I ask.

"We've been working out too," Christina laments, "But I guess that's what Coach means about being in good shape versus

176

basketball shape," she says, hanging her head and putting an icy towel on her neck.

"No shit," I reply.

"What do you have now?" Christina asks, her breathing finally returning to normal.

"I have Econ and Gender & Society and a study group for Philosophy; all are south campus. What about you?" I ask.

"Islam in History and then Catholic Social Ethics, but my first class isn't until eleven. I think I may go back to my dorm and try to take a nap after my shower," she says. Christina is a religious studies major. All of her classes sound more interesting than mine, but I have no idea what she is ever going to do with that major after graduation.

"I wish I could go take I nap," I complain, already dreading my day. "Although maybe I'll be so busy that I won't have time to worry about my mom," I sigh.

"What's going on with your mom?" she asks.

"She keeps calling, and I won't call her back. And now she's started calling Kerry!" I exclaim.

I can tell from the look on Christina's face that she's about to make a joke at Kerry's expense, but then decides against it; instead, she hesitates for a minute and then replies, "Sorry, that must suck. Can you just text her or something and tell her you'll call her when you're ready? That way she'll leave you alone?" she suggests.

"Maybe," I say, half-heartedly.

"How's everything going with Jen and Lynn?" Christina asks.

"It's really good," I reply. "I mean, totally surreal and weird a lot of the time, but good. There's definitely something going on between the two of them, but I'm not sure what it is. Neither one has said very much, but I can tell," I say, as I strip off my sweaty jersey, grab the minuscule towel provided by the athletic department and decide which part of my body I want to cover.

"But you get along with both of them, right?" Christina questions. She is already naked, and although she is taller and a little bigger than I am, she has somehow figured out how to strategically position two towels and looks perfectly natural.

"I do. They're really different, but I like them both a lot. Lynn seems like a lot more fun, but Jen feels gentler; I don't know if that makes sense," I try to explain.

"Sure," Christina says, but she sounds a little distracted.

"I'd love for the three of us to get together. Kerry always talks about what it's like when she's home with her sister and her two brothers, and you have your sisters. I always wanted a big family. I hated being an only child, and now I want to know what it's like to have siblings," I say, picturing again a fantasy of all of us around the dining room table at Thanksgiving or opening Christmas presents under the tree or some other vision from a movie.

"Let me tell you; it's not always as great as you think it is. My sisters and I fought all the time growing up," Christina says, shaking her head as if remembering some fight from her youth.

"I know," I reply, but I don't believe her.

***

I put my AirPods in and select a "Top Hits" playlist from Spotify for the walk to south campus because I can't decide what I want to listen to, even though I know I'll hate half the songs and need to skip most of them. I smile and wave at some familiar faces of other students walking to their nine o'clock classes, but most people have their heads down and aren't interested in much more than a head nod at this early hour. I notice The Rock is painted with bright colors and musical notes, and I assume it was painted last night by one of the acapella groups. The Rock is a Northwestern landmark that student groups paint over every night with crazy themes and colors representing their individual groups – it's a sanctioned and encouraged form of vandalism.

As I get closer, I see Preston talking to another guy from the football team. I give him a casual wave and walk toward my building, but seconds later, I feel a tap on my shoulder, and I know that it's him. I pull the AirPod out of my ear and say, "Hi."

"Were you just going to walk by and not say anything?" Preston accuses.

"You were talking to Zeke; I didn't want to interrupt," I say defensively.

Preston is close enough that I can smell the Arctic Ice scent of the deodorant I bought with him a few weeks ago, mixed with his shaving cream and natural Preston-smell and I make myself take a step back because it makes me want to press my face into his neck and inhale and that's not something I should want to do.

"Since when do you worry about interrupting?" Preston challenges. "You've been avoiding me all week," he accuses, pouting his full lips and making a show of batting his long eyelashes over his hazel eyes.

"I have not," I claim, but I'm not a very good liar. "It's just all this stuff going on with my mom and my sisters," I tell him. I feel bad using that as an excuse, but there is some truth in it.

"Oh shit, what's going on?" Preston asks, his tone shifting to concern, and I feel even guiltier.

"It's not a big deal. I'm not ready to deal with my mom, and she doesn't understand that," I tell him. It feels good to talk to him after pushing him away this week, and I take a tiny step closer to increase my chances of getting another whiff of deodorant or an accidental brush against his sweatshirt.

She comes out of nowhere, but suddenly the petite freshman girl with the shiny black hair and the affinity for tequila shots appears behind Preston and wraps her arms around him from behind with a lame attempt to cover his eyes since she could barely reach his shoulders on her tiptoes. "Guess who?" she squeals.

"Hey Marie," Preston chuckles, removing her hands from his face.

"I gotta go," I tell him, turning abruptly to walk up the stairs to Swift Hall.

"Wait, Courtney," Preston calls after me.

"I've got class," I call back, without turning around.

"Want to meet up by The Rock after your class?" he calls back, but I can hear Marie's giggles and see her hand on his sleeve out of the corner of my eye.

"I can't," I reply as I march inside. I know I shouldn't care. We're just friends. He can date whomever he wants, and it's not like he'd ever be interested in me, but it's started to bother me more recently. It's probably just a protective friend instinct,

180

but it's starting to feel like something else, and I don't know how I'm going to handle it if I feel one way, and I know Preston doesn't feel the same.

***

"That smells great," I call to Jen, as the smell of grilled meat wafts into the playroom adjoining the kitchen.

"Thanks!" she calls back, "Dinner should be ready in about fifteen minutes."

"It smells gross," Harper says and puts her tiny fingers over her nose.

"Shhh, don't say that," I tell her, but it's hard to keep from smiling. Jen called this morning and asked if I'd like to come over a little earlier so I could have some time with the kids before dinner. The last two times I've been here, the kids had already eaten and went to bed shortly after I arrived. I was unsure at first, but it felt rude to decline her offer, so I said I would be here by five. After an hour of play-doh with Harper and some Lego consultation with Ryan, I can't believe I ever questioned it. They are both so sweet and innocent and full of wonder, and they say the funniest things. It also doesn't hurt that they fight over who gets to sit in my lap, although Ryan gives up pretty easily. My relationships with Jen and Lynn are coming along, but they are complicated and still a little bit weird, but these two tiny instant relatives carry no baggage and don't seem to desire more than hugs and silly banter.

"Mommy made us mac and cheese; we don't have to eat the yucky grown-up food," Ryan tells his sister, seeming happy to be able to provide this top-secret information.

"Yay!" Harper says, clapping her little hands together and returning to massage her multi-colored play-doh cupcake, relieved that her dinner fears have been assuaged so easily.

181

"Let me go see if your mom needs any help," I say to Harper, unfolding my legs and using the small but sturdy (and probably very expensive) play table to pull myself up.

"No! Don't go, Aunt Courtney!" Harper whines. This is the first time that either child has referred to me as "Aunt," and I swear I can feel my heart start to melt, whatever that means. I lean down and kiss her lightly on the top of her head, also my first kiss to any of my new family members. "I'll be right back," I promise her.

***

Dinner with the five of us is mass chaos but in a good way. Every time Mark or Jen tries to ask me a question, Ryan interrupts with his own observation, or Harper needs help with her fork or something drops on the floor. We finally give up and let the kids take over, which I imagine is what happens on every occasion that they eat dinner as a family. As an only child, I have no memories of chaotic dinners or interruptions by siblings. Thinking about it now, dinners always centered on me; my mom and Brian always focused the "conversation" around things I wanted to talk about, whether I was three or thirteen. I have a pang of sadness as I think about Brian and my mom sitting together at their table right now; my mom worried about me, but then I remind myself that she lied to me for twenty years, and the guilt vanishes.

After dinner, Mark takes the kids upstairs to get ready for bed because Jen says she has something she wants to talk to me about. I have an uneasy feeling in the pit of my stomach as I follow her into the immaculate dining room, decorated in shades of gray and burgundy, looking like it's been staged to sell the house rather than for someone to actually eat in. I take a seat on the surprisingly comfortable upholstered chair, and Jen takes the chair next to me and produces a manila folder that I didn't even realize she was carrying.

"Has your mom talked to you about any of the financial arrangements?" Jen asks.

I'm not sure where this is going, but suddenly I feel much younger than my twenty years and very much in over my head. "I actually haven't talked to my mom in a while," I admit.

"Oh," Jen says, tapping her slender, manicured fingers lightly on the table.

"It's not a big deal. I just haven't been in the mood to talk to her. You know, since I found out about all of this," I say, gesturing to the two of us as if our situation needs further explanation.

"I get it," Jen says. "This must be really hard," she empathizes.

"Yeah," I acknowledge.

"We don't have to do this now, but I did want to share with you some of the information from the will since you are receiving a third of it, and we do have to move ahead with finalizing a lot of this for tax purposes, financial statements, etc.," she says, waving her hand as if this is all run-of-the-mill stuff.

"So, what do I need to do?" I ask.

"Take a look at this," she says, opening her folder and placing it in front of me. "This is a summary, but it gives you an idea of what your share will look like. The money will go into a trust until you graduate from college, or turn twenty-five if you don't graduate from college, but that doesn't seem to be an issue," Jen says and laughs.

I stare at the charts, and although I'm quite comfortable with numbers, I'm not sure I understand what it all means. I'm embarrassed to ask, but it seems better than pretending, especially with something so important. "Can you walk me through it?" I ask, using a phrase I've heard adults use before.

"Sure," Jen says. "Basically, this is what your share is," she tells me, pointing to a number that seems absurd. "It will grow, depending on how you choose to invest it for the next few years, but you should really talk to your mom or get a financial advisor to discuss that."

"Wow," I exclaim, trying to process the seven-digit figure.

"There is a decision you do need to make," she says, and I realize that this is probably the catch I was worried about all along – I mean, this type of thing only happens in movies. "The company was left to all three of us, but Mark and I aren't sure that makes sense. Mark has been running the business for years, and I can't imagine you would want any part of it – also, owning a business comes with ups and downs. We went through a few scenarios, but the number I just showed you would assume that we bought you out of your share of the business, and you just got cash now," she pauses and then flips the page. "If you want a share of the company, the amount of money you got would be this," she says, pointing to an amount that is a lot more money than I could ever imagine having but significantly smaller than the number I had just seen on the first page. "It's up to you, but if I were twenty and had my whole life ahead of me, I would take all of that money and do whatever I wanted with it! You can use it for graduate school, and a house, and whatever else you want. With smart investments, you'll be set for a long time," she says enthusiastically.

"Gosh, this is so much to take in," I say, sinking back in my chair.

"I know, it's a lot," she confirms. "Take some time and think about it and let me know," she says.

"Is Jen boring you with all that paperwork?" Mark asks, appearing in the grand archway.

"No," Jen says defensively, but she's smiling.

"Let's talk about something interesting, like the comments on ESPN after your friend Preston's game last weekend," Mark offers.

Hearing Preston's name gives me butterflies, and then I think about him with that tiny girl's arms wrapped around him, and the butterflies are replaced with knots. I haven't talked to Preston since the story came out on Sunday, so I don't have his exact opinion on it, but it's hard to imagine he's not pumped about the attention. "Yeah, it was pretty cool," I offer.

"I know he still has two seasons after this, but it will go by quickly. I'd love to help out if there's anything he wants to know about the NFL, although he's got Charlie, so I'm sure he's all set," Mark concludes.

"I'm sure he'd love to talk to you," I say, and I know this is true because Preston mentioned it about five times after the game when I introduced them.

"Why don't you invite him to dinner next week?" Jen offers as if this is the most natural thing in the world.

"That would be great!" Mark says.

"Um, okay, let me check with him," I reply, feeling like I've dug a hole I can't get out of.

"And no pressure, but maybe next week when you're here, we can finish up the paperwork," Jen suggests.

"Sure, sounds great," I reply and try to offer a smile to cover the fear of suddenly facing these major life-altering decisions all by myself.

Chapter Twenty-Three
Mark

As I'm pulling out of the Starbucks drive-thru with a Grande Flat White in the cup holder, I get a call from an unknown local number on my cell phone, ringing through to the Tesla's speakers. I rarely pick up calls from unknown numbers, but with all the weird family stuff going on right now, it feels like a bad idea to ignore it. "Hello?" I say, with great trepidation.

"Mark, it's Charlie Hill; how're you doing?" he asks. It takes me a millisecond to remember that Charlie's last name is Hill and to connect the dots that it's my former teammate and now the Northwestern coach I ran into last week. My first thought is wondering how he got my cell number, but that doesn't seem like the appropriate response.

"I'm good. Good to run into you last week. Small world, right? What can I do for you?" I ask.

"I was hoping you might be free to meet for a drink one night this week," Charlie suggests. "Bat 17 on Thursday night to catch the game?" he offers, naming the popular sports bar in downtown Evanston.

I'm about to accept when I have a vague recollection of Jen telling me that we had something one night this week, and I can't remember what it was or when it's happening. I'm sure Charlie wants to see if I can get him a deal on a policy, and although I would much rather go over coverage terms in a bar watching football, it's probably more practical to do it in the conference room during office hours. "I can't do Thursday, but I'm sure I can make time any day this week if you want to swing by the office," I suggest.

"I don't think you're going to want to talk about this at the office," Charlie says.

I don't even stop to consider what else he could want to discuss before my curiosity takes over. "Why not?" I blurt out.

"This has to stay between us," Charlie begins.

I nod my head but then realize that he can't see me, so I say, "Of course."

"Darrel's been having some health problems, and unfortunately, he just received more bad news about his condition," Charlie says. I can only assume he is referring to Darrel Jones, the offensive coordinator, who has held the job at Northwestern for the past eighteen years.

"I'm so sorry to hear that," I say, trying to figure out why he called me to share this information.

"Yeah, it was tough news. He's going to finish out the season, but he won't be able to coach after this year," he says.

"Such a loss for the team," I add.

"It really is," Charlie says, and then pauses as if he's reflecting further on the loss and only wanted to call and inform me to share in his sadness.

I'm only a couple of minutes from the office, and although I'm still curious why Charlie called and wanted to meet, I'm starting to sense that this conversation isn't really going anywhere.

"So, I wanted to talk to you about taking his position," Charlie says casually.

Thankfully I'm already stopped at a light because I might have had an accident if my foot had been on the gas. I must not have heard him correctly, but it sounded like he wanted to talk to me about a Division one coaching position at a Big Ten school, located twenty minutes from where I live – there's no way this is actually happening. When the light turns green, I pull over and park in the gas station because there's no way I can process this safely while driving. "Are you suggesting that I would take Darrel's spot as the offensive coordinator?" I ask cautiously.

"That's what I wanted to talk to you about," Charlie laughs, "I told you that wasn't something you wanted to discuss at the office, man," he says, and I can see the grin on his generous lips.

"Wow." I say, and then because I can't help it, I say it again, "Wow!" I know I should give it some more time before I say anything, but that's always been a weakness. "Why me? I've been out of the game for so long. Why wouldn't you promote one of your other offensive coaches? I don't have the experience for this. I'm an insurance salesman for Christ's Sake," I say, the words tumbling out of my mouth before I realize what I'm saying.

"You're not doing such a great sales pitch right now," Charlie jokes. "First, let's not get ahead of ourselves. We *are* promoting our Receiver Coach, Johnny Foster, to Darrel's position, and I would be recommending *you* as the new Receiver Coach. You may not be the obvious choice, and

189

maybe not even the best choice," Charlie adds. "But I know you're great with college players. You get them, and they look up to you, and you love the game," he adds.

It shouldn't, but it takes me a second for my ego to recover from thinking I was being considered for the bigger job, which would be ridiculous, to the slightly smaller job, which is still pretty absurd. I know that I should tell Charlie that I can't do it. I'm the CEO of an insurance company, and I can't take a massive pay cut to go run around with a college football team, especially when things are so up in the air at Summer Risk Management. But it also seems too good to be true that Tom Turner called a couple of weeks ago with a potential offer at the Bears, which was filled instantly after I declined a meeting, and now I'm getting a second chance?

"What does the timing look like?" I ask.

"Coach is going to want to move on this pretty quickly," Charlie says. "I'd like to bring you in as the top recommendation in the next couple of weeks," he adds.

"Let me give it a little more thought, and let's meet next week for that drink. Does that work?" I ask, hoping to have bought myself some time.

"I'll talk to you soon. Don't think about it too long," Charlie advises before he hangs up.

Chapter Twenty-Four
Jennifer

It's entirely preposterous that I am sitting in a parked car, on this quiet street in Evanston, across from Nick's empty house waiting for him to arrive home from work. It was far easier than I thought to find his home address, only requiring a couple of phone calls to former New Trier classmates who have the unfortunate task of maintaining the alumni directory. However, I still feel like a spy, or maybe even a stalker, sitting across from his beautiful early twentieth century Tudor, waiting to pounce when he pulls into the driveway. It's even more absurd because I had to get a sitter for Ryan and Harper because Mark wasn't going to be home in time. I have no idea what time Nick gets back from work, so I showed up just after five, and I've been sitting here for over ninety minutes. There's no guarantee that he's even coming straight here after work, but it's a Tuesday night, and that feels like decent odds of a stay-at-home night.

I'm about to turn on the engine and give up this foolish charade at seven-thirty when a silver Audi pulls into the driveway, and a man who looks like an attractive version of the Nick I knew in High School gets out of the driver's side of the fancy sedan. Not wasting any time to lose my nerve, I scamper

191

out of my car and across the street to catch him before he goes inside the house. As I approach him on the blue slate walkway, it occurs to me that I haven't fully thought through my opening line. I've been in the car for two and a half hours, and I've been planning this for days, yet I haven't actually determined what I'm going to say.

"Jen Summer? Is that really you?" Nick says with pure disbelief before I can open my mouth. I like to think that I look a hell of a lot better than I did in high school, but I actually don't look that much different, and Nick's instant recognition is continued proof of this fact.

"It's me," I reply, forcing a smile, trying to pretend that this is a social call or perhaps a happy coincidence.

"What are you doing here?" Nick asks, not sounding particularly pleased to see me.

"I know this is going to sound crazy, but I thought there was something you should know," I tell him.

"Does it have something to do with Lynn?" Nick asks, crossing his muscled arms protectively across his chest as he turns to face me.

"Look, I know it's been a really long time since we've seen each other, but we used to be friends, and I thought you deserved to know this," I tell him, soldiering on with the task at hand.

It's obvious from the skeptical look on Nick's face that Lynn has told him something about me that is less than flattering. "I know you and Lynn have some issues to work out, but I really don't want to get in the middle of it," Nick says.

"I don't want that either," I say, but even *I* know it sounds like bullshit. "I thought you should know that Lynn is married and

192

has a son. She lives in California, and she's only here until we settle things with our dad's will, and then she's heading back to them in California. I don't want to see you get hurt," I say lamely, thankful to have everything off my chest.

Although there was a chance Lynn had been honest with him from the beginning, the stunned look on Nick's face tells me that this is the first he's heard about Trevor *or* Declan, and although I feel bad for causing him pain; I know that Lynn is really the one at fault for deceiving him.

"Thanks for coming by, but I think you should go now," Nick says as he turns his back on me and walks toward the front door, not even stopping to pick up the briefcase he left lying on the ground.

***

Guilt gnaws at me as I drive home, but I try to remind myself that I'm only the messenger; Nick would have found out eventually when they were further along, and then it would have been even worse. The ache in my stomach doesn't seem to agree with my logic, but I ignore it as I drive home toward Winnetka, hoping the kids are still awake so I can tuck them in.

The drive home is just long enough that I can quickly call Lynn and deliver the basic information for the will and then politely excuse myself when I get home to rush inside for bedtime. I despise my own cowardice as I direct my phone to, "Call Lynn's Mobile," and hold my breath until she answers.

"Hey," Lynn says, with zero enthusiasm in her voice as she picks up the phone.

"Do you have a minute?" I ask.

"Sure," she says, and I swear I can hear her roll her eyes as she answers. "Where are you?" she asks.

"I'm in the car; I'm driving home," I tell her, attempting to sound breezy.

"Woah, late night," she jokes, but I don't find it particularly funny. The dashboard clock reads seven forty-five. I'm already trying to figure out the best response if she asks where I've been, but all she says is, "What do you want to talk about?"

"I just wanted to run something by you about Dad's will, it shouldn't take long, but there is a decision you need to make," I say, doing my best to sound casual, even as a trickle of sweat drips down my back.

"Okay, what is it?" Lynn asks, but her voice is different now, and I can tell I have her full attention, just as I had hoped.

"You'll be getting a third of the estate, as you remember from the meeting, I'm sure. I'll send you an email with all of the numbers when I get home," I promise."

"And?" Lynn prods.

"Well, the company was left to all three of us, but Mark and I aren't sure that makes sense. Mark has been running the business for years, and I can't imagine you would want any part of it – also that comes with a lot of financial ups and downs," I say, repeating exactly what I said to Courtney. "If you take partial ownership of the business, then you will get *a lot* less cash," I say, emphasizing my words carefully. "I'll send it all over, but you'll see the different scenarios. I assume you just want the cash and don't want to be bothered with a family-run business in Illinois when you're all the way out in California," I say, laughing and hoping she'll laugh with me at the absurdity of the idea.

"Let me think about it," Lynn responds, but it's difficult to read her reaction.

194

"Oh shoot, I just pulled into the driveway, and if I don't hurry inside, I won't be able to say goodnight to the kids. I'll talk to you later," I say cheerily as if we speak on a regular basis.

"Sure," Lynn says, sounding doubtful. "I'll let you know if I have any questions about the will," she adds.

"Right! I'll send that over as soon as the kids are asleep," I tell her and hang up the call, exhaling loudly the moment the phone disconnects.

Mark is sitting on the navy Belgian linen sectional in the living room, with a copy of Golf Digest open on his lap. The house is strangely quiet, so I know I've missed seeing the children.

"So?" he says, looking at me expectantly. Although he thought my stake-out plan was ridiculous, it doesn't seem to stop him from wanting to know what happened.

"I saw Nick and told him. He definitely didn't know about Trevor or Declan," I share, feeling a new wave of shame wash over me as I picture the look on Nick's face. "And then I called Lynn and told her about the will," I say.

"How did she take it?" he asks.

"She said she would have to think about it. We'll see what happens with Nick, but my guess is that it doesn't go well, and then she'll probably just want to take her cash and head home," I tell him. Although this scenario is exactly what I was angling for, I don't feel excited by the prospect of it; I only feel miserable and guilty.

"I guess that's good," Mark says, but oddly he doesn't sound as enthusiastic as I might have imagined.

"Yup. It will be more important than ever now to concentrate on the company," I say. "With the inheritance, plus savings, we have the cash to buy both of them out, but it does mean we are putting all our money into Summer Risk Management. I wonder if this is how Dad thought it would play out?" I wonder aloud.

Mark looks up at me and purses his thin lips as if he's going to say something meaningful, but then thinks twice and slumps back against the nubby fabric and sighs instead.

"What is it?" I ask him.

"Nothing," he replies, picking up his magazine.

"I'm going to go upstairs and take a shower and go to bed," I tell him.

"It's barely eight o'clock," Mark admonishes.

"I know, but it's been a long day," I say.

"Tell me about it," he replies.

I know I should ask what he means by that, but I just don't have the energy. I want to crawl into bed and go to sleep, so I don't have to spend any more time with myself today; maybe I'll wake up a better person tomorrow?

Chapter Twenty-Five
Lynn

An older man stops in the aisle right next to me and gives the customary head nod to indicate that his seat is located in my row. I squeeze past him into the aisle, narrowly avoiding a teenage boy trying to shove his gigantic backpack into the overhead compartment in the row behind me. Thankfully, the gentleman moves all the way to the window, leaving the middle seat empty. A glance up the plane's vacant aisle gives me hope that everyone is already on board, and the seat will remain empty for the four-and-a-half-hour flight from O'Hare to LAX.

I must have dozed off because the next thing I know, we are in the air, and the perky brunette flight attendant is asking for my beverage selection. "I'd love a Bloody Mary," I say, handing over my credit card and trying to forget that when I used to fly with Trevor, it was always in First Class, and he would laugh at the commoners in the back of the plane who had to pay for their drinks.

"Would you like a snack?" she asks kindly.

I contemplate the selection of unappetizing boxed meals and minuscule bags of free pretzels, but none of it sounds appealing. "No, thanks," I reply, and she smiles and moves her cart to the family in the row behind me. Out of habit, I grab my phone from my bag to see if I've gotten any texts before I remember it's on airplane mode. It's just as well since I know Nick won't ever be texting me again. It's hard to believe that a few days ago, I was naïve enough to think we might have a real future together; to think that I finally had a chance at my own happy ending. But that was before he called and accused me of lying to him. It doesn't matter that he got his facts screwed up – whoever gave him his information was quite out of date, but the accusations and lack of trust are too much. I know that I should have told him about Declan, but I was working my way toward telling him the whole story; in fact, I was planning on telling him on our next date. And then he calls and accuses me of adultery and infidelity, and I was so hurt and angry that it wasn't even worth it to refute his crazy claims. I scroll through the selection of in-flight movies for distraction, but I can't get Nick out of my head for the rest of the flight, no matter how hard I try.

***

Ali is waiting for me at our favorite bar in Malibu that night, and I feel tears spring to my eyes as I see her waving at me. "I've missed you so much!" I exclaim as I wrap my arms around her narrow shoulders.

"You too!" Ali squeals, returning the hug, and I feel a bit of tension release as I'm next to my best friend for the first time in almost a month.

"So, what happened?" Ali asks after our margaritas are delivered to the table, and we each take a generous sip.

"It just fell apart. Nick didn't turn out to be prince charming after all," I tell her, staring into my icy goblet.

"What did he do?" she questions.

"He found out about Trevor and Declan; although he thought we were married and still living as some sort of happy family. He said I cheated on him and was playing some sort of sick game when he was actually falling for me," I say sadly.

"Why didn't you explain it to him? Tell him that you've been divorced for almost two years?" Ali asks, incredulous.

"You should have heard him," I reply. "He was so hurt. And so mad at me," I explain.

"Okay, but still..." Ali says, looking confused.

"I know I should have told him about Declan, but it's so complicated, and it certainly doesn't paint me in a very good light – what kind of mother doesn't have any custody of her child?" I ask, gulping down my drink.

"Exactly. But now that he found out about it, why didn't you just explain that part? Tell him that Trevor is a massive asshole, and you're divorced, and tell him about Declan," Ali tries to reason.

"I don't need someone else that doesn't trust me," I say simply.

Ali is quiet for a minute, as if thoroughly contemplating her reply. "How do you think he found out?" she asks.

"I don't know," I say, "Does it really matter?"

"Do you think it was Jen?" Ali asks, tentatively.

"I don't know," I say quietly, although the same thought has been going through my head nonstop for the past forty-eight hours.

"Why would she care? How would she even know about Nick?" Ali asks.

"Again, I have no idea," I reply. "I'm pretty sure she wanted me out of town," I tell her. "I don't know how she knew about Nick or how she could have told him; when I met Nick, he said he hadn't seen her since High School," I tell her. "But I have no clue who else could have told him."

"Does Jen still not know the truth about Trevor and Declan?" Ali asks, looking at me intently over her frosty glass.

"No," I say sadly. "I was going to finally tell her on this trip, but that never happened."

"Oh, Lynn," Ali says. "I know she's a bitch, but if she doesn't know things are bad, she can't help," Ali reasons.

"I don't think she'd care even if she did," I say.

"Really?" Ali questions.

"I don't know," I shrug, seemingly my mantra for the night. "But I know she thinks she screwed me over by trying to buy me out of the family business and giving me more cash, but it's exactly what I want," I say with a grin.

"You don't want any part of the company?" Ali questions.

"I want the cash. If I have money, I don't need to depend on Trevor. He still has control, and I hate that! I think I could even go back to a judge again for joint custody if I could prove that I'm self-sufficient," I say.

Ali raises her eyebrows, and I know she's skeptical of that possibility since Trevor seems to have every family court judge in his pocket, but this impending influx of money is giving me the first glimpse of optimism I've had in years.

"As long as you know what you're doing," Ali warns. "From what you told me about your dad, his company was worth a fortune, and you have just as much of a right to it as Jen does," she says. I don't remember telling her that, but I guess I must have mentioned it at some point.

I laugh at the idea that Jen and I share something equally, as that has never really been the case. I came out to California as soon as I could get away to get out of the shadow of her brilliance and flawlessness, especially where Dad was concerned. "I promise, this is better," I tell her. "I signed the paperwork and sent it to Jen yesterday. Good riddance," I say.

"What about Courtney?" Ali asks.

My shoulders slump as I think about Courtney and the two un-returned texts sitting on my phone. "That's the only part I feel bad about," I confess. "But there isn't much I can do about it. Honestly, I don't know why I thought it would be different this time around; I just don't belong there," I say sadly.

***

The next morning, I get up earlier than normal and go for a long run on the beach. Until a few days ago, I started to think about what it might be like to spend the winter in the Chicago suburbs, something I haven't done since my senior year in high school. Although I was dreading the prospect of snow and relentless wind, of hats and gloves and giant coats, it felt like it would be worth it if I could be cuddling with Nick. But the smell of the ocean air and glorious sun with a temperature of seventy-two degrees in late October reminds me that the Midwest sucks, and this is where I belong, or at least that's what I tell myself.

My thoughts drift to the call with Nick as my feet pound the packed sand over and over again. What would have happened if I told him that he was wrong? Obviously, he wasn't entirely

201

wrong. I did lie by omission by not telling him about Declan. But would that have made a difference? What would he think of me if he knew I had a teenage son who barely spoke to me and whom I hadn't been allowed to see in months? I told myself, and Ali, that it was because Nick accused me of cheating and assumed the worst about me; but I know that isn't the reason. There's no way he would look at me the same or want to be with me if he knew *everything*.

Unable to stop the series of "what ifs?" running through my mind, I settle on Justin for a minute and replay our high school relationship like a John Hughes Chicagoland romance. In one version, I never break up with Justin, and I never go to California or meet Trevor. Another scenario I like to envision is one where Justin follows me to California, and I'm already dating Trevor, but Justin comes to fight for me, and he kicks Trevor's ass, and then I become a famous movie star with him by my side. But the story that keeps playing in my head is the one where I was a foolish teenager who didn't realize how perfect he was, so I went out to California on my own. I made a series of terrible mistakes and married an awful man (although I will never regret having Declan, no matter how much pain it brings); and then years later, we both end up in the same bar in our hometown, and we realize we're still in love and we have our happily ever after. Only the movie isn't going to end that way because Justin is engaged to someone else, and he doesn't love me anymore. I realize I don't love him either, but the idea of him is hard to shake, especially when I have nothing else to hold on to.

My throat is burning, and my legs are on fire when I stop to catch my breath and realize that I've been running for over four miles, and I had no intention of an eight-mile run today, especially without any water. I obviously have my phone with me, and the twenty-dollar bill I always carry in my bra, so I could get something to drink, or even throw in the towel and call an Uber to take me home. But without any real plans for the rest of the day, other than figuring out how to get out of my short-term rental agreement on the apartment in Evanston, I decide to sit down on the sand and enjoy the relative peace and quiet of the beach on a weekday, and I'll make the return trip when my legs and lungs feel ready.

Because it's impossible for me to sit here and simply appreciate the beauty of the Pacific for more than five minutes, I slide my phone out from the sport case around my arm to scroll through my emails and texts. There is another new text from Courtney inviting me to a pre-season basketball game, and my heart aches as I read it. I vow to respond to her later because I certainly don't have the right words to do so now. I texted Trevor last night to let him know I was back in LA and asked if we could arrange a time for me to see Declan, but he hasn't replied. I'm sure I will regret it, like always, but I decide to call him, so it's harder for him to ignore me.

His assistant puts me straight through to him, and I wonder if that means I'm going to get his voicemail; that seems like something he would instruct his staff to do, but instead, I hear his smarmy voice on the first ring, "Go for Trevor."

"Hi, it's Lynn," I say, aiming for a neutral tone.

"Oh," Trevor mutters, clearly surprised to hear my voice; I'm guessing the assistant who put my call directly through won't have a job by this afternoon.

"I'm back in town. And I want to see Declan," I say firmly.

"Welcome back," he sneers, "I hope you had a good time on your vacation."

"My father died!" I yell, losing my cool far earlier than I hoped, but Trevor knows how to push all my buttons.

"We'll have to see. You left the state without telling anyone, and you were gone for over a month. That hardly makes you a model guardian, although you weren't one before, were you?" he mocks.

I close my eyes and breathe deeply before speaking, hoping the ocean air will have a calming influence over my emotions. Trevor deserves every bit of my anger, but as always, he holds all the cards. "What's it going to take?" I ask.

"That's the spirit," Trevor chides playfully. "Technically, I could require that you have supervised visits, but I'm feeling generous today."

I want to scream, but instead, I ball my free hand into a tight fist, so my nails dig into my palm, and this gives me the ability to reply, "I appreciate that," through tight lips.

"Does Saturday work for you?" he asks.

Saturday feels like it is way too far away, and it will give him too much time to change his mind, but it's not like I have options. "Saturday is perfect," I reply.

"Come to the house around one to pick him up, and you can take him for the whole afternoon," Trevor instructs.

It seems too easy, but maybe one area of my life is finally going to work out. "I'll see you then," I say, cautious but optimistic at the chance to finally see my son.

Chapter Twenty-Six
Courtney

"I think I've finally stopped sweating," Christina says as she pushes open the sports center's doors and a chilly breeze hits us in the face.

"Didn't you shower?" I ask her, glancing at her over my shoulder.

"I sweat *during* my shower," she laughs. "Practice today was ridiculous!"

"I know," I agree. "Maybe once we have our pre-season opener next week, she'll let up a little bit," I suggest.

"Not a chance," she says. "Don't you remember how it was last year?" Christina asks.

"I think I've repressed it," I joke. "I heard some of the girls planning a little something at Lisa's apartment next week after the game," I tell her, unsure why I'm mentioning it since Christina was with me in the locker room when the seniors were talking about it.

"My mom and dad are coming up next week for the game, so I don't think I can go," Christina says, but she doesn't seem upset. "There will be other parties,' she adds.

"I asked Jen and Lynn if they could come to the game," I say.

"No way! I'll finally get to meet them!" Christina exclaims. The enthusiasm in her voice is over the top, and I can tell she feels bad that her parents are coming up from St. Louis when I don't even want mine driving half an hour from Lake Forest.

"Actually, Jen said there is some teacher thing at school that night, so she can't come, but she said she would come to the next home game," I say, readjusting my backpack and zipping up my sweatshirt as we pass through Shakespeare Garden.

"What about Lynn?" Christina asks, pausing momentarily to zip up her own sweatshirt, our body temperatures have finally cooled down, and the wind has picked up.

Lynn's text was waiting on my phone when I got up this morning. I read it three times because I was sure I was missing something, but it was succinct and quite clear.

"She moved back to California," I say quietly.

"What? When did that happen?" Christina asks, pivoting on her pink Nikes to face me.

"A few days ago. She didn't even say goodbye," I say sadly, hating how pathetic I sound.

"Oh my God! I'm so sorry," Christina gushes.

"Whatever," I say, wiping away a stubborn tear from the corner of my eye. "I barely know her; it's stupid to even be upset about," I say, trying to sound convincing.

"Why did she leave?" Christina asks.

"I don't really know. I haven't heard back from her for a few days, and then I got this," I say, pulling my phone out of my back pocket to show her the text.

Lynn: I would love to come see your game, but I had to go back to LA. I wish I could explain it better, but I can't be in Winnetka or anywhere near there – it just doesn't work. I hope you can forgive me. Jen will be there for you in ways that I can't, but I hope we can still stay in touch. xoxo

"Wow, that's rough," Christina exclaims, handing me back my phone.

"Whatever," I say again, no longer in the mood to talk about it. "Maybe I'm better off with Jen, like Lynn says," I say, trying to sound indifferent. As soon as I say her name, a text from Jen pops up on my screen, and I actually turn to look over my shoulder, like she might be behind me and heard us talking about her.

Jen: Hi! Confirming for dinner on Sat night. Can Preston still make it? Mark says no game this weekend, so he should be good. Lmk

"Oh shit," I sigh as I read Jen's text and shove my phone back in my pocket.

"What is it?" Christina asks.

"Nothing. I forgot I told Jen I would go over there for dinner this weekend, and I have a paper to write," I fib. I feel bad about lying, but I know Christina will give me crap about Preston, and I'm just not in the mood.

"It's just dinner; it won't take that long," Christina says. "And you got to eat," she reasons.

"You're right," I agree because that's easiest.

"I've gotta get to my study group," Christina says as we approach the turn off for the library, "I'll talk to you later," she adds and then disappears down the curvy tree-lined path.

I don't have class again for another four hours, and although I should go to the library and lock myself in a pod or go back to the house and buckle down in the study room, neither option is remotely appealing. Without officially making the decision, I veer toward Norris student center and decide that I'll find an empty table and work on my econ homework with my headphones on to drown out the noise.

There are plenty of available tables when I arrive, but as I scan the sea of students, I'm disappointed not to see a familiar shaved head. I knew it wasn't a guarantee, but Preston eats lunch here several days a week and then stays to study or hang out, so it wasn't impossible that he would be here. Even though I pretended he wasn't the reason for my venue selection; it's particularly pathetic when I have to lie to myself.

I settle myself at the plastic table and arrange my notebook, textbook, calculator, and pencil at right angles (a habit that goes back to elementary school) and select a playlist that Spotify has kindly created of my recently listened-to songs. But moments into the first problem, my thoughts keep wandering to dinner on Saturday. I wonder if it's better to show up without Preston and leave Mark and Jen speculating and deprive Preston of the opportunity, or if I should suck it up and ask Preston to go and let everyone think that everything's fine – including Preston.

I dial Preston's number before I can reconsider. After three rings, I'm about to hang up when I hear his voice, and just the way he says, "Hey darling," in his warm southern drawl, sounds like a hug.

"Hey," I reply dreamily, momentarily forgetting why I called.

208

"What's up?" he asks.

"I'm having dinner at my half-sister Jen's house this Saturday night," I explain.

"I know who Jen is," Preston admonishes me.

"Mark invited you to come along," I spit out. "If you're free, but it's not a big deal," I add while doodling concentric circles furiously on my notebook, something *I* rarely do and hate when I watch others deface their papers this way.

"I'd love to. What time should I pick you up?" Preston asks.

"Oh, um, she said dinner at seven, so maybe six forty-five?" I offer, surprised at how easy this is.

"Perfect. Can't wait," Preston says. I can see the corners of his mouth turning up as he speaks, and there is a flutter in my stomach that makes me want to stab my abdomen with my mechanical pencil. But then I hear something in the background of his apartment, and I swear it sounds like a girls' voice.

"Is someone there?" I blurt out.

"Hunter is in his room," Preston says, referring to his roommate and teammate.

I know I heard a girl's voice, but I'll sound crazy if I ask again, and it isn't like it's any of my business. I can picture that tiny brunette lying in tiny underwear and one of Preston's t-shirts on his couch, trying to suppress her laughter while Preston has to take my call so that he can hang-up and rip off her clothes and...

"Are you still there?" Preston asks, interrupting my masochistic thoughts.

"I'm here," I reply, although I'm closing my eyes to try to get the images of Preston and the naked freshman out of my head, and it still isn't working.

"I'll see you on Saturday night," he says enthusiastically. "Thanks for the invite," Preston inserts.

"You can thank Mark," I say snidely, and I hang up before I say anything worse.

***

Preston is right on time and texts me from the car where he is double-parked on Emerson. He even apologizes that he can't come to the Kappa door to get me, but there's nowhere to park. I'm not sure why this kindness annoys me further, but I try to let it go, or this night is going to be unbearable. On my way out, I glance in the oversize mirror that lines the entryway to the sorority house, and I'm not displeased with my reflection. Kerry convinced me to let her do my makeup; although it's more than I usually wear, I like that the smoky eye and mascara makes my eyes look bigger, the hint of bronzer brings out my cheekbones, and the tiniest bit of pink lip gloss makes my lips look shiny, but not wet. Kerry described them as "kissable," but I smacked her for it since I know my lips aren't the ones Preston wants to kiss. If I glance quickly, I look the tiniest bit like a less pretty brunette version of Lynn, but I put that out of my mind because thinking about Lynn just makes me angry.

Preston smiles at me from the open window of his canary yellow Jeep Wrangler, and I silently curse him, his perfect car, and my own body for betraying me as I smile right back, and my stomach does mini summersaults in anticipation of being inches away from him. The car smells like soap and men's deodorant – a mix of sandalwood and the ocean, with a tiny hint of lemon; I hate how much I love it. Preston is wearing freshly pressed khakis and a blue and white checked button-down shirt. I'm about to tease him that it looks like he's dressed for church, but it's nice that he made the effort, even if I am upset with him.

We pull into the circular driveway, and if Preston is impressed with Jen's enormous house, he doesn't show it. I've never visited his house in Houston or even seen a picture, and he doesn't talk much about money, but I get the sense that Preston's family is wealthy. He's mentioned that his mom is a lawyer and his Dad's job has something to do with oil, but I've never paid much attention. I think he's also self-conscious about his family because many of the guys on the football team would never be able to afford a school like this if it weren't for their scholarships (just like there is no way I would be able to afford to go to school here if it weren't for charity from my guilt-ridden birth father). But Preston's complete lack of reaction to Jen and Mark's multi-million-dollar lakefront home makes me think Preston is a lot more comfortable with money than I previously realized.

Ryan and Harper are already bathed, and in their pajamas when we arrive, but they are ecstatic to see us. I'm a little hurt that they seem equally, if not more, excited to meet Preston than they are to see me, but he is a captivating guy, and not surprisingly, even kids are drawn to him. Preston and I take turns reading bedtime stories while Jen and Mark finish getting dinner ready downstairs, and I wonder again if this is really what Preston wants to be doing on a Saturday night. After begging and pleading for us to stay longer, we finally make our escape and head downstairs to the dining room.

"Sorry about that," I whisper, hoping the kids can't hear me.

"Why are you sorry?" Preston asks.

"I'm sure this isn't how you pictured your Saturday night," I apologize, twisting and re-twisting my hair up into a bun, a nervous habit left over from middle school. "I'm sure dinner won't take too long, and then we can leave so you can go out or do *whatever* you have planned tonight," I say, pushing past him on the stairs.

"What is your problem?" Preston says, reaching for my shoulder, but I slip out of his grasp just as Jen appears at the bottom of the curved staircase.

"How did it go?" she asks hopefully.

"They were great," Preston responds before I have a chance to speak. "I learned all about the StoryBots," he laughs.

"That was so sweet of you," Jen gushes, and she raises her eyebrows when she looks at me, but I shake my head vigorously to ensure she knows the answer to whatever question she's asking is "no."

"What smells so good?" Preston asks as we enter the dining room with a beautifully set table.

"It's Jen's famous beef stew," Mark says, walking into the dining room carrying an enormous orange Dutch oven, that I recognize as Le Creuset and very expensive because my mom always ogled those pots and pans and insisted, we couldn't afford them.

"It's *Ina Garten's* Beef Bourguignon, not mine," Jen corrects. "I hope you're hungry," she says, as Mark returns with a matching, slightly smaller pot and opens it to reveal creamy yellow mashed potatoes.

We're too busy eating for a lot of conversation at the beginning of the meal, other than a few comments regarding the delicious food or the last time either of us ate this well (for me, it was the last time I was here, for Preston it was in September when he was home in Houston). We all agree to pause before having seconds, although I'm quite sure Mark and Preston are the only ones who will actually have additional helpings.

Mark and Preston are seated across from each other, and it doesn't take long for their conversation to turn to football. Mark is asking about their game plan for Indiana next week, and Preston says they need the most help with their offensive strategy. I could easily listen to them and make polite interjections, but instead, I choose to capitalize on this time with Jen and get far more than I bargained for.

"I'm going to miss Lynn," I say, watching Jen closely for her reaction. They've both made it clear that they have their differences, but I've only been in the picture for a month, so I'm sure Jen knows more about what's going on with Lynn than I do – they're *sisters*.

The color drains from Jen's face, and she leans her elbows on the table as if her body needs the support. "I know," she replies. "And I'm sorry about that, but it's not like she didn't know what she was doing," Jen says, sighing loudly and then exhaling upward to blow the loose hairs off of her forehead.

I'm unsure how to respond. It feels like Jen knows exactly why Lynn left, and she seems to think I do as well, so if I play my cards right, maybe I can get her to fill me in. "Hmmm," I murmur, hoping she reads that sound correctly.

"Nick was going to find out about Trevor and Declan eventually," Jen sighs. "I mean, what was she planning to do? Hide her husband and son forever?" she exclaims, looking to me for confirmation of this absurdity.

I'm dumbfounded, and I have no idea what to say or even how to shape my face, but fortunately, it seems that Jen is on a roll and not paying any attention to me. I let her continue to vent while I try to process the tidal wave of new information. "Maybe it wasn't my place to tell Nick," she muses, as if entertaining this thought for the first time, "But she was obviously going to have to go back to her real life in LA sooner or later, and I did know Nick from high school, so I kind of owed it to him..." she trails off.

"What the hell are you talking about?" I blurt out, my voice loud enough to grab Mark and Preston's attention.

Instantly Jen realizes her "mistake" but also realizes that it's too late to do anything about it. "I thought Lynn would have told you," she says quietly, wringing her periwinkle blue linen napkin with both hands.

"She told me she had to go back to California because it doesn't seem to work when she's here," I say through tight lips. "And she said you would be a better sister for me anyway, but I'm pretty sure that won't be the case," I sneer.

"You didn't know she was married or had a son?" Jen asks quietly.

"No," I reply, unsure what else to say.

"I'm sorry you had to find out this way," Jen says.

The dining room is quiet, and it seems that the entire house is holding its breath, except for a distant ticking sound coming from the kitchen, like an annoying clock that didn't get the memo. I'm staring into the remnants of my beef stew, trying to figure out my next move. I want to catch Preston's eye because I can feel him staring at me, but I'm pretty sure I will burst into tears if we make eye contact. Instead, I opt for anger as I try to put the pieces together.

"So, *you* were the one who ran her off to California? You told Nick about her husband, and then she had to leave? Is that right?" I ask furiously, although I'm sure I know the answer.

"I thought it was the right thing to do," Jen replies, but even I have to admit her face looks pained – not that it excuses anything she's done.

"I need to go," I say, standing up and throwing my napkin on the table. Thankfully Preston took my lead, and he is by my side in an instant, *and* he's even retrieved my purse from the chair in the corner.

"Please stay so we can talk about this," Jen pleads, rising from her chair and following us into the front hall with Mark following close behind.

"I don't think so," I retort, grabbing my denim jacket from the empty front hall closet where Jen put it away – who the hell has an entire closet that sits empty waiting for guests" coats?

"I'll call you tomorrow so we can talk about this when you've had some time, okay?" Jen asks.

"That won't be necessary," I say curtly. "Oh, this is yours," I spit, grabbing a handful of papers from my purse and shoving them in her direction.

"What's this?" Jen asks.

"It's the papers for your dumb company. Thank God I signed them; I don't want anything to do with this family," I say angrily and walk out the door that Preston has already opened for me, and then listen as he slams it shut behind us.

"Are you okay?" Preston asks as he pulls out of the driveway.

"I can't believe I ever wanted to be part of that family. They're all a bunch of liars," I say indignantly, trying to keep my voice from shaking.

"I'm so sorry," Preston says, glancing over quickly at me and then turning back to look at the road.

"Lynn doesn't even trust me enough to tell me she's married or that she has a son! And she's having an affair – I guess the apple doesn't fall far from the tree," I scoff. "And Jen is a total bitch! She betrayed her own sister and now thinks I'm going to be on her side!" I exclaim. "Why does everyone lie?!" I scream, a strangled sob escaping from my mouth. "My dad, my mom, my sisters – I hate my entire family!" I exclaim, collapsing into a fit of tears.

Preston pulls the car off to the side of the road and cuts the engine. "Hey, hey, come here," he says gently, unbuckling his seat belt and reaching across the front seat to wrap his arms around me. The seatbelt cuts uncomfortably across my neck as I try to respond to his hug but feeling the tight warmth of his chest under my cheek is a worthwhile trade-off. I can feel the salty tears making a damp spot on his oxford cloth shirt, but I don't make a move. Preston is making shushing noises as if I'm a cranky infant, and it's oddly soothing.

"Why did they all have to be so awful?" I ask when I finally stop crying.

"Nobody's perfect," Preston offers, still rubbing my back.

"Ha!" I laugh. "I think this is pretty far from perfect. Maybe this is why my mom kept me from that family all this time? Maybe she knew," I wonder aloud.

"Family is tough," Preston says.

"Your family is great," I mutter into his chest.

216

"Not all the time," he says.

I raise my head slightly to look at him like I can't really believe what he's saying, and he nods his head and continues. "I'm pretty lucky, but my family is far from perfect as well. And I can't say that I would have done what Jen did, but sibling relationships are hard too. You don't know their history," Preston says.

"That's not *my* fault," I cry, removing myself from his grasp.

"I know. Of course, it isn't. I shouldn't have said it like that. I just meant that there can be a lot of baggage with siblings," he offers, trying to make amends.

"I didn't think it would be like this," I sigh, leaning my head back against the rigid headrest, which is fitting for the rugged car, but right now, I could use something soft and padded. Preston reaches his left arm back over, and as annoyed as I've been with him, I'm happy to accept his hug and the comfort of his strong arms. Without warning, his mouth is on mine, and his soft lips, surrounded by tiny bits of stubble, are rubbing against the top of my lip. I've thought about this moment for so long that I can't help from parting my lips as he slips his tongue inside. Suddenly, I'm kissing him back with an urgency I didn't know I possessed. Not surprisingly, Preston knows exactly what he's doing. It's the perfect amount of pressure and moisture, and unlike the boys in high school, it doesn't feel like he's trying to count my teeth with his tongue. But then it hits me. Preston's kiss is so perfect because he has so much experience. In fact, he was probably just kissing that tiny freshman this morning – she likely even woke up in his bed! The thoughts swirl in my head, and I know that he doesn't want to kiss me; he just pities me after this disastrous dinner and all of the crying over my pathetic family.

I pull away, and Preston looks at me with a goofy smile, but it only lasts for a split second. "What's wrong?" he asks, after seeing the look on my face.

"Please take me home," I say impatiently, buckling my seatbelt and crossing my arms tightly across my chest.

"Are you okay?" he asks. The look on his beautiful face displays total confusion, most likely because he's never kissed a girl who wasn't thrilled to receive his affections.

"I just want to go home," I say, staring straight ahead out the Wrangler's windshield.

"Okay," Preston says warily, starting the engine with a loud roar and pulling out into the street.

We drive in silence, and when we reach north campus, about a block from Preston's apartment, he says hopefully, "It's still early. Do you want to come over for a little bit?"

I don't know if he wants to pretend like the pity kiss never happened, or if he really can't read signals and he thinks he's got a chance at an actual pity fuck while my spirits are so low, but either way, there's no chance. "No. I'm tired. The whole night has been a disaster; I just want to go home," I tell him, turning my head even further to stare out the passenger side window.

Preston doesn't answer; he simply makes the appropriate turns and stops the car in front of the arch to the sorority quad, exactly where he picked me up three hours ago; before I realized my entire family was a pack of liars and that my best guy friend didn't view me any differently from the rest of his conquests.

"Call me if you want to talk," Preston says as I get out of the car.

"Thanks," I manage to reply because I was raised with manners, and it feels impossible not to say anything.

Once I'm through the stone arch and out of his sight, I run the last sixty feet to the door of the Kappa house and don't stop until I'm locked in my room, face down on my bed; I barely make it in time before the first sob escapes, but it's a Saturday night, and the house is empty anyway. The only thing I want to do right now is talk to my mom. Or better yet, to be home in my own room, sitting on my bed, with my mom lightly rubbing my back and telling me everything will be okay – but that's another relationship I've messed up. I've never felt so alone.

Chapter Twenty-Seven
Mark

"Well, that went well," I say as I hear the car peel out of the driveway.

"Shit," Jen mutters, shaking her head and walking back toward the dining room to start clearing dishes from the table; I follow behind her to lend a hand. We take several trips in silence back and forth to the kitchen before the table is clear, and it's time to start doing dishes. It's been a while since we've had more than a few plates to clean up after a meal. Rose does the majority of the cooking, and every surface is spotless when she is done – as if we had gotten delivery, only without the waste of plastic containers, and the food is better.

Jen starts scrubbing the filthy ceramic pot with burned-on bits of meat and onions. It would be ten times easier if she let it soak, yet she continues the arduous task. Although I've also gotten quite accustomed to having help, I didn't grow up this way. I did the dishes every night until I left for college. Most nights, I made dinner as well, and I think I have a lot more experience with burned-on food than Jen does, but I don't think she'd appreciate my advice right now. Instead, I stand beside her, holding a blue-checked dishtowel, and wait in silence for her to hand me something to dry.

"Didn't you think Lynn would have told her?" Jen finally says as she hands me the heavy pot that still has flecks of brown on the bottom, but I pretend not to see them.

"I guess so," I reply, bending down to put the Dutch oven away in a cabinet with the complete set of matching orange pots and pans.

"I get that she didn't tell Nick, but she was getting so close with Courtney. I can't believe she wouldn't have told *her* she was married!" Jen says, raising her voice to convey her despair.

"I don't really know," I say. "I've never been able to figure out your sister," I explain, desperately wanting to get upstairs and take off this collared shirt and put on an old t-shirt and climb into bed.

"Do you think I should call Courtney tonight or wait until tomorrow?" Jen asks.

"I'd give it at least a few days. I'm sure this was a pretty big shock to learn that her sisters are lying to each other and to her," I offer, surveying the kitchen to see how much work is left to be done before I'm excused.

"This was your idea too!" Jen accuses, her light green eyes are almost glowing like a cat's, filled with fury.

"I have my issues with Lynn. A lot of them," I add. "But I never told you to rat her out to Nick," I say.

"Are you fucking kidding me with this?" Jen asks, starting to laugh in a maniacal way that means she finds this anything but funny. "You were the one who told me about Lynn and Nick in the first place!" Jen yells.

"I know I did," I say, trying to keep my composure. "I told you because I thought you should know, but mostly because I was so fed up with watching her cheat. I thought you might talk to her about it," I say, although hearing it out loud sounds unlikely. "I didn't tell you to go track down her lover."

"So, you wanted her to stay here and take over the company?" Jen asks, twisting things around.

I'm so sick of thinking about Summer Risk Management. I just want to tell Jen that it *is* what I want. I want to be free of this albatross, and if Lynn is the one to free me, then so be it! But I'm not mad enough to go that far; I don't know if I could ever be angry enough to say something like that to her.

"There's just something about Lynn," I say, biting on my top lip and clenching my fists as I avoid her question.

"I know," Jen retorts. "Remember, I grew up with her!"

"I didn't actually *meet* Lynn before I met you, but I ran into her at a few parties while I was playing, back in 2006," I say calmly, unsure where I'm going with this story but convinced it's one I need to tell.

"What are you talking about?" Jen asks, looking at me like she's been slapped.

"Come sit down," I say, pulling out two chairs at the kitchen table. It looks like Jen is going to refuse, but then she walks over and accepts the chair, although she perches on the edge, like she wants to be in a position to flee at a moment's notice.

"The first time I saw her was at an after-game hotel party in San Francisco; I never actually met her. She was with a group of models. I didn't think anything about it, but she slept with one of my teammates and then appeared at a few parties over the next few months," I say, pausing to calibrate Jen's reaction.

222

"When was this?" Jen asks, and I can tell she is trying to do the math.

"Fall of 2006," I reply.

"Before Lynn and Trevor got married?" Jen asks, but it's not really a question.

"She was engaged. She had a ring," I tell her.

"I guess that's not a shock," Jen says. "But why didn't you tell me?" Jen asks, starting to get upset again.

"It gets more complicated," I say, trying to figure out the best way to say it, but now that I've said this much, it seems like I have no choice.

"How so?" Jen asks. "You pretended like she was a total stranger when I told you about her!" Jen accuses.

"When you told me about her and showed me her picture, you also told me about her three-year-old son," I say, running my hands through my hair to stall for time.

"Why did that matter?" Jen asks, but after the words leave her mouth, I can see the wheels turning in her head.

"Because Declan looked a lot more like my former teammate than he did like Trevor," I manage to say, finally getting the words out that I've been holding on to for nine years.

"Holy shit!" Jen says, staring at me. "Holy shit!" she says again. "You've known all this time, and you didn't tell me!" she says, glaring at me.

"I've thought about it so many times," I say, putting my face in my hands, so I don't have to look at her. "But as much as I hated Lynn for cheating, I also didn't want to break up their family. I wasn't going to take a father away from his son and destroy a family for a mistake she made a long time ago. It made it worse when I saw her cheating again in Vegas and then doing it again here, but I still don't want to ruin their family, and most of all, I can't do that to Declan. He deserves to have both of his parents," I say, trying not to get too emotional.

"Fuck," Jen declares, shaking her head as she shoves her chair away from the table and storms out of the room.

Chapter Twenty-Eight
Jennifer

I'm not usually the one to open up the shop, but Stephanie had a doctor's appointment this morning, and I was happy to have an excuse to get out of the house as early as possible. Ever since dinner on Saturday night, there has been tension, and I know Mark isn't happy with me. I feel like *I* deserve to be upset that he's been holding back secrets about Lynn all these years, but somehow that's gotten lost along the way.

Monday is usually a slow day, especially in the morning, as the ladies in town are shuttling children to school and running to the gym and the grocery store to re-stock the pantry from the chaos of the weekend. I've learned over the years that whether it's shopping for a gift or for themselves, people tend to be more interested in spending money later in the week. So, I busy myself folding and refolding cashmere scarves and merino wool sweaters, and I change the outfit on the faceless linen mannequin in the center of the store to showcase new items that arrived over the weekend. I glance at my watch and am dismayed to see that it is only eleven o'clock; merely one hour has passed without a single customer, and Stephanie won't be in until one.

I try to remember the feeling I got when I first opened the boutique. Am I just imagining it, or was I really excited to come here every day and rearrange jewelry and make small talk with customers? The very early days were exciting. Finding the location, negotiating the lease, getting the business loan, designing the plans for the store, and deciding what to sell. But now that it's a well-oiled machine, the only thing for me to do is swipe credit cards and fold sweaters – which is similar to a job I had after school when I was sixteen.

The bell chimes, and I perk up a bit at the idea of a customer, or at least another human being to chat with for a few minutes. When I look up, I see that it's Mitchell, red-faced and sweaty from the two-block walk, even though it's a cool fifty-five degrees outside.

"Good morning Jennifer," Mitchell says, trying to catch his breath.

"Hi, Mitchell," I reply. "What brings you here today?" I ask him.

"I have most of the paperwork ready. I just need the signature page from Courtney, and then we can get everything tied up," he says, handing me a thick envelope.

The knot in my stomach grows as I think about the papers that Courtney thrust at me on Saturday night and the look of disdain in her eyes. I actually have the pages at the bottom of my purse, but it feels wrong to turn them over in our current situation. "I'm waiting to get it back from her," I say to Mitchell, "I'll let you know as soon as I have it," I tell him.

***

After two more days of unreturned texts and calls from Courtney and a civil but cold shoulder from Mark, I decide it's time to reach out to Lynn and see if it's possible to repair any of the damage I've done. I start on Wednesday morning with a simple text:

226

Jen: How are you doing? How's LA?

Although I'm slightly disappointed, it's not surprising that I don't get any response. A few hours later, I try again:

Jen: Checking in – how is everything?

And then an hour later, I write:

Jen: Do you have time to talk?

I know that I shouldn't expect much *and* that my texts are rather lame, but it's hard not to keep checking my phone to see if she's written back. Once the kids are home from school and settled at the counter for a snack of graham crackers and strawberries, I leave them with Liliana and go to my office. I know it's completely unreasonable to expect a reply, but now that I've decided to initiate contact with Lynn, I'm anxious for her response. I begin to craft a fourth text message and then abandon the effort and decide to call her instead. After five rings, it goes to voicemail, and I hang up without leaving a message. It's only two-thirty in the afternoon in California, and I will admit that I have no idea what her days look like; she could be doing any number of things that make it impossible for her to answer her phone, but I think it's more likely that she's screening my calls. I dial again, and this time I get her voicemail on the first ring, and I hesitate but still don't leave a message.

The rest of the afternoon and early evening pass slowly. Even though Liliana is here to help, she has to leave at six, and Mark is out late tonight, so dinner and baths and story time feel particularly onerous. It's not their fault, but I can't help my mood impacting my interactions with Ryan and Harper, and they are the unfortunate recipients of my short temper this evening.

When they are all tucked in, I make my way back downstairs and pour a large glass of red wine and fill a bowl with almonds and dark chocolate chips in lieu of dinner and head back to my office. Not surprisingly, there is still no response from Lynn. I know I don't deserve a response, but the guilt is starting to overwhelm me, and even if she won't talk to me, I need to make sure she's okay.

If we were a more functional family, I would have contact info for Trevor in my phone with his work and cell numbers and probably multiple email addresses – considering he is my brother-in-law. But I have none of those things. I have a closer relationship with the guy who sold me sliced ham a few times at Whole Foods than I do with my own family member. I can't remember the name of the firm where Trevor works, or if I did, he might not even work there anymore. I Google "Trevor Henkel" in the hope of finding his office number so I can call and ask a few vague questions and make sure Lynn is okay.

I'm not prepared for the amount of material that pops up seconds after I send my search into the universe. There are dozens of images of Trevor at the top of the page: headshots of him in a suit and tie, full-length pictures in a tuxedo, standing aboard a yacht, in a golf shirt with a bunker behind him – and in each one, he looks slightly older than I remember, but his gleaming white teeth, bronzed skin and movie star good looks remain the same.

The first website must be his law firm; it is called "Henkel, Schmidt, and White" and lists him as the managing partner. The next entry is his LinkedIn profile, and the third is a link to a company where he seems to sit on the board. I'm about to click on his firm website to get his office number and declare my fact-finding mission successful when something in the description of the fourth website catches my attention; it reads: "Attorney-To-The-Stars Trevor Henkel and actress Missy Green announce their engagement."

I'm sure that this is a different Trevor, but I click on the link anyway out of curiosity, and I see a picture of my brother-in-law with his arm around a very young-looking blonde girl and a short story of their engagement on Catalina Island and their planned nuptials for the coming year. I read the paragraph three more times before I can even begin to make sense of it and then type frantically, trying to find out the rest of the story.

It takes a bit of digging, but it seems there's no real privacy anymore, and once I figure out what I'm looking for, it doesn't take long to find all of it. Each one I read is worse than the next, but it's a massive train wreck, and I can't tear myself away. After half an hour, I've pulled most of the pieces together, and from what I can tell, Trevor and Lynn have been divorced for two years, and Trevor has full custody of Declan. Lynn had one DUI five years ago and another one a few months before they got divorced, and Trevor used that to declare her an unfit mother. I'm sure there is a lot more that I can't read about from the LA gossip columns and police blotters, but I'm pretty sure I have the basic idea.

I slam my laptop shut as if closing the screen will erase the images of what I've just seen. Nausea comes quickly, and I'm reminded of the early days of pregnancy as I run down the hall and barely make it to the toilet before all the red wine and pieces of almonds come right back up and splash into the bowl. I wrap my arms around the white porcelain fixture and start to weep as I think about what a monster I am and the pain I've caused my sister.

Chapter Twenty-Nine
Lynn

The house looks slightly different, but it only takes me a minute to figure out what's changed; the lemon tree is gone. I planted that right after we first moved into the house when Declan was just a baby. Trevor thought it was dumb when I brought it home from the nursery, but he was actually impressed when it started producing full-sized unblemished lemons that rivaled anything we could get at a farmers market. I wonder if Missy didn't like it or if it reminded Trevor too much of me, but either way, there is now a patch of baby grass on the front left side of the lawn where my tree used to grow. Oh well, I think, as I turn off the engine. I abandon my car in the circular driveway and begin my trek down the path to the monstrous Mediterranean style villa that I called home for nine years.

I ring the bell, and the familiar five bell chime brings back way too many memories. I expect to be greeted by one of the uniformed maids, but instead, Trevor appears. "Come on in," he says, holding open the heavy wooden door.

Cautiously, I step inside and look down the long hallway and into the study on the left and the sitting room on the right, trying to see what else had changed in the past two years.

"Is Declan ready?" I ask hopefully.

"Not quite," Trevor replies. "Why don't you have a quick drink while you wait," he offers, flashing me a smile that most would read as charming.

He is using the tone he uses for clients and celebrities, and it is incredibly off-putting. He used to talk to me this way on rare occasions when he was apologizing, but it's been a long time since I've heard him sound this way, and I'd prefer he yell and shout obscenities because this façade is even scarier. "That's okay, I'll just wait here," I tell him, taking a step back towards the door.

"Don't be silly, Lynn. You know how boys can be; he'll be a while. Just come in and have a drink. I've been under a lot of stress lately, and I know I haven't been at my best. I also want to hear how everything went in Chicago with Jen, and I'm sorry about your dad. Let's just sit and talk," he says. "Please?"

It's so unnerving for him to be this contrite, and as much as I hate myself for feeling this way, I've felt so alone this past week that there's something comforting about talking to the person I've known since I was eighteen – the person who knows me best – even if things have been pretty bad recently.

"Okay, just one drink," I relent, and I follow him down the Spanish-tiled hallway and through the curved archway to the chef's kitchen and great room, which used to belong to me.

"What can I get you?" Trevor asks, sauntering over to the full wet bar that lines the back wall, behind the red leather couch.

"Where are all of your *people*?" I ask him. "It's rare that you make your own drinks," I comment.

"Everyone's off today," he says casually.

A chill runs down my spine at his words, but I take a deep breath and reassure myself that Declan is here, and we will be leaving shortly. "I'll have a gin and tonic," I say.

Trevor busies himself at the bar, and I reluctantly take a seat at the kitchen table, accepting that I'll be here for a short while. I may as well sit down and enjoy the view of the backyard, the free-form rock-ledged pool surrounded by twelve identical lounge chairs, where I used to try to get the perfect tan to please Trevor and my agent.

The next thing I know, Trevor slides an overflowing eleven-ounce martini glass in front of me (I know the size since I got them for him for a previous birthday). "I asked for a gin and tonic," I say, looking up at him with confusion.

"I know these are your favorite," he says, slipping into the seat next to me with a martini glass of his own. "I made yours extra dirty," he says, winking at me.

I sigh and bend down to take a small sip from the glass since it's way too full to pick it up without spilling all over the reclaimed wood. It's easier to do it his way, but I'll only have a few sips while I wait for Declan.

"How was Chicago?" Trevor asks, relaxing back in his chair like we are old friends catching up.

I struggle to think of the best way to answer his question. I'm obviously not going to tell him that I thought I found the perfect guy until it exploded in my face. Even though he never liked Jen, I'm not going to tell him that she ignored me for most of the trip and then stabbed me in the back. And I'm not ready to tell him that I found out I'm about to inherit a lot of money from my dad because I need that leverage. Also, I'm too ashamed to admit that Jen would rather pay me to disappear than have me in her life. I settle for the simplest answer I can think of, "It was really sad, but I'm glad I was there."

"I thought your dad would outlive us as all," Trevor laughs, taking a generous sip of his martini. I give him a small smile and decide to interpret his comment as deferential to the deceased, even though I know Trevor never liked Dad.

"Why aren't you drinking?" Trevor asks, gesturing to my full glass. "You don't like the way I make a drink anymore?" he asks, but there is an edge to his voice that wasn't there a moment ago.

"I'm driving," I shrug.

"That never bothered you before," he says, with a wicked smile.

"I'm going to go check and see if Declan's ready yet," I say, rising from the table.

"Give him a little longer," Trevor urges, placing his hand firmly on the back of my chair.

"Five more minutes," I say politely, settling back in at the table and taking a sip from the goblet of pure gin; it's bigger than I intend, but it succeeds in calming my nerves.

"Are you still going out on calls?" Trevor asks, which feels out of the blue.

"Occasionally," I tell him. "I'm in the process of switching agents," I say, which is technically true, but I don't disclose that I'm switching because my agent of the past ten years told me he doesn't have work for someone my age, and it's unlikely I'll get any work in the future. I also don't dare tell him that I've been researching real estate courses.

"How's work for you?" I ask him. It is surreal to sit in this kitchen and shoot the breeze like we're friends when just last week he was screaming at me over the phone, and he hasn't allowed me to see our son for two months. But I'm so close to seeing Declan now that I'm just going to smile and keep up the charade until I get out of here.

"I'm going to see what's taking him so long," I say firmly, pushing my glass away, but before I can get up, Trevor grabs my wrist and pulls me towards him.

"Do you miss me?" Trevor says, his voice starting to slur slightly, and I suddenly realize from the familiar thickness of his voice that although this is *my* first drink, it isn't his.

"We had some good times," I reply, trying to figure out where this conversation is going.

"It doesn't have to be this way," Trevor says, grinning at me, although he hasn't released his hold on my wrist.

"What do you mean?" I question.

"We don't have to fight all the time. We could get along much better," he says, his words getting slushier by the minute.

"I'm all for it," I say as I try to pull my arm away from him unsuccessfully. "Why don't we talk about it after Declan and I come back. We can figure out a way to all get along better," I suggest, attempting to stand up again.

"Declan's not here," Trevor says nonchalantly.

"What did you say?" I spit, glaring at Trevor's smug face.

"He's at an overnight school trip; he'll be back in the morning," Trevor says, laughing as he sees the look of shock on my face.

"What am I doing here?" I yell. "What kind of sick game are you playing?" I shout at him, pushing back from the table with both hands finally free and knocking the chair over in the process. We both stare as the wooden chair slams into the ceramic tile and comes dangerously close to the glass patio door, but just misses it.

"I wanted to see you," Trevor says simply.

"So, you tricked me and lied to me about getting to see our son?" I say, seething with anger.

"I've missed you," Trevor says, taking a step toward me and putting his hand on my lower back, about half an inch above my ass.

"I highly doubt that," I quip, trying to gauge my reaction carefully, as Trevor continues to prove that he still holds all the cards. "And you have Missy now," I throw in, hoping that a reminder of his perky fiancée will be a helpful hint.

"All she wants to do is get pregnant," Trevor groans. "She's taken all the fun out of it. Sex is all about timing and taking her fucking temperature – it's ridiculous! I don't even remember agreeing to have another kid. But with *you,* it wouldn't be that way," he says creepily, lowering his hand, so it rests firmly on my ass and then giving it a hard squeeze.

I scream and jump into the air at the unanticipated pinch. "What are you doing?" I accuse, staring at his red-rimmed eyes.

"Come on. For old time's sake," he chuckles, moving towards me again, this time grabbing for my breast.

"I'm leaving," I say, grabbing my purse from the end of the table.

"Don't you want to see your boy?" Trevor asks, settling back into his seat and finishing the remaining swallow of his martini.

"He's not here. We've already covered that," I say indignantly.

"Right. But I'm the one who gets to decide when you get to see him," he says casually. "So, it seems it would be in your best interest to be on my good side," Trevor suggests, getting up and walking back to the bar to refill his drink.

"Are you seriously suggesting that I sleep with you in order to get my custody back?" I say, incredulous.

"Woah, woah, woah, don't get ahead of yourself. You're not just going to get joint custody from one fuck. But it would certainly improve your odds on visitation," he laughs wickedly, making his way to the ostentatious red sofa and collapsing backward onto it, spilling a significant portion of his drink in the process. My jaw drops open, but nothing comes out; I can't begin to find the words to respond to his depravity.

Trevor pats the spot on the couch next to him, "Come join me," let's see what we can arrange," he says like this is one of his settlement agreements.

"I'm not doing this," I say, starting to slowly back out of the kitchen, although I want to turn and run as fast as my legs will carry me.

"Are you sure? I guess I'll just have to tell Declan that his mom still doesn't want to see him. I can make this better, or I can make it much, much worse," Trevor smirks.

"You Bastard!" I yell. "I'm calling my lawyer. I won't let you do this!" I threaten, my voice shaking with anger, as I turn and run down the hallway toward freedom.

"Good luck," Trevor calls out, and I can still hear his cackle echoing in my ears as I slam my car door and race home, sobbing the whole way.

Chapter Thirty
Courtney

I have five new voicemails on my phone. I know who they are from because I watched the calls come in, and I don't need to listen to the messages to know what they will say. Coach wants to know why the hell I wasn't at practice and if I have any possible explanation for my unexcused absence.

I've been sitting on my bed in my basketball clothes all day because I *did* get dressed for practice this morning, but then I couldn't make myself walk out the door. And I couldn't make myself leave two hours later for Econ, or for my TA's mandatory weekly discussion group for my Women's Studies lecture. So, I'm still sitting here at three-thirty in the afternoon, and I'm going to miss the afternoon practice if I don't get out of here in the next ten minutes.

My phone rings again, but this time it's Christina. She may be genuinely concerned, or Coach may have asked to her call and find out what's wrong since I've never even been late to an off-season team run, let alone skipped an in-season practice. But instead, I silence the ringer, strip off my basketball clothes and put my pajamas back on and climb underneath the soft duvet on my twin size bed, trying not to think about the day I picked out the bedding with my mom at Bed, Bath & Beyond, and I close my eyes.

"Are you sick?" Kerry asks the second I open my eyes.

"What time is it?" I ask, rubbing the sleep out of my eyes and trying to get my bearings.

"It's six forty-five," she replies, turning on the larger lamp in the room to provide more light.

"At night?" I ask, trying to remember what time I fell asleep.

"No! In the morning!" She declares. "You were passed out when I got back from classes, so I left you alone, but you hadn't moved when I got back at ten from the library. I checked to make sure you were breathing but figured you must be sick," she says. "I hope I don't get it," Kerry throws in, "I have a big chemistry test this week."

"I'm not sick," I assure her. "I just really needed to sleep."

"Okay," Kerry drawls, sounding skeptical. She sits up in bed and pulls her long blonde hair into a twist, securing it to the top of her head, and I marvel yet again at how glamorous she looks first thing in the morning with zero effort.

I glance over at my phone on the desk next to my bed and see fifteen new voicemails and forty-seven unread texts. I don't have the heart to look at them, but I know if I want any chance of keeping my spot on the team, I better get dressed and haul ass up to the court so I can be the first one there and attempt to explain myself to Coach.

***

"What the hell happened to you?" Christina hisses as we're gulping water during our two-minute break.

239

"Sorry," I reply quietly.

"Sorry?!" she exclaims. "What does that mean? I thought you might have died! On Sunday, you said you had work to do and couldn't talk, and then you disappeared yesterday and skipped both practices!" she cries. "What is going on?"

"I don't really want to talk about it," I say, tossing my water bottle to the ground and jogging back out to the free-throw line for the next drill. I know Christina deserves so much better than this, but I'm mortified at what happened on Saturday, and I know if I even think about it, I will fall apart again.

After practice, I decide to skip my usual shower in the locker room and go straight to the Kappa house. It isn't solely to avoid confrontation with Christina, but it's certainly part of the reason. She calls to me as I'm packing up my gym bag on the bench, and she's walking toward the ladies' locker room, "You coming?"

"Nah, I'm going to shower back at the house today," I reply, trying to sound like it isn't a big deal, even though I *always* shower here.

"Whatever," Christina says, with an attitude that's impossible to miss, and turns on her heel to jog toward the locker room without looking back.

Back in my room that night, I draft several texts to Christina but delete all of them after only five or six words because I know they're totally lame and don't come close to offering the necessary explanation or apology. I'm sure she would be understanding and compassionate about my messed-up family because that's the type of friend she is. However, I've been so excited about my new sisters for the past month and a half that I can't bear to do a post-mortem with her on everything I no longer have; especially since she'll never really understand as she comes from a home with loving, truthful parents and siblings.

I also can't bear to share the additional embarrassment of what happened with Preston. She's always teased me about liking him, but now I've finally realized that I do like him, and worse than not liking me back – he pities me! It's just too much.

Kerry comes in from the library and sits down at the end of my bed, which is highly unusual. Her evening studying and bedtime routine is so precise, I could write it out in bullet points, and when she comes in from the library, she generously applies hand sanitizer from the pump on her desk and then methodically unpacks her backpack into her bookshelves and desk.

"What's up?" I ask, looking up from my highlighted copy of *The Handmaid's Tale*.

"Is everything okay?" Kerry asks, her sweet southern drawl making her especially nurturing.

"Of course," I reply quickly, brushing her off.

"Alright," Kerry says, pausing. "You seem a little down," she states, patting the top of my foot, although I almost don't feel it through my heavy wool socks.

"Just busy," I say, picking up my book and highlighter to indicate the end of our chat.

Kerry sighs as she gets up from the end of my bed and then initiates her evening routine. I feel bad shutting out another close friend, but I know no one will understand, and that will make it even worse.

***

I'm able to avoid all social interactions other than basic pleasantries for the next few days by spending all my free time at the library at Garrett Theological Seminary. Christina introduced me to it last year when she was researching a paper; it's right on campus, but I think only loosely affiliated with Northwestern, and it is always quiet and empty. Christina hates studying at the library, so even though *she's* the religious studies major, I know I won't run into her here or anyone else! It's weird not talking to her much at practice, but for now, it's for the best.

On my third day in hiding, I find that I'm remarkably caught up in all of my classes and even ahead on the reading in two of them. The librarian is starting to give me weird looks, but so far, he just smiles at me and seems satisfied that I don't make any noise and don't leave a mess. I'm still miserable, but at least I feel good about schoolwork, and I know I'm ready for my statistics test tomorrow. I'm almost smiling and not paying attention when I walk out the library doors into the chilly fall afternoon and practically run into Preston's shoulder.

"Watch yourself," he laughs, "Someone's gonna get hurt," and he flashes me a smile that would melt the heart of most of the girls on campus, and I use all of my self-control to ignore the flutter in my stomach and force myself to remember his pity kiss the other night and the girl he actually likes.

"Sorry, my bad," I say, taking a step backward and changing direction as if I had just bumped into a perfect stranger.

"I was just kidding," Preston says, making a few quick strides to catch up with me. Even with my long legs, he's taller and faster, so it's not a challenge. "Why are you ignoring me?" he asks, walking beside me toward south campus, even though I know he was previously headed north.

"I'm not. I'm just busy," I say, keeping my gaze straight ahead, even though I can feel him looking at me.

"That's bullshit," he says, "And you know it."

"I just need to figure this all out on my own, okay?" I ask although it's hardly a question.

"Why are you being like this?" Preston questions. "We just want to help."

"Who's *we*?" I ask, faltering slightly but then regaining my stride.

"I ran into Christina the other day, and she said you wouldn't talk to her, and you were being really weird. Why didn't you tell her about what happened at Jen's house?" Preston asks

I stop in my tracks and jerk my head in his direction, "So you told her?" I ask, raising my voice, so people walking around us on the path turn to stare.

"I thought she already knew," Preston protests. "Why wouldn't you tell her about it – she's your best friend!" he maintains.

"And it's my business who I tell," I yell at him. "Did you tell her about the pity kiss *too*?" I say angrily, and then clap my hand over my mouth as I realize what I said.

"What are you talking about?" Preston asks, bewildered.

"Nothing. Forget it. I've got to go," I say, and I take off running, my heavy backpack slapping against the top of my butt the entire way.

When I get back to the Kappa house, it only takes me a few minutes to pack my overnight bag. I'm not sure what I need to pack, but I know I have to get out of here. I throw in pajamas, jeans, underwear, workout clothes, a sweatshirt, a hairbrush, and a toothbrush and hope that's enough. I grab my backpack, which already has almost every book and notebook I own, and head outside to wait for my Uber.

I almost wish the ride was longer because it would give me time to plan out what I want to say. I probably should have called first, but I've been on the receiving end of the deception for so long, this time, I want a bit of a head start. I'm still working on my opening line when the Uber pulls into the driveway. I'm not sure if I should start on the offensive by calling her a liar and rattling off my list of grievances or if I should give her a chance to explain – something that I haven't really done yet. But before I can decide, the front door opens, and I burst into hysterical sobs, unable to catch my breath, let alone move forward with a plan. My mom runs to me and gathers me up in her arms, even though she is several inches shorter than I am now, and I collapse into her, barely able to make it up to the porch. She guides me to the swing and sits next to me, putting my head in her lap so she can brush the hair off my face and sing Blackbird, the way she always did when I was little.

"I've missed you, Momma," I say quietly when I can finally speak. "I'm so sorry."

"I'm sorry," she says. "You're here now; we can fix it, no matter what's wrong."

I know that she can't fix any of this, but my body still relaxes for the first time in weeks.

Chapter Thirty-One
Jennifer

"Are you sure this is a good idea?" Mark asks as I'm zipping my smallest suitcase. I think the last time I packed this lightly was when I was still taking business trips; I almost forgot how easy it is to pack when I'm by traveling by myself.

"I have no idea," I reply, "But I have to do something. I've fucked up so badly; I can't begin to try and make it right with a phone call or a text." Mark and I have been discussing my internet findings for the past few days, and though there are still some gaps, we know things aren't good – and we've only made them worse.

"Are you sure you don't want me to come with you?" Mark offers again, even though we discussed it ad nauseam last night.

"I have to do this myself. I know she didn't tell me about the divorce in the first place or that she lost custody, but I need to find out what's going on and try to make things right," I tell him. "And you need to stay for the kids. Liliana and Rose can be here during the day, but they have their own families, so you have to be here at night," I remind him.

"What if the address is wrong?" Mark asks, even though we discussed this issue last night as well.

"I don't know," I admit. "This is the address she gave Mitchell for her paperwork, and it's a mid-priced condo in a decent neighborhood, at least according to Zillow. So it seems pretty likely that this is where she's living now, but if it's not, then I'll just have to figure it out," I tell him, anxious to get to the airport, even though I still have four hours until my flight to LA.

"Did you hear back from Courtney?" Mark asks as we're walking down the stairs; even though it's light, Mark still carries my suitcase because that's how he is.

"Care to rub any more salt in the wound? I'm well aware that I'm the world's worst sister," I say, taking the bag from him as we reach the front hall.

"I take it that's a no," Mark says. "Text me when you land," Mark adds, bending down to give me a kiss on the cheek. I turn my head slightly, so our lips meet. The kiss rates low on the passion scale, but hopefully conveys love or partnership or something positive to Mark. Although I'm still mad at him for keeping the secret about Lynn all these years, I'm mostly just furious with myself, and the last thing I want to do is let my thoughtlessness ruin my marriage as well.

***

I slept fitfully for most of the flight. I was up all night fretting about what happened if I couldn't find Lynn and then worrying even more about what would happen if I actually found her. I sprung for a first-class ticket, so I can't blame my accommodations. I was plenty tired, but I woke up every fifteen minutes from a different version of the same terrible dream - Dad crying and telling me how much I've failed him.

Hertz upgraded me to a black Yukon, even though I insisted the mid-size sedan was fine, and in fact, preferable; however, the woman at the counter insisted that as a valued corporate member, she couldn't let me drive away in anything less. Now that I'm heading north on the 405, I realize that half of the cars look like the one I'm driving, and I'm the only one that isn't an Uber. I suppose it doesn't matter, but I realize the Hertz lady's desire to give me the car probably had a lot more to do with excess inventory than my special status.

I reach the Mar Vista address in record time, and against all odds, I find a parking spot in front of Lynn's building. I've been thinking about this moment for days, and I've had at least eighteen hours since I bought the plane ticket last night and another five on the plane and almost an hour since landing, and I still have no idea how to handle this conversation. It's early afternoon, so Lynn may not even be home, but it's not like I have anything other to do than sit here and wait. There's always the chance this isn't even her apartment, but I'll have to deal with that challenge if it arises.

When I left O'Hare early this morning, it was in the high forties with clouds and drizzle and a chance of reaching fifty-two degrees by noon. But here in California, the sun is shining, and in this first week of November, it is seventy-three degrees, and I can practically smell the saltwater, even though I know the beach is a couple of miles away. As much as I love my hometown, it's surprising that anyone would choose to live in the Midwest if they knew this kind of weather was an option. I lock my oversized taxi and slowly make my way up the short sidewalk to the front of her building. It's similar in style to most of the complexes I've seen on television, shades of muted yellows, and pinks with external stairs and apartment doors that open to outdoor hallways. In most other parts of the country, this style is reminiscent of a motel and would signify inexpensive housing, but here in the sunshine state, I know it's just an excuse for more vitamin D.

Lynn's apartment is 2F, which I assume means it's on the second floor. I climb the metal staircase and walk down the expansive external corridor until I find her door. I know it wouldn't be safe for her to have her name on her door, but part of me was still hoping there would be an indication I was in the right place, rather than the sterile yellow door with a peephole and multiple locks. I hold my breath and knock twice, uncertain which outcome I'm hoping for.

I wait a minute, and nothing happens, so I knock again, slightly louder this time. I uncross and re-cross my arms as I wait for a response, moving slightly closer to the door, so I can tell if there is any noise coming from inside, but I don't hear anything. I decide to give it one more try before going back to sit in my car, and I rap my knuckles loudly on the door three times, feeling emboldened by the likelihood that no one is there, but this time, just as I've turned to walk away, a very familiar voice calls out, "Coming!" and I freeze in my tracks.

***

Lynn opens the door without checking the peephole or asking for my name, and the smile on her beautiful face turns immediately to a scowl when she sees me. Lynn's blonde hair is damp, and her face is bare, which results in her looking even more gorgeous than the last time I saw her painted and sprayed to perfection, and she doesn't look much older than she did in college.

"What are you doing here?" Lynn spits, her tone filled with venom. "And how did you even know where to find me?" she adds.

"I got your address from Mitchell," I admit. "Can I come in?" I ask, hopefully.

"I'm not sure," Lynn replies. The part of the apartment I can see over Lynn's shoulder is not particularly large but appears to be enough space for one person to live comfortably. It's a modern open-plan design with the kitchen, living, and dining

248

area all in one place, and it seems to have been recently renovated. I had never been to Lynn and Trevor's house in Bel Air, which is crazy when I think about it, so I don't know what Lynn's decorating style is, but the apartment is done mostly in white with some gray and blue accents and feels slightly sterile, but mostly just lonely.

"I know you don't owe me anything, but now that I'm here, please let me come in so I can try and explain," I say, growing more anxious with each second I wait for her reply.

Lynn puts her hand on her slender waist, and she stares at me so hard, I think she might burn holes right through my forehead. "You want to explain how you ruined the only good thing that's happened to me in years? You want to explain how you went behind my back and lied about me to Nick?" Lynn says, raising her voice as her anger grows.

"I know it was a terrible thing to do," I groan, "but I thought you were still married," I try to reason.

"Why would that make it any of *your* business?" she asks, hands on both of her hips now, with her heart-shaped chin jutted out defiantly.

"You're right. I'm so sorry," I say. "Can I come in for a few minutes so I can apologize and try and figure out what's going on? I read about what happened with Trevor and Declan in some articles online; I'm so sorry," I say quietly.

"Ten minutes," Lynn says crossly and holds the door open just wide enough so I can pass by her.

Even though it's a perfect temperature outside, the air conditioning is on full blast, and I find myself wishing I hadn't left my sweater in the car, leaving me with only a sleeveless silk shell. However, I know I'm not in a position to complain or ask Lynn to turn down the air, and it seems I'm not going to here long anyway unless Lynn has a massive change of heart.

"I love your apartment," I say as I make my way over to one of the two white sofas. I almost make a joke about how clean they are and that I couldn't have anything like this because of the kids, but then I remember the situation with Declan, and I'm thankful I kept my mouth shut.

"Cut the bullshit," she says, taking a seat on the other sofa and tucking her long tan legs underneath her.

"What happened with Trevor?" I ask.

Lynn flinches but recovers quickly. "Is that your version of an apology?" she questions, resorting to sarcasm.

I take a minute to try and get the words right, but no matter how many times I practiced saying it in my head, it never sounded right, so I can't imagine it's going to sound any better now that I'm here. "I'm so sorry. I should never have said anything to Nick. It wasn't my place. I don't have a good excuse, but I'm really sorry. I'll do anything to make it up to you. I'll talk to Nick, or…" Lynn cuts me off and holds up her hand in the universal stop sign.

"That's over," she says bluntly.

"But it doesn't have to be," I plead. The look on her face tells me not to proceed, so I don't. We sit in silence for a minute, and I contemplate asking again about Trevor, but I'm sure it won't go any better. I wasn't sure if I would have the opportunity to bring up Mark's paternity theory, but at this point, that seems impossible. Before she kicks me out, I decide to throw my last card on the table. "I'm sorry about asking to buy you out of the company; it wasn't right," I spit out.

"What are you talking about?" Lynn asks.

"Summer Risk Management belongs to all of us. Dad wanted all of us to have it, and I shouldn't have convinced you to sell," I say humbly.

"What am I going to do with part of an insurance company?" Lynn questions. "Besides, doesn't Mark run it anyway?"

"He does," I say, chewing on my bottom lip. Mark has been acting weird for a while now whenever I ask him about work, and he seems more and more checked out recently, but I don't know what's behind it. "I know that you're an actress, and you aren't interested in insurance, but it's part of our family, and you should still own a piece of it," I say sincerely. "I'll talk to Mitchell, and he can change the paperwork," I begin, but again, Lynn puts up her five finger stop sign.

"Don't bother," Lynn says. "I'm fine with it as it is," she says coolly.

"But we can change it, and we can get Courtney back in too, just like Dad wanted," I say, pausing to gauge her reaction.

"Stop pretending we're one big happy family," Lynn says. "I'll just take the money and be done with it; I'm going to need it for legal fees anyway," she says, under her breath.

"What do you mean?" I ask her, putting my elbows on my knees and leaning toward her.

"Nothing, never mind," she says hurriedly, pulling her feet out from under her and placing them on the floor. "Look, I don't think we have much more to say," Lynn says, getting to her feet.

I stand up with her and look up to her, as I've done since her twelfth birthday when she shot past me in height. "Is there anything I can do? Can I help?" I implore.

"You've done enough already," Lynn says snidely as she walks across the apartment to open the door and send me on my way.

Chapter Thirty-Two
Mark

"Where's Mommy?" Harper asks. I'm drumming my fingers on the counter, waiting for the coffee to brew, so I can pour it into my thermos and get out the door. Liliana is standing behind Harper, pulling her baby hair into an elaborate braid without eliciting a single cry, something Jen can barely manage when gently brushing our daughter's hair.

"She had to take a quick trip to California," I reply, even though I've explained this to her at least three times already this morning.

"Mommy doesn't take trips," Ryan says while delicately stabbing his waffle.

"Sometimes she does," I reply, anxiously reaching for the coffee pot. Liliana arrived right on time this morning, but I didn't factor in how much time it would take to get the kids up and dressed after Jen left at the crack of dawn for the airport. I came upstairs from my workout at my regular time and then realized the kids are usually up and dressed before Liliana meets them in the kitchen for breakfast and the school run, but Jen normally handles that. I hadn't paid much attention to these logistics until today. Now we are all running late, but Harper and Ryan don't seem to be bothered by it. Other than my

253

general aversion for tardiness in all situations, I wouldn't care too much about missing a bit of time at the office, either.

"No, she doesn't," Ryan replies stubbornly. He puffs out his little chest and purses his lips, unwilling to give any ground.

"She doesn't travel much *anymore,* buddy," I concede, "But she used to travel a lot before you guys were born," I say, but Ryan is focusing on his breakfast again, now that he's won the argument – he doesn't give a crap about what his parents did before he was in the picture.

"I'll see you tonight," I tell the kids, walking around to their side of the counter to kiss them each on the head.

To Liliana, I say, "I'll try to be home by six, but Rose will be here if you need to leave early."

"Don't worry about it, Mr. Olsen. I can stay as late as you need me to. Mrs. Olsen texted me everything, so I'm all set," she smiles, and I back out of the room with a wave knowing that things here will probably run better without me, similar to the office – I'm really just a figurehead.

***

Charlie calls while I'm driving to the office. He called twice yesterday, and I meant to call him back, but the day got away from me.

"Hey, Charlie," I say.

"You're a tough guy to get a hold of," Charlie laughs, and his voice rumbles through the car on the Bluetooth speaker

"Sorry about that," I apologize. "What's going on?"

"We want you to come in for a practice," Charlie says.

"Oh. Wow!" I reply, unable to censor my response before it comes out.

"I've been talking you up, but they're bringing in a few other guys to interview, and you need to come down and talk to the coaching staff and meet the guys. They'd love to see you in action," he jokes.

I'd be lying if I said I hadn't thought about the Northwestern coaching position. I've thought about it almost every day since Charlie mentioned it, but it's been more like the idea of the job, how it would be in a dream. I haven't seriously considered what it would be like to take the job, or even to properly interview for the job. Going to an in-season practice and running drills with the team are almost too tangible. What happens after I go for the interview? It won't be a dream anymore. What if I get the job – what happens to Summer Risk Management? Honestly, they'd be fine without me, but it's not like I can simply quit. And what if I don't get the job? Do I just go back to insurance and pretend it never happened? The thoughts are swirling in my head so quickly, it's hard to grab onto a single one, but I've obviously been lost in my own thoughts for too long because Charlie pipes up. "Mark? You still there?" he asks.

"Yeah, I'm here," I reply.

"You can come in and meet the other guys and then sit down and talk to Johnny and Darrell. You can come to practice the same day, or you can come back another afternoon and do that. And if all goes well, you'll come back and sit down with Kurt," Charlie says, referring to Kurt Watkinson, the head football coach for the past fifteen years, the one who turned the entire Northwestern program around.

"What day were you thinking?" I ask him.

"We're away this weekend at Iowa, so let's do it next week when we're back. Let's say Tuesday. Is that good?" Charlie asks.

"Sure," I hear myself say, although it feels like I'm listening to someone else rather than hearing my own voice. "Text me and let me know where to be and what time," I say, surprising myself again.

"Sounds good," Charlie replies.

"Good luck this weekend!" I tell him.

"Thanks! See you Tuesday," Charlie says, and then the morning sports show returns immediately to fill the car as if the call never happened.

I'm almost giddy with excitement as I pull into the parking lot, wondering how I'm going to focus on work, or anything else, until next Tuesday. But a bigger question is what to do about Jen... Should I talk to her about it before the interview? That's presumably the smart thing to do, but if nothing comes of it, then it could be a big fight for no reason. Mostly for self-preservation and the desire to delay, I decide right then and there that I won't say anything until at least after the first interview; maybe I'll even wait to see if I get the offer. Besides, she already has enough going on with Courtney and Lynn; I don't need to complicate things further.

***

The next few days are pure agony. Waiting for the coaching interview while still going about my normal routine is painful enough, but that's only a small part of the misery in our house. Jen returned from California less than twenty-four hours after she flew out there, and she's been a mess ever since. I told her that Lynn might just need more time, but I'm not sure that's true. I've always had my issues with Lynn because she cheated on Trevor when they were engaged, and I've been sure she was lying about Declan's real father; but looking at the mess everyone's in right now, I'm having trouble finding anything but sympathy for all parties involved – except for Trevor of course. I was so angry for so long because her betrayal somehow reminded me of my parents and my own broken family, but I can't find that anger anymore, and I'm not sure it was fairly placed to begin with; however, that's a different story.

From the second I met Jen, I envied her family. It was really just her and her dad by that point, not so different from me and my mom in a way, but I know it's ridiculous to try and equate our twosomes. I built them up to be perfect because of the fancy house and David's fatherly yet commanding demeanor during dinners at the country club and brunches by the pool. But now the polish is off, and nothing looks shiny anymore, either from the inside or the outside, and Jen seems to be feeling it most intensely.

Jen is moping around the house on Sunday, fending off Harper's request to help her with a puzzle for what feels like the thousandth time that day. When the doorbell rings, I'm closer to the door, so I call out that I'll answer it, but Jen runs in from the playroom and beats me to it – I guess she was anxious to have a plausible excuse to turn Harper down.

I stand back behind Jen so I can see who it is, and on the other side of the door is a tall, skinny guy, somewhere between the ages of sixteen and twenty-five. I'm sure when I was younger, those ages seemed drastically different, but now there are kids in high school who are bigger than I am with full beards, and then there are guys working at the firm that I swear are part of a bring-your-kid-to-work program until I find out they are new associates a few years out of college.

"This is for Jennifer Olsen," the guy says, holding out a legal-size white envelope but waiting for confirmation before releasing it.

"I'm Jennifer. What is this?" Jen asks.

The guy looks flustered at the simple question, and I immediately adjust his age downward; there's no way he's more than twenty. "I was just supposed to hand it to you," he says, looking nervously over his shoulder. "It's from Courtney," he says quietly, looking over his shoulder again, and this time I see that he's looking at the white Honda Civic parked on the street, where Courtney is sitting in the passenger seat, staring straight ahead.

"Is she okay?" Jen asks immediately.

"Yes, she's fine," he answers, and then corrects himself, "I mean, she's doing okay."

"Are you a friend from school?" Jen asks.

"We went to high school together," the boy replies. "I go to Lake Forest College, so I live close to Courtney. Well, close to her parents," he adds.

"Do you think I could go talk to her?" Jen asks hopefully.

"I don't know," he says, shifting his weight from side to side, clearly uncomfortable; this is a lot more social pressure than this kid appears to be ready for.

"She'd probably have come up here herself if she wanted to talk to us," I offer, and Jen turns around and shoots daggers at me with her eyes, letting me know I should keep my mouth shut.

"These are some papers she forgot to give you," he says, slowly backing away, trying to make his escape.

"Thanks," Jen says sadly. "Can you tell her that I say hi and I miss her? Tell her I've been trying to reach her," Jen says, sounding crazier and more unhinged with each word.

"Um, okay. I'll let her know," the boy says, turning around and breaking into a jog for the last several yards to the car. He pulls away as soon as he gets in, even before he buckles his seatbelt, and I'd be surprised if he relayed anything we said back to Courtney.

Jen opens the envelope, and there is only one piece of paper inside. She scans it quickly and then hands it to me before running upstairs and slamming the door to the bedroom. There are legal-sounding terms sprinkled throughout, but it's immediately clear that this is something Courtney has prepared herself in a Word document. The gist of the letter is that Courtney doesn't want any part of David's estate. She will regrettably continue to use the money that was set aside for her college education, but beyond that, she wants nothing to do with David's will or the Summer family – ouch.

***

It's hard to temper my enthusiasm as I leave the meeting with Johnny and head toward the field for practice. My first meeting was with Darrell, and even though he's retiring, he is very protective of the offensive program he's created, and he wants to know it's in good hands moving forward. I was nervous for the first few minutes, but it didn't take long to break the ice and start swapping war stories from our college days – he played at the University of Illinois as well, although he was there long before me. If possible, my meeting with Johnny went even better. We got along like a house on fire from the moment I sat down, and we didn't stop until one of the

259

assistant coaches knocked on the door to remind us that practice was about to start.

As we approach the field, the players abandon their personal conversations and quickly snap into formation for warm-ups, spacing themselves out evenly across the ten and twenty-yard lines. It's hard not to feel a pang of jealousy for these boys; they get to play football every day, go to parties, hang out with friends, date multitudes of girls, and they have their whole lives ahead of them, maybe even playing in the NFL. But I stop my wandering mind before I fall down that rabbit hole; it's easy to do, completely futile, and clearly requires rose-colored glasses. Instead, I take a deep breath and inhale the familiar smell of grass, dirt, sweat, and pure grit and remind myself how lucky I am to be here.

I saw Preston in the second row as soon as I stepped on the field, and I gave him an almost imperceptible head nod in acknowledgment, but as he's a defensive player, I didn't encounter him for the remainder of the two hours of practice, which seemed preferable considering the current situation with Jen and Courtney. But at the end of practice, as I'm high-fiving and fist-bumping my future players (if I let myself dream of this becoming a reality), Preston runs over, and things get a bit more difficult.

"Hey, *Coach*," Preston says with a smile. Given the circumstances, I was hoping they might just introduce me as a former player stopping by to watch practice, but Charlie killed any potential misconceptions right off the bat when he introduced me as, "Mark Olsen, former Chicago Bear, and hopefully our new Receiver Coach."

"Hey, Preston," I reply. "How's it going?"

"It's okay," he says. "I didn't expect to see you here," he says.

"Yeah. It all happened kind of quickly, but Charlie's exaggerating quite a bit. It's really early in the process; I just came to check it out," I tell him, hoping to downplay my presence here and minimize the chance he tells Courtney before I have a chance to talk to Jen. But then I realize that the odds of that happening are slim to none, and I'm going to need to be explicit if I want to control the flow of information. "Jen doesn't know about it yet, since it's still so early," I fib, "So it would be great if you didn't mention anything to Courtney quite yet," I say, hoping he gets the picture.

"Oh sure, no problem. Courtney isn't really talking to me right now anyway, so that shouldn't be a problem," he says, with a dry laugh, but it doesn't look like he finds it funny. "I was actually going to ask you if you knew how she was doing?" Preston asks, looking awkward and uncomfortable, which is not a look he wears well.

"I don't know too much. She still seems pretty mad," I tell him. "But she did stop by the other day to drop off paperwork," I add, trying to be helpful.

"How did she seem?" Preston asks, looking at me intently.

Now I wish I hadn't said anything, since I don't have much to report. "Well, she stayed in the car. The guy she was with was the one who came to the door to hand Jen the papers; he wouldn't let us near her."

"Oh," Preston says, taking a step backward and exhaling heavily through his nose. "I've got to go," Preston says. "Bye," he calls out halfheartedly as he jogs toward the clubhouse.

I jog over to the endzone to catch up with the coaching staff before it's time to go home; however, the euphoria that I had moments ago is gone. It's been replaced by feelings of unease and regret, but I can't quite put my finger on what changed.

Chapter Thirty-Three
Lynn

After a couple of days sulking in my apartment following Jen's bombshell visit, I finally accept Ali's offer to meet up and go for a walk. She initially suggested drinks or dinner, but I need the exercise and fresh air. We meet a few blocks away from my apartment with a plan to wander toward the beach in Venice. It's a beautiful afternoon, just cool enough to warrant leggings instead of shorts, and I grab a sweatshirt in case we walk long enough that the sun goes down, and it really cools off.

Ali is already waiting on the corner when I get there, but she is talking animatedly, waving her hands and gesturing to the street sign in sync with her moving lips. Her long hair is covering her ears, but I'm assuming she's wearing AirPods and is on the phone. Sometimes I still see people chatting away without any visible form of communication, and my first thought is that they are talking to themselves. Ali sees me crossing the street and mouths the word "Hi" and points to her phone, tucked into the side pocket of her leggings. I smile in return and stand a few feet away from her, so it doesn't seem like I'm eavesdropping, but it's hard not to hear her side of the conversation.

"Sorry about that," Ali says, and she walks toward me and stands on her tiptoes to give me a hug. Ali isn't short like Jen, but I still have roughly three inches on her, so this puts us almost eye-to-eye.

"Is everything okay?" I ask, referring to her agitated attitude on the phone call.

"It's fine," Ali says, rolling her eyes. "Wade didn't remember that I told him I was going out tonight."

"Do you need to go?" I ask.

"Hell no," she replies. "He'll go out another night. You know how men are," she laughs, and then she bites her lip, "Sorry."

"Don't worry about it,' I assure her. "Just because it wasn't like that with Trevor doesn't mean I don't understand."

"Have you heard from him?" she asks as we start walking toward Venice, and we have the added freedom of walking side by side and not having to stare at each other while we speak.

I want to tell her about what Trevor did and said when I went to the house last weekend, but I can't bring myself to do it; I'm too ashamed. I know she would tell me it isn't my fault, but I keep playing the afternoon over and over in my head and wonder if I gave him the wrong idea or if I could have done something differently; it's simply too mortifying to let her know that this is the depths my life has sunk to, even if she is my best friend. "He's still being a total ass about custody and visitation," I tell her, which is completely true, even if it isn't the entire truth. "As soon as I get the money from my dad's will, I'm going to hire a lawyer. I'm going to get a shark this time," I say fiercely.

"I wish I could help," Ali says supportively. "I don't really know any lawyers, other than the woman who looks over my contracts," she says.

"Thanks. I'm sure I'll find someone," I say with much more confidence than I feel. "I bet Jen would know someone. She always has connections to the right people," I say, without really thinking about it.

"That's a great idea!" Ali cries, clapping me on the shoulder as we cross over onto a more crowded street on the edge of Venice, and we have to sidestep a few teenagers sitting on the curb to avoid stepping on them.

"No way!" I yell at her, and we walk to the end of the next block in silence before I quietly apologize for my outburst. "Sorry," I say meekly.

"It's okay," she replies, but I still feel guilty.

"She came out here," I say, keeping my eyes on the ground in front of me, even though I can feel Ali's head swivel in my direction as soon as the words are out of my mouth.

"Jen did? When?" she asks, clearly confused.

"A few days ago," I reply.

"To see *you*?" she asks.

"She showed up at my apartment without any warning," I say.

"What did she say?" Ali questions.

"She claims she came here to apologize for ruining things with Nick. Apparently, she found out about the divorce online and some of the details from the trial that made it into the news."

264

"Wow!" Ali exclaims, reducing her pace as if she needs to slow down to let the news sink in.

"I know," I reply. "I guess it's good that she finally knows, but it doesn't really matter."

"What do you mean?" Ali asks.

"She still fucked me over with Nick," I say angrily. "And it's too little too late."

"Is that what you told her?" Ali questions.

"Basically. I told her to leave," I say.

"How long was she here?" Ali asks.

"I don't know, maybe fifteen minutes," I reply.

"Seriously? She flew out here, and you kicked her out after fifteen minutes?" Ali says, the shock evident in her voice.

"Yes," I say, feeling awkward.

We continue down Palms Boulevard in silence, each lost in our own thoughts or trying to figure out how to repair the conversation until we reach Abbott Kinney and Ali breaks the ice by suggesting we get some coffee. "What do *you* think I should do?" I ask as we're waiting in line at Tom's Flagship store for our takeaway iced coffees.

"You really want my opinion?" she asks.

"Yes," I say. "I'm sorry if it hasn't seemed that way."

"I know she screwed things up for you with Nick, and that was seriously messed up. But you've also kept a lot from her, so it's not exactly a level playing field. She's your sister. You've both lost your parents, and you both have this new sister and all of your dad's baggage that comes with that; I think that you need each other right now, and maybe she can help you with Trevor. You won't know if you don't give her a chance," Ali says, looking up at me with her big brown eyes. Although it sounds like a speech from a bad Lifetime movie, possibly even something she was in a few years ago, I have to admit that the idea of accepting help and no longer being alone is very appealing; I can almost feel some of the tension leave my body at the idea of having *someone* on my side – assuming Jen means what she says.

"Thanks," I say to Ali. "I really appreciate it. I need to think about it, but you may be right."

Chapter Thirty-Four
Courtney

I'm still disoriented when I wake up and see my chipped white Pottery Barn Teen dresser across the room, covered with basketball trophies and framed photos from high school dances. I've been home for almost a week, but I still expect to see Kerry's purple floral comforter when I open my eyes, and it's a mix of relief and disappointment when I don't see them. There are slivers of light framing three sides of my room-darkening shades, but it's enough to let me know that the sun is starting to rise, and that means I have to get up and dressed and drive to Evanston for morning practice. Coach was moderately understanding when I missed practice last week but also let me know that if it happens again, I'll be on the bench for the rest of the season.

"Knock, knock," my mom says, lightly tapping the door as she says the words and pushes open my bedroom door.

"I'm up," I sigh, throwing the duvet cover off my legs and stretching my body into the shape of a starfish, so I cover the entire queen-size bed.

"I was just checking," she says, hovering in the doorway, dressed in her flannel bathrobe, clutching a mug of coffee.

"Can you make me a couple of hard-boiled eggs?" I ask her. "Please," I throw in.

She opens her mouth as if to say something but then closes it and simply sighs. "Sure," she says, turning around to walk back down the stairs.

This past week hasn't been easy for either of us. I'm still having a tough time coming to terms with Mom lying to me for my entire life. However, in light of recent revelations with Jen and Lynn, it doesn't feel like my options are much better with my long-lost sisters. Mom and I talked the first day I got home, but now we are both acting as if things are back to normal, even though it's obvious they aren't.

When I get to the kitchen, I find an old green canvas lunch bag on the counter. I think the last time I used it was in eighth grade, but Mom isn't big on throwing things away. Although for all I know, she's been using this to bring her lunch in for years, and she's simply letting me borrow it today. I peek inside and see a Tupperware container with four hardboiled eggs, a banana, two apples, three granola bars, and a bottle of Gatorade.

"Thanks," I say to her. She's sitting at the kitchen table, still in her bathrobe, but now fully immersed in the front page of the Chicago Sun-Times.

"You're welcome," she replies without looking up. "Sorry, that's all I have to offer. I bet the options are better at the Kappa house," she throws in.

"This is perfect," I reply, but it isn't hard to pick up on her not-so-subtle hint.

"Will you be here for dinner?" she asks casually.

"I was planning on it," I reply.

She looks up from the paper this time when she responds, and without any makeup and her grayish-blonde hair hanging limply to her shoulders, she suddenly looks older and wearier. Even though I've been around my mom all week, it feels like this is the first time I've truly seen her. "Courtney, you are welcome to stay here as long as you want. This is your home. But hiding here isn't going to solve your problems."

"I'm not hiding," I protest lamely.

"You're running back here as soon as you're done with practice and classes, and you aren't seeing any of your friends. You can call it whatever you want," she says, folding her arms across her chest.

I let out a noise that sounds like "hmmph," and is reminiscent of one of my wittier teenage replies.

"And you're ignoring your sisters as well, and that isn't going to solve anything either. They're your family, and you don't quit when something doesn't go your way," my mom says firmly.

"That's different!" I argue. "I know I need to fix things with my friends," I admit, "But I don't want anything to do with Jen and Lynn," I tell her. "I've got to get to school, or I'm going to be late to practice," I say, catching a glimpse of the clock on the wall.

"I'll see you tonight," she says, turning back to look at the paper, but her disappointment hangs in the air.

**

For the past week, I've been miserable every day. My goal has been to avoid seeing as many people as possible, so I scurry back to the seminary library between classes and hide at a table in the corner until it's time for my next class. Christina and

Kerry, and most of my other friends have finally given up on trying to talk to me, and although it's entirely my fault, it still hurts.

As I'm sitting in the library in the early afternoon, having eaten my second apple and third granola bar as my lunch on the walk over, I keep returning to my conversation with my mom from this morning. Somehow, just admitting out loud that I needed to fix the issues with my friends made it seem increasingly urgent. It will take a while to get back to normal or a new normal with my mom, but I'm pretty sure we will get there. But as I sit here hungry and alone, I'm not able to remember why I was so adamant that Christina and Kerry be kept in the dark. At the time, it felt too embarrassing to share, and my jealousy for both of my friends' traditional large families clouded my judgment; however, now all I want to do is tell them about it and cry on their shoulders. I'm tired of being alone, and I'm getting tired of living at home too.

Christina will be harder to win back because I was a much bigger bitch to her, and she's also not one to easily forgive, so I decide to start with Kerry. I can't quite remember her Wednesday class schedule, but I know she has labs most afternoons, so I sit outside the entrance to the tech building and decide to wait here until I have to leave for afternoon practice. There's always a chance she'll take one of the back exits to the building, but I'm feeling lucky.

At three-twenty, Kerry walks out the front door of the building, bundled in a white ski jacket and grey cashmere hat, even though it's barely in the forties, but her Southern blood doesn't take well to the cold – I saw it firsthand last winter.

"Kerry, wait up," I call out, jogging across the massive front pavilion to catch up with her.

Kerry turns when she sees me and gives the faintest of smiles, but I can tell that she's pissed.

"I'm really sorry," I say, as soon as I reach her – it seems best to get right to it.

Kerry looks at me with her big brown eyes and raises her perfectly arched eyebrows but doesn't say a word. I knew it wasn't going to be easy, but it looks like it might be harder than I thought.

"I'm sorry that I disappeared. I'm sorry that I didn't tell you what was going on. That was really shitty," I say to her.

"It was," Kerry says, stopping to face me and put a hand on her non-existent hip.

"I found out something about my sisters. They both lied to me and to each other, but it had nothing to do with you or with us, and I'm sorry about how I acted," I say, hoping I sound as sincere as I feel.

The look on her face changes, and I can tell that I've broken through. "It's a lot quieter in the room when you're not there," she smiles. "I might get used to having a single if you don't hurry up and come back," she teases, but her tone is playful.

"Don't get too used to it. I'll be back soon; I forgot what it's like to live at home," I joke, and we both smile.

"Sorry about your sisters," Kerry says.

"Thanks. It's okay. I went my whole life without having them and only had them for a few months, so it won't be too hard to adjust to life without them," I explain.

"What do you mean?" Kerry asks, scrunching up her face in confusion.

"They weren't honest with me, and they were mean to each other…" I say, but Kerry cuts me off.

"Seriously? That's what sisters do. Not all the time, but sisters can lie or be mean or keep things from each other – it happens. But they can also be your best friend!" she exclaims.

"You and your sister aren't like that," I accuse her, trying to remember the stories she's told me and her half of the conversation when they talk on the phone.

"We're sisters; of course, we have problems!" she says. "We happen to have a great relationship, and I love her more than anyone in the world, but she's also the person I want to strangle more than anyone," she says.

"Would you lie to her?" I ask, still stuck on Jen and Lynn's betrayals.

"It depends. If I thought it was going to help her, then I would. Or if I had a good reason, then I would do it too," she adds.

"I just don't know," I say, shaking my head.

"So, you never talk to them again?" Kerry asks, her eyebrows raised in doubt.

It sounded perfectly reasonable when I was locked away in my childhood bedroom, staring at my Taylor Swift posters, but saying it out loud makes it all sound a bit ridiculous. "I guess I need to think about it," I admit. A vision of the letter I wrote and had Andy deliver to Jen last week pops into my head, and a massive feeling of regret, along with dizziness and nausea, washes over me. I was so mad and hurt that I wanted to distance myself from both of them, and I decided that refusing the inheritance would be the clearest way to send the message. But now, it seems like yet another rash decision and one that my mom will certainly kill me for when she finds out.

"Are you okay?" Kerry asks.

"Yeah, why?" I question.

"You just looked a bit pale there for a second," she comments. I have no doubt Kerry will be a great doctor because she's so smart and such a diligent student, but she also notices things like this, which seems like a special talent.

"No, I'm fine," I reply, although it's not quite true.

"Have you talked to Christina yet?" she asks.

"No, I still have to do that," I say, feeling queasy again at the prospect of that difficult discussion but knowing how much better I'll feel when it's done.

"Good luck," Kerry giggles and flashes me a smile, letting me know that at least one part of my life is back on track.

Chapter Thirty-Five
Jennifer

I've always categorized the people who ask their dead relatives for guidance as flat out crazy; but recently, I find myself wishing I could ask my dad for help, and today must be the day I've reached my low point because I'm sitting here at the cemetery, right next to the spot we buried Dad only a few months ago. There's no headstone yet, because that's another Jewish custom we are following, and the people in charge at the synagogue insisted on it since he is buried in a Jewish cemetery. There will be a headstone unveiling in a year, where family will gather again to say goodbye, but seeing what a shitshow this year has been so far, I can't even begin to imagine that gathering. I'm honestly not even sure if I'm supposed to be here before there's a headstone, but in all the movies, people go to the cemetery to talk to their dead relatives, so I figured I should go all in.

"Hey Dad," I say, feeling ridiculous as I speak to the ground, and even more ridiculous when I pause and wait for him to reply.

"Ha," I laugh at myself and quickly look around to make sure no one saw or heard me. "I guess this will be pretty one-sided," I say, pausing again and then shaking my head as I try to decide if this is even worth doing. "Okay, here goes," I say, steeling myself for my confession, as if he really can hear me.

"I fucked up, Dad. I mean, I really fucked up. You asked us to all get along, and I ruined everything. I've been a terrible sister to Lynn, and now she's got all sorts of problems, but she hates me, so she doesn't want my help. And I messed up with Courtney too. She doesn't trust me, and I can't really blame her. And things with Mark aren't going so well either," I admit sadly, but I barely registered how much it had weighed on me until I said it out loud.

I continue before I lose focus. "I'm not exactly sure what's wrong, but he doesn't seem happy, and I know I'm not happy, but it's like we want to pretend everything is fine. Is that what it was like with you and Mom? I mean, I know there were other issues, of course, but is that what marriage is like?" I ask, and stupidly I pause again as if he's going to reply.

Then I change course and say the words I've been holding onto since that day in Mitchell's office, and the tears start to flow as soon as the words tumble out. "I'm so mad at you," I cry. "How could you keep that secret from us for all those years? How could you know we had a sister only a few miles away and never tell us about her?" I weep, not even bothering to wipe the tears or snot as they run down my face. "How could you do that to Courtney? Maybe everything would have been different if we had known? Maybe Lynn wouldn't have run off to California and married that asshole if she had a little sister? Maybe I wouldn't have been so mean and jealous if there had been three of us," I say, although even that sounds a little far-fetched to me. "But now we'll never know. And now it's just a disaster, and I don't know what to do," I say forlornly, slumping down to the grass, having lost much of my intensity from just moments ago.

I sit for a minute on the hard ground, thinking about what I've said. The grass is starting to turn brown and is sprinkled with crunchy leaves. The trees above still hold a few of the glorious autumn reds, yellows, and oranges, but in a week or two, they will be bare, and the idea of sitting outside like this in a light jacket and jeans will seem insane. I've always loved the seasons, especially the months leading up to the holidays. The idea of Thanksgiving and Hanukah and Christmas without Dad this year has been especially painful. But it's been even worse the past couple of weeks when I've started to put the tacky seasonal decorations up in the shop (way too early, but I have to keep up with the trends), and I've realized just how lonely it's going to be when I could have been spending it with two sisters, and now I won't have any.

I'll never be convinced that there can be communication from beyond the grave or any of that nonsense, but just as I'm feeling particularly sorry for myself, a massive gust sweeps through, causing leaves and grass and dust to blow everywhere. I'll never admit it to anyone, but I swear, it feels like a sign from Dad. Right after the wind dies down, I felt the strangest shift in my outlook. It sounds crazy, but it's as if the wind blew away some of the anger and negativity and carried in a puff of hope.

***

Mark texted that he would be home a little late for dinner that night, and we should go ahead and eat without him, but I told him I would have the kids eat early, and I would wait to eat with him. Mark arrives around eight-thirty, and the kids are already in bed. I debated about setting the table in the dining room for the two of us, but the last time we ate there (with Courtney and Preston), it was a disaster, and I need good mojo.

"You didn't have to wait for me," Mark says as he walks into the kitchen and sees the table set for two.

"I wanted to," I reply, crossing the room to give him a kiss as he shakes off his overcoat.

"What's the occasion?" he questions, gesturing to the white linen placemats and napkins that we only use for holidays because the kids stain them three minutes into any meal.

"I just thought it would be nice," I reply, feeling nervous and ridiculous at the same time.

"It smells great," Mark offers, loosening his tie, and then removing it completely and tossing it onto the kitchen stool.

"Rose made Chicken Marsala this afternoon, and she gave me instructions to warm it up," I admit, only slightly embarrassed that I have to rely on Rose to make Mark's favorite dinner. "But I did stop at Hewn to get bread," I tell him.

"Did you get the olive bread?" he asks hopefully.

"I did," I smile, pleased that this makes him happy. "And I picked up some cookies and brioche too. Not that I need it," I add, patting my stomach.

"Oh, stop. You're perfect," he says, enveloping me in a hug, and I melt into his arms, trying to see myself the way Mark seems to see me.

"Why is this so good?" Mark asks, pulling off a piece of the country olive bread and stuffing it in his mouth.

"I don't know. Everything at Hewn is delicious. I had to stop myself from buying more," I say. I'm about to make another disparaging comment about limiting the amount of carbs I eat, but I change my mind and silently pat myself on the back.

Once we're halfway through our meal and have covered the usual topics of kids and mundane events of the day, I bring up the question I've been holding back for a long time. "Are you happy?" I ask him, and Mark looks up at me with eyes wide and a mouth full of chicken.

He can barely finish chewing before he responds. "What is that supposed to mean?" he asks anxiously.

"I feel like something is bothering you, and I don't know what it is. But I want you to be able to talk about it with me," I offer.

Mark takes a sip of wine and then looks at his plate for a minute as if contemplating his answer. "I have you and the kids and a great job. Why wouldn't I be happy?" Mark asks, smiling at me across the table, but it seems like the smile takes a bit of effort.

"I don't know," I hesitate. "It just feels like something's been off lately," I offer, taking a hefty sip of my sauvignon blanc.

"Are *you* happy?" Mark asks, turning the question back on me.

I should have been prepared for this, and this *was* the discussion I wanted to have, but now that I'm faced with the inquiry, my initial reaction is to mirror Mark's answer and tell him everything's fine and put on a happy face like we usually do. But I think back to my revelation at the cemetery this morning and decide to plow ahead.

"Not really," I say, shaking my head. "Of course, I know I'm lucky to have you and the kids, and I know I should be happy, but I'm not. I'm bored at work. It was a novelty at first. I enjoyed the challenge of designing and creating the store, but now it feels frivolous," I tell him. Mark's about to say something, but I put my hand up to stop him because I want to get it all out at once. "And then there's this nightmare with Courtney and Lynn. I want Courtney to give me another chance. I want to help Lynn with whatever is going on with Trevor and Declan. And I want to make it up to her for how awful I've been, but she won't even talk to me," I say, relieved to have put some of my feelings on the table.

278

Mark is quiet for a minute and lifts up his hand to rub the stubble that has grown on his face since his early morning shave. "What if I try to talk to Lynn?" Mark asks.

"She doesn't like you either," I say, trying to make a joke.

"I know, but I have an idea of how we might be able to help. And if I can get her to listen to me for long enough to hear the idea, I think it could work," Mark says.

"What is it?" I ask anxiously.

"Let me talk to James first, just to make sure. I don't want to get your hopes up if it won't work," Mark says.

"Too late," I reply.

"I'll go give him a call now," Mark says. "As for Courtney, why don't you give Mary a call and see if she has any thoughts?" Mark suggests.

"You mean the woman my dad had an affair with and then kept from us for twenty years?" I ask, clarifying her identity, even though we both know exactly to whom he's referring.

"She's Courtney's mom," Mark says as if that's all that needs to be said on the matter, and he's probably right.

Chapter Thirty-Six
Mark

I never have trouble falling asleep; I'm always out the second my head hits the pillow. But tonight, Jen is snoring softly beside me, and I've been staring up at the rotating ceiling fan for over an hour. I'm trying to quiet my racing thoughts, but I keep returning to Jen's question at dinner and my stubborn reaction. She gave me the perfect opportunity to tell her about the coaching position, or at the very least, to tell her that I don't think running an insurance company is for me. But I didn't say any of that. Now I'm thinking about everything I should have said, as well as worrying about how I'm going to convince Lynn to listen to me. I made it sound like I had it all figured out, but I've only begun to think it through with James; and if Lynn won't talk to me, then it's all futile.

It's only nine o'clock in LA. Rather than waste more time on the counting and breathing methods that Jen swears by for insomnia, and are doing nothing for me, I go downstairs to reach out to Lynn – no time like the present.

My initial plan was to call her. However, if for some reason, she does have me programmed in her phone, then she won't pick up. And she likely won't pick up an unknown number either, so a call seems like a bad choice. I don't expect her to reply to my text, but as long as I can get her to read it, or at least read *enough* of it, I'm confident she'll reach out.

Mark: Hi Lynn. It's Mark. I think I can help you get custody of Declan.

I hit send and wait to see if she'll reply, but I know it's unlikely at this point, so I give her more material.

Mark: I was on the Bears with Tim Larkson in 2006

I wait again to see if this is enough information for her, but there are no blinking dots yet to indicate a reply.

Mark: Declan looks a lot more like Tim than Trevor…

It seems that I've finally hit a nerve, and Lynn starts to type her response.

Lynn: What do you want?!

Mark: I want to help you

Lynn: Why?

Mark: Because Trevor's a total dick. Because we're family. Because it's time I start acting like your brother-in-law.

Mark: Because we should have known you needed help, even if we didn't.

Mark: Because you deserve to be with your son.

Lynn starts typing and then stops three times before her reply finally pops up.

Lynn: How?

Mark: I work with a guy. His best friend from Yale Law is now in LA and makes Trevor look like an ambulance chaser

Lynn: And he'll help me?

Mark: Yes

Lynn: I don't have the money yet...

Mark: Don't worry about it

Lynn: The fees will be outrageous if he's anything like Trevor

Mark: seriously, don't worry about it. The only thing we will need is a sample of Declan's DNA for testing. Can you get that?

Lynn: I don't know

Mark: You need to get that from him. We'll take care of tracking down Tim

Lynn: Are you going to tell Tim about Declan??

Mark: We don't have to. This lawyer will take care of it, whatever that means

Lynn: You can tell him

Mark: Are you sure?

Lynn: Yes

Mark: I'll have the lawyer get in touch with you

Lynn: Thank you Mark

Mark: You're welcome – it was all Jen's idea

***

Jen's already in the kitchen with Rose and the kids when I get downstairs. I slept like a rock once I finished my conversation with Lynn, but it was still two hours later than I usually go to sleep. I was only able to squeeze in a quick workout this morning, but I'm so excited to tell Jen about what transpired with Lynn that it doesn't matter.

"Good morning," I say, addressing everyone in the kitchen together. The kids each murmur replies between bites of Cheerios, and Rose and Jen echo my greeting in unison.

"How are you doing this morning?" I ask Jen, walking up behind her at the sink and brushing her hair to the side so I can plant a kiss at the nape of her neck.

"I'm okay," she shrugs.

"I texted with Lynn last night," I say quietly. The kids don't hear us when we're talking directly to them, but they have ears like bats when we don't want them involved.

"Really?" Jen says, turning abruptly, so her face is inches away from my chest.

"She's all in. She's going to let James's friend help her," I say.

"What?" she asks, sounding shocked. "She wouldn't even talk to *me*."

"I told her that I knew Trevor wasn't Declan's dad," I whisper, realizing it's risky to have this conversation ten feet away from Ryan and Harper.

"But you didn't *know* that?" Jen accuses.

"I took a guess, and it seems I was right. I told her that we would take care of the lawyer, and she accepted," I tell her, with pride.

"Oh. That's great, I guess," Jen says, turning back around to give her full attention to scrubbing an apple harder than any piece of fruit should ever be scrubbed.

"I thought you'd be happy," I say, confused at her reaction.

"I am," she says, finally turning off the water. "It's just...it's not...this isn't how...never mind," Jen says.

"What's wrong?" I question.

"Nothing. It's great," she says, forcing a smile. "Maybe you should call Courtney too?" she says, with a frosty laugh.

"Don't look at it that way," I request, my emotions torn between sympathy and irritation.

"Sorry. I'm glad she wants you to help her. Really, I am. It's just one more thing that makes me feel separate from my family," Jen laments. "Everything's different, and so much has changed since Dad died; it's just a lot to take," Jen says, tears springing to her eyes.

"I know," I say, pulling her close to my chest and rubbing her back as she sobs into my blue dress shirt, leaving wet patches uncomfortably close to my nipples that make us both laugh when she pulls away. "It'll dry," I assure her as I say goodbye and kiss the top of her head, as well as the sweet-smelling heads of my children, even though they barely glance up as I go.

***

After the team practice and interviews, I got a call the next morning informing me that it had gone well, and they wanted me to come back and meet with Kurt for a final interview. Kurt played for Northwestern and then spent three years in the NFL playing for Tampa Bay before he came back and took a job as an assistant coach, and he quickly moved up to assume the role of head coach, making him the youngest ever Division One coach. Now he's been here for fifteen years and the name Kurt Watkinson is synonymous with football in Evanston. I've seen plenty of interviews with him on ESPN, but I've never met him in person.

Charlie prepped me for the interview as best he could. He told me he was an affable guy who took the program very seriously but was also a genuinely good guy, and he gave me a couple of talking points and areas to steer clear of. However, I wasn't prepared for how much I was going to like him and how easy it would be to imagine working together every single day. Kurt reminded me of my old high school coach and my best friend from college, and the uncle I never had, all wrapped into one. I know it was only a ninety-minute meeting, but by the end of it, I could see myself as a college football coach more clearly than I'd ever seen myself before.

So even though it's been several days since that interview (Charlie told me that they were still interviewing other coaches), I'm not surprised when Kurt calls my cell phone after lunch today to offer me the position. "Someone will get the paperwork over to you this week so you can have your lawyers look at it, and all that crap, but we're really excited to have you on board," Kurt says, right after he tells me that I'm their first choice for the job.

"Thanks," I reply. "I'm flattered. But I'm not sure that I'm going to be able to accept," I tell him, and my heart sinks with each word.

"Seriously?" Kurt says, sounding stunned.

"There's a lot going on with my family right now, and I'm not sure if it's the right time to make this big of a change," I say, essentially repeating the words Jen sniveled this morning.

"This is not what I was expecting to hear," Kurt says, but he doesn't raise his voice or add any emotion.

"I really appreciate the opportunity. And if the timing was different..." I say, trailing off.

285

"We have a second choice, and I guarantee he'll say yes," Kurt says confidently. "I'm going to give him a call in exactly one week," he says, conveying his message loud and clear.

"Thanks, Kurt, I appreciate it," I say, although I don't know if I'm thankful for another seven days to agonize over the decision or if it would be better if he would let me slam the door now and get on with it.

"Hope to hear from you," Kurt says as he ends the call.

Chapter Thirty-Seven
Lynn

I feel a glimmer of hope for the first time in ages. I'm trying not to get too far ahead of myself, but it's hard. Mark and I have had a few conversations since his initial text message, and it's as if he's an entirely different person than he was before, or at least the person I had created in my head. I was always sure he hated me, and perhaps he did - it wasn't like I gave him a lot of reasons to like me. Finally, telling him the truth about Declan feels like an enormous weight has been lifted off of my shoulders. I'd gotten so used to carrying it around with me for the past thirteen years that I forgot how light I felt without it. Jen listened in on the call with Mark the first time, the day after Mark initiated everything with his text. It's nice that she's trying to be supportive, but I've felt more comfortable sharing the whole story when it's just Mark, or Mark and James – I appreciate her effort and realize I need all the help I can get, but I'm not ready to forgive her yet.

This morning I have a conference call with James and his friend, the hot-shot lawyer who is supposedly going to be the answer to my prayers. Mark said he would try to join the call, but he has an urgent meeting, so he warned me that it would be unlikely. I'm a jumble of emotions as I log in to the secure video conference website and wait for Ray and James to appear on the screen.

James pops up first. Until now, I've only spoken to him on the phone, but he looks exactly as I pictured him; he should be holding court in a leather club chair of some exclusive men's club with a drink in his hand. His glossy brown hair is gelled back, and he's wearing an expensive-looking suit and gives me a smile that reveals years of high-priced dental work. James reminds me of a benign version of Trevor, but maybe that's the look I've come to associate with all wealthy, even reasonably attractive lawyers – it's hard not to be biased. I'm expecting more of the same when Ray emerges onto my screen, but Ray couldn't be more of a surprise.

Mark didn't tell me too much about him, because he's never met him either, but James promised he was the best there was. Apparently, they were roommates at Yale, and then Ray went on to clerk for some famous judge before moving to the DA's office in New York. He was there for a few years before joining a big firm in Manhattan and then moved to Los Angeles to take on the position of partner in a firm that specializes in criminal cases for the rich and famous. Based on this background, I expected a slimier version of Trevor, but the person grinning back at me from my laptop definitely doesn't remind me of Trevor.

First of all, Ray is a woman. I silently reprimand myself for assuming that this fantastic, shrewd lawyer had to be a man. I think back on my conversations with Mark when he described Ray to try to remember exactly what he said, and now I wonder if Mark also assumed that Ray was a man – so typical. Ray is a powerfully built Black woman with dark wavy hair down to her shoulders and a smile so wide and welcoming it covers most of the lower part of her face. She's wearing a light-yellow shift dress, revealing toned arms and shoulders, and I can see a matching jacket hanging on the back of her chair. Trevor insisted on rolling imaginary lint off his gleaming Zegna and Armani suits before every meeting, which ensured he looked more like a mannequin than a man, while Ray's slightly laid-back attire makes her look approachable, and she automatically appears to be less of an asshole. Although I have a moment of hesitation before she starts to speak because only a total sociopath can go toe-to-toe with Trevor, my doubts are quickly quashed.

"It's a pleasure to meet you, Lynn," Ray says, her voice as warm as her smile promised it would be. "Good to see you, buddy," she says to James, and James tips his head in response.

"Let's get right to it," Ray begins. "James has briefed me on your situation, and my team pulled your case files from the initial custody hearings, so I'm mostly up to speed," she says, her voice already sounding more serious as she gets down to business. "And I've had the *pleasure* of trying a few cases against your ex-husband before, so I know what I'm up against," she says, winking at me.

I'm relieved that she's familiar with Trevor, so I don't have to prepare her for that, but I'm also worried about her chances; as far as I know, Trevor's never lost a case. "How did that go? I mean, when you tried cases against him?" I ask timidly.

"I crushed him every time," Ray says with a chuckle. I cautiously exhale and wonder why I'm surprised, considering Trevor's track record for lying.

"We have some good news," James interrupts, trying to keep the conversation moving.

"Right," Ray agrees. "Tim Larkson retired a few years ago, but he's working in San Diego now, running a surf shop, and my guys tracked him down yesterday, and they had no trouble getting a sample to run his DNA," she tells me.

"Wow!" I reply, sinking back in my chair and feeling the wooden slats press firmly into my spine. "Just like that?" I question, wondering how it could possibly be that easy. "Did he have a lot of questions? Did he want to know about Declan?" I ask.

"It wasn't quite like that," Ray chuckles. "Let's just say we got the sample we needed. If it's a match and you decide that you want to pursue it, then we can figure out how to loop him in," she says confidently.

"Is that even okay? If he doesn't consent to give the sample, or whatever he needs to do?" I ask, concerned for the case and questioning her practices.

"Don't worry about Ray," James chimes in, trying to make me feel better.

"He definitely consented to provide the sample; he just doesn't have all the info yet. Let me worry about it. I promise you it's airtight," Ray says, and I realize as different as she seemed from Trevor initially, maybe deep down, they're more alike than I thought, but if we're going to win, it might be my only option.

"The next thing we need is a sample of your son's DNA, so we can run the test. It would be great if we also had Trevor's so we can rule him out as the father, but as long as Tim is a perfect match, we won't need that," Ray promises.

I've been worried about this since the moment Mark brought it up; I have a pit in my stomach like I used to get in school when I wasn't prepared for a test. "I definitely can't get Trevor's," I confirm. "But I'm not even sure how I'm going to get anything from Declan. Trevor won't let me near him! That's why I'm here talking to you!" I exclaim.

"I know, I know," Ray says in a soothing voice. "I can always send someone from my team if we get to that point, but I really don't like doing that with kids, and if we want this to be a surprise attack, we don't want Trevor to know we're sniffing around," Ray advises.

"Let me think about it," I reply, but I've been thinking about it for days, and everything leads to a dead end. "So, what happens after we do the DNA test?" I ask, trying to be optimistic.

"Assuming it's a match, there are two approaches we can take. We can file in court and re-open the custody discussion now that we know Trevor isn't the biological father," Ray says.

"But what about everything that happened last time?" I ask nervously.

"What do you mean?" Ray asks, and I can't tell if she's being kind or if she genuinely doesn't know what I'm referring to, but I'm pretty sure it's the former.

"Because of the DUI's. They said I was an unfit mother. That's how I lost custody in the first place. Why would they give it to me now?" I question, sadly, images of the disastrous first trial popping into my head.

"Your last attorney was a joke," Ray says, not mincing words. "You have grounds to go after him for negligence," Ray adds, "But you shouldn't need to do that since I plan to win this for you."

"What's the second option?" I question.

"We can bring the test results to Trevor informally and see what he has to say," Ray suggests.

"How would that work?" I ask, squirming in my seat to find a more comfortable position, but the hard chair isn't my problem.

"I have a feeling Trevor won't want this to become part of the public record in a grand fashion," Ray says.

"But I'm the one who slept with someone else when we were engaged. Won't it just make me look bad?" I ask, voicing the fears that have sat with me for years.

"No, honey," Ray says kindly. "He cares about appearances, you know that, and my guess is that he won't want any of this publicized. I'm not a betting woman, but I would wager that Trevor has a long history of infidelity that *he* would like to keep under wraps," Ray says and winks at me.

She continues, "He was fine when he bullied you in court and got to look like the big winner, but now that I'm here, it's different. He knows that those DUI's are from ages ago, and they're bullshit. He also knows that he has no evidence to support his preposterous claims of your drinking problem. And we have dozens of photos of him in highly compromising positions with one of his summer interns, which I'm pretty sure he wants to keep private," Ray says with a flourish, having saved the icing on the cake for last.

I gasp as she says it, unable to absorb all the information at once. "Holy Shit!" I shout, watching as Ray is clearly pleased with my reaction. "Isn't that blackmail?" I ask her, as it starts to sink in.

"We'll win in court. I have no doubt. But my approach would be to set up a meeting where we share the DNA findings and see how he reacts, and if necessary, we have some leverage with our intelligence, but we don't need to *blackmail* anyone," she says confidently, and I try very hard to believe her.

"So maybe we don't even need Declan's DNA?" I ask hopefully.

"No. We have to have that. The photos are in my back pocket just in case I need a little nudge, but I want to know this is a slam dunk, and we need the test for that," she says firmly. "Call my office as soon as you have it. We can get the results within a day once we have the sample," she adds.

"Okay, will do," I reply, trying to muster some enthusiasm. "Thanks for all of your help," I say to Ray and James, but the website is already informing me that the host has ended the meeting, off to bigger and better things.

I'm elated at the prospect of having Declan back, even though I'm sure it won't be easy to win him over after years of Trevor poisoning him against me, but no use worrying about that yet.

***

It's been two days, and I'm no closer to a plausible idea on how to get close enough to Declan to get his DNA. I even watched old episodes of Law & Order last night for inspiration, but even with my best acting skills, I know I won't be able to pull any of those stunts off in real life.

Ali suggested I join her and Wade and the kids at the beach this afternoon, and although I'm not exactly in the mood to spend quality time with her lovely husband and adorable children, it might be a good distraction. Not surprisingly, almost all of our beach stuff stayed in the house with Trevor, along with almost everything else I owned; however, somehow, I ended up with a collapsible beach tent that Ali asked if I could bring along today to provide shade for the kids.

My two-bedroom unit has a surprising amount of storage space, considering the overall square footage, and there are two humongous closets in the second bedroom that hold all the miscellaneous items I stubbornly refuse to part with. I'm not sure when I last opened this closet before today; luckily, I spot the tent as soon as I turn on the light. I pull the turquoise strap, but the bottom appears to be wedged underneath a duffle bag on the floor. I nudge the duffle bag with my bare foot, and it doesn't budge, so I have to bend down to pick it up. With a bit of effort, I toss the red bag onto the floor of the guest bedroom and grab the tent. I don't remember storing that bag in the closet, and honestly, I'm not even sure I recognize the bag. I'm already running late, but out of curiosity, I bend down to unzip the nylon bag and audibly gasp when I see what's inside. It's an overnight bag that Declan used one of the first and only times he stayed here; it was shortly after the divorce when Trevor was slightly less psychotic. I rifle through the bag and pull out a worn pair of pajamas, a t-shirt and shorts, three hardback books, and then a toiletry bag containing a hairbrush, a tube of toothpaste, and a toothbrush.

It's a Saturday morning, but if Ray is anything like any of the lawyers I've ever known, she never stops working. I dial the number she gave me the other day and hold my breath while I wait for her to pick up and tell me if this discovery is as amazing as I think it is.

Chapter Thirty-Eight
Jennifer

"You'll never believe what just happened!" I say to Mark as I walk into his home office and find him absorbed in a video game, yelling obscenities at the small figures on the screen.

"What?" Mark asks, glancing up quickly before returning his gaze to the screen.

"Lynn called and said she's going to be back in town for a few days," I say.

"Really?" Mark asks, skeptically, pausing his game to engage in a conversation.

"Crazy, right?" I ask.

"Why?" Mark questions.

"Her lawyer said they got the DNA test back, and it's a match, so they're going to deliver the news to Trevor tomorrow. She suggested Lynn leave town for a few days while they see how Trevor reacts," I tell him.

"Wow! James told me things went well with her and Ray, but I haven't talked to Lynn since then," Mark clarifies. "Is she staying with us? Does she want to see you? It's a good sign that she called, right?" he asks, rattling off questions.

"I think so. It's all so weird. She is still renting that apartment in Evanston, so she's going to stay there. But she wants to talk. I don't know what's going to happen, but I'm glad she's coming here *and* that she wants to see me, that's a lot of progress," I say.

"That's great," Mark concurs, shifting his attention back to his video game, my cue to leave.

***

I offered to pick Lynn up at the airport, although it's probably best that she turned me down; I don't think I've driven to O'Hare since Uber and Lyft were created. Lynn did ask about Courtney when we spoke yesterday, and I failed to pass this along to Mark, but I promised Lynn that I would reach out to Mary to see what we could do. I told Mark I would think about it when he suggested it initially, but I couldn't bring myself to do it – until now. It wasn't as if Lynn laid out a list of terms for her visit but reconciling with Courtney is important to both of us. And I certainly played a big role in fucking it up, so it was implied that it would be a good idea if I followed through here.

This means it's my job to call my dad's mistress. I know that I shouldn't think of her that way, but it's still hard for me not to. I decide to direct my anger toward my dad, instead of Mary, to prevent sticking my foot directly into my mouth. As far as I know, Courtney still isn't speaking to her mom, and Mark found out that she isn't talking to Preston either, so I don't know that Mary will be any help, but I'm not sure of any other options.

She answers on the second ring with a pleasant "Hello," and I barely get my words out, "Hi Mary, this is Jennifer Summer,

296

well Jennifer Olsen. I'm Courtney's half-sister, I mean, David's daughter," I offer, completely flustered.

"Hi, Jennifer. I know who you are," she says sweetly.

"I hope I'm not bothering you, but I was hoping you could help me," I begin.

"If I can, I'd be happy to. What can I do for you?" Mary asks.

"It's about Courtney. I'm not sure what she's told you, but Lynn and I would like the chance to apologize to her," I say.

"Uh-huh," Mary says, letting me know that she's not completely in the dark.

"It's no excuse, but she got wrapped up in an old argument of sorts between Lynn and me, and we'd like the chance to explain and let her know that we want it to be different with her and with us as well," I add.

"That's what I told her," Mary says, taking me by surprise.

"Oh. Okay, thank you. What did she say? I question.

"She said she wasn't ready, but I think she could be convinced," Mary says. "This has been a lot for her to process," she adds.

"Right, of course."

"It's a lot for *all* of you," Mary adds quickly, and I soften the tiniest bit at her recognition.

"Do you have a suggestion of what we could do? I've been trying for weeks, but she won't return my texts or my calls," I assert.

"She just returned to campus this past weekend..." Mary says, but I interrupt her mid-sentence.

"What do you mean? Where was she? Is everything okay?" I ask, alarmed.

"She's fine. She was having a tough time, so she came here for a week or so, but she's still been going to school during the day. But now that she's back in Evanston, I don't know her schedule quite as well, that's what I was saying," Mary explains.

"Ah," I reply, trying to make sense of this new information.

"Wait!" Mary exclaims. "Courtney has a home game tomorrow night. Brian and I were planning to go, but he has an event at school, and I'm not so sure she's ready for me at her game," Mary admits.

"And you think she wants to see *me*?" I scoff.

"Actually, I do," Mary says. "I'm sure it will take a little while, but I think she would love it if you went to the game, even if you don't end up talking to her. You can show her that you support her, and then maybe next time she'll be ready," Mary says.

It's not exactly what I was hoping to hear, especially with Lynn only in town for a few days, but it's better than nothing. "Thanks, I appreciate it," I say. I'd be lying if I said my animosity had disappeared, but after I hang up, I recognize that Mary's not the monster I'd made her out to be in my head, and also simply a mom who loves her daughter and is trying to do what's best for her; as if on cue, the tears spring to my eyes and I think of my own mom and my dad and Lynn, and I miss them all.

***

298

I've been pacing around the house all afternoon, too nervous to sit or eat, and I couldn't even focus on the story I was reading to Harper, so I gave up and sent her to watch television. Mark came home early from work to be here when Lynn arrived. He's supposed to serve as a natural tension breaker, but unfortunately, he's in his office on the phone when Lynn's car pulls up in the driveway.

I race to open the front door and then doubt myself as I swing it open. I must look like a stalker, watching for her to arrive instead of waiting patiently while she rings the bell, but it's too late now. "Hello," I call out, willing my voice to sound natural.

Lynn waves to me as she closes the door of her generic rental car and emerges carrying two large gift bags. She looks beautiful, as always, but even from a distance, she looks tired, the way her shoulders are slightly slumped and the sluggishness of her pace. As she gets closer, I swear I can see the hint of purplish circles under her eyes that she couldn't quite conceal, but it doesn't look like it's the result of a long flight or a late night out; she looks genuinely drained and sad.

"I'm so glad you came," I say, as soon as she steps over the threshold.

"Thanks for having me," Lynn replies. "These are for the kids," she says, holding up the bags, one green, and one purple. Their bulkiness prevents us from having to decide if we are going to hug, and I think we're both relieved.

"You didn't need to do that," I tell her, but follow it with, "Let me go get them."

"Wait," Lynn calls, and I pause on my way to the playroom, but I don't say anything.

"I'm sorry about how I acted when you came to visit in LA," Lynn says.

She barely gets the words out before I jump in, "No. No, it's all my fault. I should have stayed out of all of it; it wasn't my business," I cry.

"You're right about that," Lynn says firmly, but then she softens. "But I should have told you what was going on. I've kept everything from you and stayed away. I pretended my life was great, and then I was angry with you when you didn't understand that I needed help," Lynn says.

Hearing the noise in the front hall, Harper and Ryan rush in and are delighted to discover their mysterious aunt. Other than a brief meeting at the funeral, they've never really met her before. And they are doubly thrilled when they learn that she has brought gifts for each of them.

The children's arrival and joy over the extravagant gifts are a welcomed interruption to our conversation and lighten the mood in the room, an unintended superpower that children carry with them wherever they go. I catch Lynn's eye over the top of Ryan's head while they are examining the back of the box for the remote-control monster truck and the corners of her full lips turn slightly upwards. I return with my own small grin and feel the butterflies in my stomach slow their wings to a gentle flutter.

The next couple of hours pass quickly as the four of us sit on the playroom floor with Ryan's new truck and Harper's new animatronic stuffed bear, which reminds me of a futuristic and somewhat scary Teddy Ruxspin. The conversation flows freely, partially because we have two natural buffers, but also because we are purposefully avoiding controversial topics. However, just being in the same room together and talking, even if our primary focus is whether or not Ryan's truck can defeat Harper's bear in a head-to-head battle, it feels like we are making progress.

Liliana enters the room, and both children run to her and pull her arms in opposing directions, fighting over who gets to share their new toys first. "What time are you leaving?" she asks me, already resting in the beanbag chair, with Harper planted in her lap.

"We should probably get going pretty soon," I say to her and Lynn together. "The game starts at seven, but we need to find parking," I say, trailing off as I start to think about the evening ahead and wonder if we're doing the right thing.

"I'm going to say hi to Mark quickly before we leave," Lynn says, rising from the floor. "I feel bad that I haven't seen him yet."

"He's just down the hall in his office," I tell her. It's still startling to hear Lynn and Mark mention each other with anything other than disgust, but this change is certainly preferable, and I attempt to keep a neutral expression. "I'll meet you in the front hall in a few minutes; I'll just grab my bag and my phone," I say to her as she wanders one way down the hall, and I go the other.

When I get to the front door, Lynn has her coat on and is waiting for me and looks somewhat distressed. "Is everything okay?" I ask her.

"Yes, everything's fine," she replies as we walk outside, but it's not convincing.

***

We each drive our own car, so it will be easier after the game since her apartment is in Evanston, not too far from the stadium. Even though the women's team has already won their first five games and is predicted to have a great season, there is still plenty of room to park in the lot by Welsh Ryan Arena when we arrive. We also have no trouble securing seats in a prime section, even though this game versus Marquette is expected to be far better than any of the men's games so far this season. We could get seats closer to the floor, but I'm nervous about Courtney's reaction, so we select seats at the back of the lower section.

With Diet Cokes and popcorns in hand, Lynn and I are seated next to each other with twenty minutes until tip-off. Marquette is warming up at our end of the court, and we can see Courtney shooting lay-ups with her team, but it doesn't appear she's seen us, which is probably for the best.

"Are you sure you're okay?" I ask Lynn. She's been weird since we left the house, and I would generally assume it's my fault, but we had been having such a nice time before that. Maybe I was too optimistic in assuming things could get better this quickly.

Lynn takes a sip from her paper straw and a handful of popcorn and stares out at the court. For a minute, I wonder if she even heard me, but then she twists her body on the bleacher to face me, and I brace for what she's about to say. "I have something I need to tell you, but I'm not sure if I should say it," she says carefully.

"Okay…" I say cautiously.

"It's about Mark," she says, biting her lip, and I feel my heart sink. I'm not sure what I expect her to say next, but a million scenarios run through my head, and they're all terrible. "I kept things from you before, and that got us into trouble. So, I think this is something you should know," she says, nervously licking her glossy lips.

"What is it?" I ask, my entire body simultaneously growing cold and breaking out into a massive sweat, running down my back and dripping into my bra.

"Mark was on the phone when I went into his office, and I overheard his conversation, even though I didn't mean to," she quickly qualifies. The sweating intensifies as I wait for her to divulge the terrible secret that will tear my family apart. I nod for her to continue.

"He saw me. I told him that I heard his call, and he said it was no longer relevant, but I feel like you should know," Lynn explains.

"What did he say?" I choke out, squeezing my cup of soda so tightly, it's a miracle it doesn't explode all over my lap.

"He was offered a job to coach the Northwestern football team. Well, to be *one* of the coaches, and he turned it down," Lynn tells me.

"What?" I ask her, completely perplexed. "What are you talking about?" My initial terror seems to have passed, and now I'm left with a clammy shirt and utter confusion.

"I didn't have long to talk to him, but I guess he's been interviewing for a coaching job, and he got the job, but he told the guy on the phone that he couldn't take it because his family needed stability right now – that's the part I heard. I'm sure I'm overstepping, but I wanted to let you know," Lynn says, exhaling as if clearing her system now that the secret is out.

"He wants to coach football?" I say aloud, although I'm not really asking Lynn.

"I have no idea if that's what he wants. I know my marriage is a shining example of what not to do, but I felt like you should know about it. I mean, he just seemed so sad," Lynn says as if picturing Mark when she says it.

"He was sad?" I question miserably, trying to remember the last time he was unhappy or if I've really been paying much attention to any of his feelings lately.

***

The Wildcats came back to win 73-66 after trailing at the half, and Courtney scored fourteen points. I waved to her once during the game when she looked up into the stands, but I don't think she saw me; however, during a timeout in the fourth quarter, she glanced up, and her eyes grew wide as she caught a glimpse of Lynn and me together. At first, she looked perplexed, but then she gave us a little smirk, barely even noticeable to her teammates in the huddle, and she finished out the game.

"Do you think we should go down there?" I ask Lynn as the team finishes up their celebration on the court and begins to split off in singles and pairs to walk to the locker room.

"Isn't that why we're here?" she asks.

"I know, I know. But what if she doesn't want to talk to us?" I offer. "Maybe simply seeing us here is enough for now," I say nervously.

"I'm going down there," Lynn says as she begins to march down the middle of the bleachers, her high-heeled boots echoing with each step on the wooden benches. I hurry to follow her but choose to take the more traditional and quieter path down the aisle instead, approaches that mirror our personalities.

Courtney sees us coming and meets us at the bottom of the bleachers. Even with her sweaty hair matted to her forehead

304

and her flushed, shiny face, she is still gorgeous, and for the first time, I notice just how much she looks like Lynn.

"Great game," Lynn says casually as if there's nothing extraordinary about our presence here.

"Thanks," Courtney says, echoing her nonchalant tone, and I feel like I'm in the twilight zone.

"So…" I say, unable to play along with the calm dialogue. "It's really good to see you. And so nice for all three of us to be in the same place! I also need to apologize again for how I handled everything that night at dinner," I say, pausing to see Courtney's reaction.

"Let me get changed. Can you wait around a little bit?" she asks. "I'll be quick," Courtney promises.

"Of course!" Lynn and I reply in unison.

"I'll meet you in the lobby," Courtney says as she jogs off toward the locker room.

The arena is practically empty at this point, with only a few stragglers left in the stands, and the cleaning crew is already sweeping the court. Lynn and I walk slowly side-by-side toward the exit. I get the feeling she is going to say something, but she remains quiet the whole time. There are so many things I want to say now that we're finally talking and that we're about to see Courtney, but I worry that whatever I say will be taken the wrong way, so I keep quiet.

Thankfully Courtney is true to her word and emerges into the lobby shortly after we arrive. She's wearing team sweats, and her dark hair is wet from the shower and hanging down her back, already starting to dampen the back of her sweatshirt.

"Thanks for coming to watch the game," Courtney says, dropping her Adidas bag to the floor with a thud.

"I can't believe how good you are," I gush.

"Thanks," Courtney says. "It wasn't my best game, but the season is off to a good start," she remarks as we continue to bullshit.

"We totally fucked up," Lynn says to Courtney, this time; she's the one who cuts to the chase first. "We don't have any excuse for lying to you, but we want a second chance," Lynn says, graciously including me in her apology.

"Have you two made up?" Courtney asks, looking back and forth between the two of us.

"We're getting there," I reply. "We're trying to work it out, and we want the chance to try again," I say to her.

Courtney sighs and shakes her head, her damp hair brushing her shoulders. I can't believe that she won't even entertain the thought of giving us another chance, but before I can object, she says, "I would like that," while staring down at the glossy floor.

"I actually have an idea that I wanted to run by both of you," I say, suddenly excited to share the fragment of a thought that's been percolating in my head but didn't start to take shape until tonight. They both look at me with anticipation, and I hesitate slightly because the idea is far from fully formed. "I don't think either of you should sell your portion of the company. I think the three of us should run it together," I say, and they both look at me like I'm crazy.

"I don't know anything about insurance, nor do I want to," Lynn replies. "I've actually been considering taking some classes to get my real estate license," Lynn says cautiously.

"Oh, wow! That's great," I reply, surprised by her announcement and genuinely thrilled for her potential second career – I bet people would line up to have her as their agent. "You wouldn't actually have to run the business or work there on a daily basis, but we could all *own* the business. I think that's what Dad would have wanted," I throw in, and Lynn gives me a look that conveys skepticism.

"I don't know what I want to do after school, but the company isn't really relevant for me anymore," Courtney says quietly.

"What are you talking about?" I ask her, puzzled at her dismay.

"I already gave up my share of the will, and anything to do with any money or the family," she says sadly.

"What are you talking about?" Lynn questions, flipping her long blonde hair so quickly when she turns her head that I get a mouthful of it.

"The letter," Courtney says, gesturing to me as if that explains everything.

"Huh?" Lynn asks, looking back and forth between the two of us.

I try not to laugh or even raise the corner of my mouth, but it's not easy. "That letter didn't change anything," I say to Courtney. "I'm so sorry we made you feel like you didn't want to be a part of the family, but just signing that letter isn't a way out – you can't get rid of us that easily," I joke, hoping to elicit a grin.

"Oh. Really?" Courtney says, looking relieved. "How would it work?" she asks.

"I have no idea," I laugh. "But I think a partnership has real potential," I say, and all three of us smile together for the first time.

***

When I get home that night, I feel better than I have in months. Mark is already in bed with the lights off, but I can tell from his breathing that he's still awake. "How was it?" he asks.

"It was great," I reply happily, sitting down on my side of the bed to pull off my boots. "I'll tell you all about it in the morning."

"Okay," he says, rolling back over.

"Wait," I say to him, stretching across the king-size mattress to reach his shoulder, clad in a threadbare t-shirt.

"What is it?" Mark asks, turning to face me.

"I've been thinking that I want to go back to work at Summer," I say, testing the waters.

"Really?" Mark says, pulling himself up with his muscular forearms to turn his whole body toward me. The overhead lights are off, but my eyes have adjusted, and with the hall light, I see the look of intrigue and concern playing on his rugged face.

"I think I should be the CEO," I say slowly, knowing that this is a risky move. I pause to see if he'll respond, but when he doesn't, I plow ahead. "You hate it there. I'm sorry I didn't see it sooner. And that's the only job I've ever really wanted," I tell him, finally sharing what I've wanted to say since I left for maternity leave. I'm waiting for Mark to respond, but he's still staring at me like he can't quite figure out what to say. I suddenly wonder if I've played this entire thing wrong, but it

308

seems too late to back out now, so I put it all on the table "Lynn told me about the coaching job, and I think you should do it. I want you to do whatever makes you happy," I add for good measure.

Mark continues to stare at me with his deep blue eyes, and I'm about to burst from the tension and anticipation, but Mark rescues me. He slips his right hand under my waist and pulls me on top of him in one swift motion. His kiss is more revealing than any verbal confirmation he could have provided. We make love like newlyweds, with sheets twisted around our ankles and clothes strewn around the room because it was impossible to remove them quickly enough. When we're done, and I'm lying on his chest, slick with sweat, Mark murmurs how much he loves me into my ear, and it feels like I'm getting a fresh start on multiple levels, and a chance to do it right this time.

Chapter Thirty-Nine
Courtney

"Those were your sisters, huh?" Christina asks, but it's a statement, not a question; the punctuation is just for decoration.

We are sitting across from each other at a table at Evanston Pub after the game, with a pitcher of beer between us on the sticky table, officially purchased by one of the seniors, but when we're out with the team, no one ever cards us. Christina accepted my apology days ago, but our friendship still feels fragile. I think about what I'm going to say before I say it, which is obviously a good habit, but I'm used to being impulsive and irreverent with my best friend. Now I feel the need to be more cautious in case I say the wrong thing, but I'm hoping things will get back to normal soon.

"Yup. I still can't believe they came," I reply, drawing a smiley-face in the condensation on my pint glass while I decide what else to say.

"Is everything cool with them now?" Christina asks, finishing the beer that remains in her glass and quickly pouring herself a refill.

I'm facing the door, so I'm the first to see the redhead from the volleyball team walk in. Christina has liked her all year, and they finally hooked up a few nights ago, but she's barely heard from her since, and it's driving her crazy. I know I need to tell Christina she's here, but she'll ditch me as soon as she knows, and selfishly, I want a few more minutes with her. I'll wait until the redhead gets her drink and finds a table, and then I'll let Christina know that will buy me a little time.

"They seem to be getting along. Lynn's in town for a little longer, and we're all going to have lunch together this weekend," I tell her.

"Cool," Christina replies, her dark eyes scanning the room behind me.

I debate whether or not to mention Jen's idea about all of us having a role in Summer Risk Management, but it still seems a little improbable at this point, so I decide to keep that to myself. Although merely the mention of it and the idea that Jen and Lynn would want to involve me in any sort of shared venture is enough to make me happy.

"Guess who just walked in?" I say to her, deciding it's time to let her know and already regretting the annoying way I've phrased the question.

"Preston," she says decisively.

"No," I reply, shaking my head and trying to shake away the idea of him at the same time.

"Yes," she says. "He just came in with that big group. They're right over there," she says, lifting her long arm to point to the back corner, and I immediately slap down her hand.

"I take it you haven't made up with him?" she smirks. Over the course of my apology, I told her what happened with Preston on the car ride home. Christina is adamant that Preston likes me and thinks my theory that he pities me is nonsense. I don't want to fight with her, so we have agreed to disagree, but her smirk isn't helping matters.

"No, I haven't talked to him," I say. "But he hasn't tried to find me either," I add.

"Whatever," Christina says, rolling her eyes but thankfully dropping the matter. "Who were you talking about?" she asks.

"Oh, right!" I say, almost forgetting. "Your *friend* from the volleyball team," I say, with an overexaggerated wink, made worse by the fact that I close both eyes when I try to wink.

"No shit, really? Where?" she asks.

"By the bar," I tell her. "She's already looked over here a few times," I say.

"Should I go talk to her? She never returned my text," she maintains.

"Go talk to her, you know you want to," I say, giving her a gentle nudge with my foot under the table, but Christina is already pushing back her chair.

"You should take your own advice," she calls playfully over her shoulder as she walks toward the bar. She looks poised and confident and sexy as she walks up to her crush, and I'm happy for her and jealous of her self-assurance at the same time.

It's impossible to tell what Christina and the redhead are saying, but judging by body language, I'm betting Christina isn't going home alone tonight. I'm so caught up watching them that I don't notice someone slide into the empty seat beside me until it's too late.

"Your boyfriend isn't here tonight?" Preston says snidely, placing his empty pint glass on the table with more force than is strictly necessary. "May I?" he says, gesturing to the pitcher but he begins filling his glass before waiting for my response.

"What are you talking about?" I say, thrown off by his question and flustered by his proximity. He's sitting so close that I can smell his shampoo and shaving cream heavily overpowered by the stench of multiple pints of beer and whiskey. It should repulse me but actually makes me want to bury my head in his chest – I loathe myself.

"You know what I'm talking about," he chastises, and although I know he's been drinking, and his speech is a little loose, I can tell he isn't drunk.

"Where's that little girl that follows you around?" I retort, hating how childish I sound but unable to control myself.

"I don't know," Preston says, rubbing his free hand nervously on the worn fabric of his jeans, stretched tightly across his thigh. But then he reconsiders and says, "She's probably here somewhere."

"I've gotta go," I say, standing up so quickly that my hip bumps into the table, and I knock over the last three inches of beer in the pitcher, the golden liquid dumping onto the table and then cascading in a stream onto the floor. I feel guilty leaving the mess, but my need to disappear is more urgent. I also have a smidgeon of remorse about ditching Christina, but she looked occupied when I last saw her.

It's cold tonight, the temperature dropped twenty degrees since this morning as if winter wanted to give us an early reminder, and I wrap my arms tightly across my chest, wishing I had worn more than my jean jacket. It's eerily quiet as I walk alone up the street; apparently, everyone else is still out at the bars or already back in their rooms. But then I hear footsteps behind me as I approach the corner of Sherman and Church; I will myself not to turn around, and instead, I break into a jog. I

313

never like walking home alone at night, but sometimes I have to do it, and I feel like I set the women's movement back every time I get scared – guys never get nervous walking alone at night.

I'm sure I'm imagining it, but the footsteps are getting closer, even with my increased pace, and as I'm about to cross to the other side, a familiar voice calls out, "Slow down already, I can't run with this much beer sloshing around in my stomach."

Although I was the one who ran out of the bar to avoid him, I stop in my tracks and wait for Preston to catch up. "What do you want?" I plead as he approaches.

He looks at me for a minute and then bites his top lip with his lower teeth, the adorable way he does when he's studying and can't remember an answer. "I don't want to fight with you," he says.

"Okay, then we won't fight," I say snidely.

"But I would rather fight with you than have you ignore me," Preston says, staring straight at me with his sparkling green eyes.

"I wasn't ignoring you," I say, but we both know I'm lying.

"Are you dating that guy that Mark saw you with?" Preston asks quietly.

"What guy? Oh, Reagan?" I ask and force myself not to laugh at the absurdity of the idea. "No, definitely not. He's just a friend from high school," I say, "Not that it matters," I add, with a slightly snotty tone.

"So why not me?" Preston asks, his eyes focused directly on me once again.

"What about you?" I ask him, hugging myself tighter to guard against the wind as well as the whirlwind of emotions coursing through me.

Preston takes a step forward, and for a split second, I think he's going to kiss me but reprimand myself for being foolish as well as letting myself accept his charity. But then he leans down, so his lips are right next to my ear, and he says, "I want you, Courtney. I've wanted you since the day we met." And then he stands back up to his full height and looks at me, waiting for my reaction.

"What about all the other girls?" I ask him.

"I don't want to be a dick and say that they didn't mean anything, but none of that was serious – and it wasn't serious for them either," he adds quickly, although I'm sure some of those girls might disagree. "We were friends, and that was fine. I didn't think you liked me that way, but as long as we got to hang out all the time, that was enough. But I can't take it if you won't look at me or talk to me," Preston says sadly, and my heart breaks into a million pieces knowing that I'm the one who's made him sad.

"I thought you just felt bad for me," I admit, and the perplexed look on his face tells me that I need to elaborate. "When you kissed me, I thought it was out of pity. Because my family was so shitty," I explain, hoping to see acknowledgment on his face so I can stop digging my hole.

Preston leans down again, but this time his lips go straight for mine, and I part them in anticipation, feeling his tongue slip inside like I've imagined every day since our last kiss. My heart pounds, and my knees actually start to weaken, something that I thought only happened in old movies, but Preston's solid arm is wrapped so tightly around me that I'm not in any danger of falling. I pull away slightly, only to get a look at his face and make sure this is finally for real. Preston grins and says, "Does that seem like pity to you?" and I wrap my arms around him as our lips find each other once more.

Chapter Forty
Lynn

I promised myself I won't check my phone again for at least another hour, but I already know I'm going to break that promise. It seems absurd that I'm renegotiating a mental contract I made with myself, but it's the only way I'm going to get through the next few hours until I hear from Ray.

Even though Ray was convinced that Trevor would want to renegotiate our custody deal after getting the DNA results, I was sure he would insist on dragging it into a long, nasty trial because that's the kind of guy he is. Ray called after she met with him and delivered the news that Trevor needed a few days to think things through, but he was not interested in taking this back to court. I was stunned, even though this is what Ray told me would happen. I have a feeling that their meeting wasn't quite as cut and dry, but I'm happy to let Ray handle the details.

Now I'm waiting for Ray to call and deliver the news that will dictate my future. Ray provided appropriate legal guidance and asked if I wanted to demand full custody, but I rejected that immediately. Although Declan isn't Trevor's biological son, it would be cruel to ask them to sever their relationship. No matter how much of an asshole Trevor is, he's still the only father Declan's ever known. I'm seeking a fair custody agreement, which is what we should have had in the first place.

I'm also seriously considering leaving California, and I need to think about how that will impact Declan, but I want the ability to have him with me in Illinois or wherever I choose to go.

I know it's only ten o'clock in California, but I can't take the waiting anymore, and decide to take my nervous energy for a run. It's much colder than when I was here a few weeks ago, but I've always preferred this crisp fall weather for running – I know I won't feel the same about Chicago-area weather in a few months, though.

I suit up in navy running tights and an orange long-sleeve shirt, which will provide some visibility on this overcast day. I lace up my well-loved Nikes and note the disparity that I wore these same shoes for a run in Venice Beach only a week ago; so much has changed since then, and in a few hours, so much more could change.

A blast of cold air hits my face as I step out onto the street, and I think back with sudden nostalgia to my running days in high school; I remember my pink down vest and purple fuzzy headband that fit snugly over my ears – I may need to invest in more appropriate winter gear if I'm really going to be spending more time here.

I push the ball of my right foot against the brick step in front of my building to stretch out my calf and then switch to the left. Unable to stop myself, I pull my phone out of the pocket on my outer thigh, just to make sure I haven't missed a call, or text, or email, and then jam the phone back, disappointed at my lack of willpower. I'm one more arm stretch away from jogging east toward Sheridan when I see a familiar silver Audi pull into the empty parking spot in front of me, and an even more familiar face exit the car.

It's incredibly childish, but part of me considers bolting. I'm sure I'm faster than he is, but even if I'm not, he's wearing loafers, jeans, and a wool pea coat – he'd never catch me. But

I'm too curious to see why Nick's here to run away, and despite how angry I've been, I've missed him too.

"How'd you know I was here?" I ask Nick. The first thing that comes out of my mouth is more confrontational than I intend, but it's what flies out as he approaches.

"Your sister told me," Nick says, looking contrite.

I'm desperate to make a snide comment about how well things went the last time he talked to Jen, but I also realize I'm not without fault. I wasn't ready to listen to Ali initially, but on further reflection, I know her points were valid. If I were in his shoes, I know I would have been hurt and pissed off to find out that he was married and had a child he hadn't told me about. It wasn't his fault that Jen didn't have the right information, but there were no crossed wires on Declan; that was all me.

"I don't know how long I'll be here," I say, blowing into my hands and hopping back and forth on my feet, trying to keep warm.

"Are you cold?" Nick says although it's obvious that I am. "Can we go inside and talk?" he asks.

"I'd rather walk, if that's okay with you," I say. I'm sure I'll still be cold, but at least some movement will help, and I'm not sure I can handle a sit-down, face-to-face conversation with what I need to divulge and apologize for.

"Of course," Nick says.

We turn in sync toward Sheridan and walk the first block in uncomfortable silence, or at least it feels that way to me. I run through all the possible conversation openers, but nothing seems right. I assume that Nick is experiencing the same ordeal, but maybe he doesn't notice anything's amiss.

"So…" I say, drawing out the word for several beats as we reach the corner and turn north on Sheridan, unable to take the silence a minute longer.

Nick laughs quietly. "That about covers it," he says warmly.

"I didn't plan for things to happen the way they did," I say quickly. Nick doesn't respond, so I continue. "Jen and I don't have the best history, although we *are* working on it," I ramble, "I should have told you about Declan, and I was working up to it, but she didn't have all of her facts straight," I try to explain.

"That's what she said," Nick says.

"Huh?" I question.

"When she came by to tell me that you were back in town *and* to tell me that she got it all wrong," he says.

"Oh," I reply, unsure what else to say.

"I admit I was shocked when she told me that you were married, but more than that, I was hurt that you didn't even explain when I tried to talk to you about it," Nick says.

"I'm sorry," I tell him, which seems to be my new catchphrase. "I should have explained. I didn't know how to react, so I just shut down. But Jen was right about Declan, and I felt terrible that you found out that way. It's such a long story, and not a good one, so it's not something I was ready to talk about," I say to him, staring straight ahead, preferring the sting of the wind on my cheeks to direct eye contact after this revelation.

"Do you want to talk about it now?" Nick asks kindly. Quickly following with, "It's okay if you don't."

"I do," I reply. I proceed to tell him the entire story as we walk through the streets of Evanston, weaving through the historic homes, a mix of stately multi-million-dollar mansions, and small carriage houses that are destined to be torn down, and everything in between. For the first time, I tell the tale from start to finish, without omitting any of the sordid details that I've tried to hide over the years. My body is mostly numb when I finish over an hour later, and I wrap up at the present day, where I'm waiting to hear from Ray.

"Thank you for sharing that with me," Nick says. At first, I fear that he's going to follow it up with a quick exit, but instead, he says, "That was very brave of you share. I'd love to be part of this with you if that's something you want."

Before I can respond or even absorb what Nick has said, my phone screeches loudly and simultaneously vibrates against my thigh. I've finally forgotten to obsess over it, and now it rings. The caller ID says, "Ray," and I hold my breath as I answer.

My end of the conversation is merely a series of "yeses," "mm hmms," and "thank yous," so when I finally hang up, Nick looks at me expectantly for details.

"He agreed!" I shriek, unable to control my enthusiasm.

"Congratulations!" Nick says, throwing his arms around me in a bear hug, the first contact we've had since I left for LA, but it feels natural. "What happens now?"

My heart is racing, and I feel like I might faint if I don't sit down, but instead, I start walking again to aid my wobbly legs. "We have a lot of details to work out, but we now have complete joint custody, and there are no restrictions on travel or when and where I can see Declan. None of that!" I exclaim.

"That's great," Nick says, but he looks slightly deflated.

"Are you okay?" I ask him, surprised at his change in mood.

"I'm really happy for you," Nick says. "It was silly. I thought you might stick around here, but I know it makes more sense for you to be back in LA so you can be with your son," Nick says.

"Honestly, I don't know what I'm going to do," I tell him. "As much as I want to see Declan, and this is a huge win for me, I know that things aren't going to change overnight. He hasn't lived with me for two years, and I wouldn't want to pull him out of school or make huge changes to his life, no matter how much I hate Trevor," I say to him, thinking it through in real-time as I'm speaking.

"So, what does that mean?" Nick asks.

"I'm not sure. I haven't been able to see him at all, so I think we do need to go slowly, but I also think I'm ready to make some big changes in *my* life," I say.

"I'm listening," Nick says, looking at me with a cautious smile.

"This is only my first idea, but I thought I could have Declan here in the summer and for all of his breaks. And I could keep my place in LA, or get another one, and fly out there a couple of weekends a month to spend with him," I say, the thoughts starting to marinate in my brain.

"And when you say *here*, what do you mean by that exactly?" Nick asks hopefully.

I can't help but laugh at the adorable puppy-dog look in his eyes when he asks the question. "I was thinking the Evanston area," I smile, gesturing with my arms to the streets around me. "Although with my inheritance and whatever partnership Jen seems to have in mind, I may upgrade from my student rental to something a little nicer," I say, already thinking of the possibilities.

"That sounds like a perfect idea," Nick says, reaching down and taking my hand; his fingers still inexplicably warm intertwining around mine until they feel like one whole. We walk most of the way back to my apartment without saying much, taking turns squeezing each other's hands, and this time it's the perfect kind of comfortable silence – a precursor of peaceful and joyous days to come.

Epilogue
Jennifer

Two Years Later

"I'll meet you all back at the house," I call over to Lynn, unsure if she can hear me over the cheers of the home crowd.

She responds with a thumbs-up signal, and Nick turns to give me a wave as well, with Harper happily beside him munching on popcorn. I take that as my sign that it's okay to leave and scurry down the tunnel and out of the stadium, hoping to avoid the crowds by disappearing with five minutes left on the clock. As the wife of a coach, I know I should stay until the end of the game, but the Cats are ahead by four touchdowns at the end of the fourth quarter, so hopefully, it's safe to go.

On the drive to Winnetka, I run through a mental checklist of what still needs to be done before the post-game gathering. It's only a small affair, but I still get nervous and excited when everyone's together, even though it's become far more routine than I ever imagined.

It's early November, and autumn already feels like it might be gone, with temperatures dropping to the thirties a few nights last week. In that spirit, I decided to serve chili today for the post-game meal. There's a huge pot that I made yesterday, and it's been simmering on the stove all morning, and now all I need to do is put together bowls for toppings and cut pieces of cornbread. I'm grating cheese when I hear a perfunctory knock at the back door, followed by the low squeak it makes as it opens. "We're here," Lynn calls out cheerfully, echoed by several other voices shuffling into the house and shrugging of outerwear and kicking off shoes.

"What was the final score?" I yell back anxiously. Although it's something I could have easily looked up for myself, I've been too busy to think about it. If someone told me a couple o years ago that the score of a college football game would have me on pins and needles, I would have thought they were crazy but now I'm one of Northwestern's biggest fans.

"Iowa scored one more field goal after you left, but we still killed them," Courtney says, appearing in the kitchen in an oversized purple sweatshirt with frayed jeans and stocking feet.

"Oh good," I say, sighing with relief. "Definitely something to celebrate!" I exclaim.

"We *do* have something to celebrate," Lynn says mysteriously, strolling into the kitchen, with Nick close behind.

I squint my eyes at her and give her a look that says I need more information, and she responds with a devilish smirk.

"Don't you think we should wait for everyone to get here?" Nick says, wrapping his arm around her waist.

"What is going on?" Courtney says, scanning the room.

"Don't ask me," I say, raising my hands in mock surrender, "I have no idea what's going on." Lynn and Nick both laugh, and if they weren't so cute together, it would be annoying.

Then Lynn holds up her left hand to display an elegant emerald-cut diamond ring that wasn't there previously, and in spite of ourselves and how ridiculously cliché it is, Courtney and I both scream as we enclose Lynn in a group hug.

"When did this happen?" I demand. "I was standing next to you all day!"

"Gloves," is all Lynn says and wiggles her fingers at me again.

"Does Declan know?" Courtney asks, which is really a more important question.

"Do I know *what*?" Declan questions, sauntering into the kitchen, with Ryan hot on his heels. An unexpected outcome of Declan's time living with Lynn in Evanston has been his relationship with Harper and Ryan, but mostly Ryan. Ryan worships Declan, the exotic older cousin, and after a period of adjustment, Declan's decided it isn't so bad having a groupie.

"About the engagement," Lynn fills in the blank.

"Oh, yeah. It's cool," Declan responds nonchalantly. "Hey, Aunt Jen, is it almost time to eat?" he asks hopefully.

At fourteen, Declan appears to be taking after his biological father and is already well over six feet tall and weighs close to two hundred pounds. To both Mark and Preston's chagrin, he has no interest in football and prefers creative writing, playing guitar, and surfing, but he still eats like a linebacker.

"We're going to wait for Uncle Mark and Preston to get here, but you can grab a snack while you wait," I tell him.

"Thanks," he says and goes straight to the pantry, reappearing with a box of crackers and a jar of peanut butter. "Come on, dude," he says to Ryan, "Let's have a pre-game snack," and Ryan dutifully follows him out of the kitchen, where I have no doubt, they will consume everything and leave a huge mess, but I wouldn't want it any other way.

"He's good with it?" I quietly ask after Declan's gone.

"Nick picked him up at the airport when he flew in yesterday, and the two of them went out to lunch," Lynn gushes.

"We talked about it, and he said he thought it was great," Nick confirms. "I casually mentioned it to him this summer when he was here, just to see what he thought, and he seemed fine. But when we talked yesterday, I needed to make sure this worked for him, and he assured me that it did."

"I'm so happy for you," Courtney says, hugging Lynn again.

"Me too," I echo, feeling tears of joy start to well up behind my eyes as I come out from behind the counter to join my sisters in our second group hug of the day.

"What's going on in here?" Mark asks, his voice booming into the kitchen, although I was so wrapped up, I didn't hear him come in.

"Lynn and Nick are engaged!" I say happily, removing myself from the embrace.

"Congratulations!" Mark cheers, clapping Nick on the back and wrapping his arms around Lynn.

"Yeah, congratulations," Preston says, the last one to enter the kitchen, but apparently, he heard the news on his way in.

"This calls for champagne!" Mark declares, heading to the wine fridge to grab a bottle.

"We need to celebrate the game too!" I say, nodding to both Preston and Mark, acknowledging their victory in light of the bigger news.

"Just sparkling water for me," Lynn says casually, sharing a quick look with Nick.

The rest of us exchange glances, but no one says a word as Mark fills glasses of champagne for the five of us and one glass of Perrier for Lynn. Hearing the commotion, Declan, Ryan, and Harper join in the kitchen, and we fill their glasses with Sprite so they can join in too.

When the glasses are full, we all raise them high in the air and toast the engagement and the victory over Iowa, and then we start adding additional items to the list, and it almost morphs into a gratitude exercise - Declan's weekend visit, Summer Risk Management's best quarter ever, Lynn's latest real estate sale, Courtney's score on the LSAT, and the list grows, but all I know is that my biggest accomplishment *and* what I'm most thankful for, is being here, surrounded by my loving family.

THE END

Acknowledgements

I wrote this book in 2020 – in some ways, that says it all. At times it was impossible to find the strength to write, and at other times writing was the only thing that provided the much-needed retreat from reality. I know I don't have to tell you that 2020 was a challenging year, although it was hard for each of us in our own ways. In addition to COVID-19 and the political turmoil in the United States this past year, it was also a difficult year for my family for many reasons; however, writing *The Last Summer Sister* helped me get through it, and for that, I am grateful.

I am indebted to all of you for reading my books and supporting me. I hope this book brings you joy and allows you to escape into the world of the Summer sisters. Thank you to all of my readers for buying, reading, downloading, and reviewing my books – your encouragement is what keeps me going.

An enormous thank you to my sister, Sarah Nelson, for being the first to read all of my work and cheering me on every step of the way. Even if I know she is slightly biased, it's wonderful to have someone who loves my first drafts.

Thank you to my other early readers and dear friends for reading and providing helpful feedback – I keep waiting for you to tell me that you're too busy (because all of you are). Still, you always make time to read and provide thoughtful advice: Aimee Kaplan, Erin Ginsburg, Hillary Pryor, and Kathy Soderberg.

I am lucky enough to have too long of a list of friends and family to thank each one individually for their unconditional support. Still, I want to send a hug (virtual, of course) to each of you, near and far, to thank you for supporting my work, promoting my books, driving carpool, or simply sharing a laugh, a walk, or a cup of coffee.

Last but certainly not least, I want to thank my three wonderful daughters, Emily, Samantha, and Lexi, and my amazing husband and best friend, Doug. You are my biggest fans, and I certainly wouldn't be able to do anything without your love and support.

Rachel Cullen is a graduate of Northwestern University and NYU Stern School of Business. She worked in consulting and marketing in San Francisco, London, and New York and currently lives in Westchester, New York, with her husband and three children, and her two large dogs. *The Last Summer Sister* is her fifth novel; she is also the author of *The Way I've Heard it Should Be*, *Second Chances*, *Only Summer*, and *First Came Us*.

www.rachelcullenauthor.com

www.facebook.com/RachelCullenAuthor

www.instagram.com/RachelCullenAuthor

Made in the USA
Middletown, DE
07 June 2022

66792752R00198